THE
HALF-MAMMALS
OF DIXIE

The
Half-Mammals
of Dixie

STORIES

George Singleton

A SHANNON RAVENEL BOOK

Algonquin Books of Chapel Hill

2002

ℝ

A SHANNON RAVENEL BOOK
Published by
ALGONQUIN BOOKS OF CHAPEL HILL
Post Office Box 2225
Chapel Hill, North Carolina 27515-2225

a division of
Workman Publishing
708 Broadway
New York, New York 10003

Some of the stories here originally appeared in slightly different versions and sometimes with different titles in the following magazines and anthologies, to whose editors grateful acknowledgment is made: "Show-and-Tell" in *The Atlantic Monthly* and *New Stories from the South,* 2002; "Fossils" as "Public Defenders and Other Fossils" in *Book;* "When Children Count" in *The Southern Review;* "How to Collect Fishing Lures" in *The Raleigh News & Observer;* "Answers" as "The Tribological Nature of Answers" in *The South Carolina Review;* "Public Relations" in *The Georgia Review* and *New Stories from the South,* 2001; "Duke Power" in *The Greensboro Review;* "Impurities" in *Shenandoah;* "The Half-Mammals of Dixie" in *Harper's;* "What Slide Rules Can't Measure" in *The North American Review;* "Page-a-Day" as "Seldom Around Here" in *Zoetrope;* and "Richard Petty Accepts National Book Award" in *New Delta Review.*

This is a work of fiction. While, as in all fiction, the literary perceptions and insights are based on experience, all names, characters, places, and incidents are either products of the author's imagination or are used fictitiously. No reference to any real person is intended or should be inferred.

Library of Congress Cataloging-in-Publication Data
Singleton, George, 1958–
    The half-mammals of Dixie : stories / George Singleton.
      p. cm.
    "A Shannon Ravenel book."
    Contents: Show-and-tell — Fossils — This itches, y'all — How to collect fishing lures — When children count — Answers — Public relations — Bank of America — Deer gone — Duke Power — Impurities — The half-mammals of Dixie — What slide rules can't measure — Page-a-day — Richard Petty accepts National Book Award.
    ISBN 1-56512-354-9
    1. Southern States—Social life and customs—Fiction.   I. Title.
PS3569.I5747 H35 2002
813'.6—dc21   2002023205

10 9 8 7 6 5 4 3 2 1
First Edition

for Glenda, with more love

Acknowledgments

First and foremost I want to thank my editor, Shannon
Ravenel. Thanks to Liz Darhansoff and Kristin Lang,
agents worthy of daily flowers. I must thank the following
magazine editors: C. Michael Curtis, Ben Metcalf, Adrienne
Brodeur, R. T. Smith, Jim Lester Clark, and Adam Langer.
Big thanks to Jerome Kramer and Mark Gleason.
And an invitation to Melissa Gray and David Molpus,
journalists extraordinaire, to come back down to Pickens
County any Wednesday morning before dawn.

Contents

"Ah well, natural laws, natural laws,
I suppose it's like everything else, it all depends
on the creature you happen to be."

—Samuel Beckett, *Happy Days*

THE
HALF-MAMMALS
OF DIXIE

Show-and-Tell

I wasn't old enough to know that my father couldn't have obtained a long-lost letter from famed lovers Héloïse and Peter Abelard, and since European history wasn't part of my third-grade curriculum, I really felt no remorse in bringing the handwritten document—on lined and hole-punched Blue Horse filler paper—announcing its value, and reading it to the class on Friday show-and-tell. My classmates —who would all later grow up to be idiots, in my opinion, since they feared anything outside of South Carolina in general and my hometown of Forty-Five in particular, thus making them settle down exactly where they got trained, thus shrinking the gene pool even more—brought the usual: starfishes and conch shells bought in Myrtle Beach gift shops, though claimed to have been found personally during summer vacation; Indian-head pennies given as birthday gifts by grandfathers; the occasional pet gerbil, corn snake, or tropical fish. My father instructed me how to read the letter, what words to stress, when to pause. I, of course, protested directly after the dry run. Some of the words and phrases reached beyond my vocabulary. The general tone of the letter, I knew, would only get me playground-taunted by boys and girls alike. My father told me to pipe down and read louder. He told me to use my hands better and got out a metronome.

I didn't know that my father—a "widower" is what he instructed me to call him, although everyone knew how Mom ran off to Nashville and hadn't died—had once dated Ms. Suber, my teacher. My parents' pasts never came up in conversation, even after my mother ended up tending bar at a place called the Merchant's Lunch on Lower Broad more often than she sang on various honky-tonk stages, waiting for representation by a man who would call her the next Patsy Cline. No, the prom night and homecoming of my father's senior year in high school with Ms. Suber never leaked out in our talks, whether we ate supper in front of the television screaming at Walter Cronkite or played pinball down at the Sunken Gardens Lounge.

I got up in front of the class. I knew that a personal, caring, loving, benevolent God didn't exist, seeing as I had prayed that my classmates would spill over their allotted time, et cetera, et cetera, and then we'd go to recess, lunch, and then sit through one of the mandatory filmstrips each South Carolina elementary-school student underwent weekly on topics as tragic and diverse as Friendship, Fire Safety, Personal Hygiene, and Bee Stings. "I have a famous letter written from one famous person to another famous person," I said.

Ms. Suber held her mouth in a tiny O. Nowadays I realize that she held beauty, but at the time she was just another very old woman in front of an elementary-school class, her corkboard filled with exclamation marks. She wasn't but thirty-five, really. Ms. Suber motioned for me to edge closer to the music stand she normally used on Recorder Day. "And what are these famous people's names, Mendal?"

Ricky Hutton, who'd already shown off a ship in a bottle that he didn't make but said he did, yelled out, "My father has a letter from President Johnson's wife thanking him for picking up litter."

"My grandma sent me a birthday card with a two-dollar bill inside," said Libby Belcher, the dumbest girl in the class, who later went on to get a doctorate in education and then become superintendent of the school district.

I stood there with my folded document. Ms. Suber said, "Go on."

"I forget who wrote this letter. I mean, they were French people."

"Might it be Napoleon and Josephine?" Ms. Suber wore a smirk that I would see often in my life, from women who immediately recognized any untruth I chose to tell.

I said, "My father told me, but I forget. It's not signed or anything," which was true.

Ms. Suber pointed at Billy Gilliland and told him to quit throwing his baseball in the air, a baseball supposedly signed by Shoeless Joe Jackson that none of us believed in, seeing as the signature was printed, at best. We never relented on Gilliland, and later on he plain used the ball in pickup games until the cover wore off.

I unfolded the letter and read, " 'My dearest.' "

"These were French people writing in English, I suppose," Ms. Suber said.

I nodded. I said, "They were smart, I believe. 'I want to tell you that if I live to be a hundred I won't meet another man like you. If I live to be a hundred there shall be no love to match ours.' "

The entire class began laughing, of course. My face reddened. I looked at Ms. Suber, but she concentrated on her shoe. " 'That guy who wrote that "How Do I Love Thee" poem has nothing on us, my sugar-booger-baby.' "

"That's enough," Ms. Suber belted out. "You can sit down, Mendal."

I pointed at the letter. I had another dozen paragraphs to go, some of which rhymed. I hadn't gotten to the word "throbbing," which showed up fourteen times. "I'm not making any of this up," I said. I walked two steps toward my third-grade teacher, but she stood up and told everyone to go outside except me.

Glenn Flack walked by and said, "You're in trouble, Mendal Dawes." Carol Anderson, who was my third-grade girlfriend, looked like she was going to cry, as if I'd written the letter to Ms. Suber myself.

Ms. Suber said, "You've done nothing wrong, Mendal. Please tell your daddy that I got it. When he asks what happened today, just say that Ms. Suber got it, okay?"

I put the letter in my front pants pocket. I said, "My father's a widower."

. . .

MY FATHER WAS WAITING for me when I got home. Like everyone else, he started off in textiles, then gave it up. I never really knew what he did for a living, outside of driving around within a hundred-mile radius of Forty-Five buying up land and then reselling it when the time was right. He had a knack. That was his word. For a time I thought it was the make of his car. "I drive around all day and buy land," he said more than once, before and after my mother took off to replace Patsy Cline. "I have a Knack."

I came home wearing my book bag, filled with math homework and an abacus. I said, "Hey, Dad."

He held his arms wide open, as if I were a returning P.O.W. "Did your teacher send back a note?"

I reached in my pocket and pulled out the letter from Héloïse to Abelard. I handed it to him and said, "She made me quit reading."

"She made you quit reading? How far along did you get?"

I told him how I only got to the part about sugar-booger-baby. I said, "Is this one of those lessons in life you keep telling me about, like when we went camping?" My father taught me early on how to tell the difference between regular leaves and poison ivy, the year before, when we camped out beside the Saluda River, far from any commode, waiting for him to gain a vision on which tract would be most saleable later.

"Goddamn it to hell. She didn't say anything else after you read the letter?"

My father wore a seersucker suit. He wore a string tie. I said, "She called recess pretty much in the middle of me reading the thing. This is some kind of practical joke, isn't it?"

My father looked at me as if I'd peed on his wing tips. He said, "Now why would I do something like that to the only human being I love in this world?"

I couldn't imagine why. Why would a man who — as he liked to tell me often — before my birth played baseball for the Yankees in the summer, football for the Packers in the winter, and competed in the Olympics, ever revert to playing jokes on a nine-year-old son of his? "Ms. Suber seemed kind of mad."

"Did she cry? Did she start crying? Did she turn her head away from y'all and blow her nose into a handkerchief? Don't hold back, Mendal. Don't think that you're embarrassing your teacher or anything for telling the truth. Ms. Suber would want you to tell the truth, wouldn't she?"

I said, "Uh-huh. Probably."

"Uh-huh probably she cried, or uh-huh probably she'd want you to tell the truth?" My father walked to the kitchen backwards, pulled a bottle of bourbon from the shelf, and drank from it straight. Twenty years later on I would do the same thing, but over a dog that needed to be put to sleep.

I said, "Uh-huh. I told her you were a widower and everything. We got to go to recess early."

My father kept walking backwards. He took a glass from the cabinet, then cracked open an ice tray. He put cubes in the glass, poured bourbon into it, and stood staring at me as if I had told secrets to the enemy. "Did she say that she's thinking about getting married?"

I said, "She didn't say anything."

I wondered if my mother stood before a group of men and women drinking house beer, if she sang "I Fall to Pieces" or "Crazy" or any of those other country songs. It wasn't but three-thirty in my father's house. There was a one-hour time change, at least, in Nashville.

"I'VE GOTTEN AHOLD of a genuine Cherokee Indian bracelet and ring," my father said the next Thursday night. "I ain't shitting you any on this one. Your mother's father gave them to us a long time ago as a wedding present. He got them when he was traveling through Cherokee County up in the Cherokee country. Your grandfather used to sell cotton, you know. Sometimes those Indians needed cotton. They traded things for cotton. That's the way things go."

I said, "I was thinking about taking some pinecones I found." I had gathered up some pinecones that were so perfect it wasn't funny. They looked like Christmas trees built to scale. "I was going to take a rock and say it was a meteorite."

"No, no. Take some of my Cherokee Indian jewelry, son. I don't mind. I don't care! Hotdamn I didn't even remember having the things, so it won't matter none if they get broken or stolen," he said. "This is the real thing, Bubba."

What could I do? I wasn't but nine years old, and early on I'd been taught to do whatever my elders said, outside of drinking whiskey and smoking cigarettes when they got drunk and made the offer, usually at Sunken Gardens Lounge. I thought, Maybe I can pretend to take my father's weird jewelry and stick it in my desktop. Maybe I can stick a pinecone inside my lunch box. "Yessir."

"I won't have it any other way," he said. "Wait here."

My father went back to what used to be my mother's and his bedroom. He opened up a wooden box he'd fashioned in high school shop, and pulled out a thin silver bracelet, plus a one-pearl ring. I didn't know that these trinkets once adorned the left arm of my third-grade teacher, right before she broke up with my father in order to go to college, and long before she graduated, taught in some other school system for ten years, and then came back to her hometown.

I took the trinkets in a small cotton sack. My father told me that he'd come get me for lunch if I wanted him to, that I didn't need to pack a bologna sandwich and banana as always. I went to the refrigerator and made my own and then left through the back door.

Glenn Flack started off show-and-tell with an X ray of his mother's ankle. She'd fallen off the front porch trying to run from bees—something the rest of us knew not to do, seeing as we'd learned how to act in one of the weekly filmstrips. I got called next and said, "I have some priceless Cherokee Indian artifacts to show y'all. The Cherokee Indians had a way with hammering and chiseling." My father had made me memorize this speech.

I showed my classmates what ended up being something

bought at Rey's Jewelers. Ms. Suber said, "Let me take a look at that," and got up to take the bracelet from my hand. She peered at it and then held it at arm's length and said, "This looks like it says 'sterling' on the inside, Mendal. I believe you might've picked up the wrong Indian jewelry to bring to school."

"Indian giver, Indian giver, Indian giver!" Melissa Beasley yelled out. It wasn't a taboo term back then. This was a time, understand, before we all had to say Native American–head penny.

I said, "I just know what my dad told me. That's all I know." I took the bracelet from Ms. Suber, pulled out the ring, and stood there as if offering a Milk-Bone to a stray and skittish dog.

Ms. Suber said, "I've had enough of this" and told me to return to my desk. I put the pearl ring on my thumb and stuck the bracelet around the toe of my tennis shoe. Ms. Suber said, "Has your father gone insane lately, Mendal?"

It embarrassed me, certainly, and if she had said it twenty or thirty years later, I could've sued her for harassment, slander, and making me potentially agoraphobic. My desk was in the last row. Every student turned toward me except Shirley Ebo, the only black girl in the entire school, four years prior to lawful integration. She looked forward, as always, ready to approach the music stand and explain her show-and-tell object, a face jug made by an old, old relative of hers named Dave the Slave.

I said, "My father has a Knack." Maybe I said nothing, really, but I thought about my father's Knack. I waited.

Ms. Suber sat back down. She looked at the ceiling and said, "I'm sorry, Mendal. I didn't mean to yell at you. Everyone go on to recess."

AND SO IT CONTINUED for six weeks. I finally told my father that I couldn't undergo any more humiliation, that I would play hooky, that I would show up at school and say I had forgotten to bring my show-and-tell gimcrack. I said, "I'm only going to take these stupid things you keep telling me stories about if it brings in some money, Dad."

Not that I was ever a capitalist or anything, but I figured early on that show-and-tell would end up somehow hurting my penmanship or spelling grade, and that maybe I needed to start saving money in order to get a head start in life should I not get into college. My father said, "That sounds fair enough. How much will you charge me to take this old, dried Mayan wrist corsage and matching boutonniere?"

I said, "Five bucks each."

My father handed them over. If the goddamn school system had ever shown a worthwhile Friday filmstrip concerning inductive logic, I would've figured out back then that when Ms. Suber and my father had had their horrific and execrable high school breakup, my father had gone over to her house and gathered up everything he'd ever bestowed upon her, from birthday to Valentine's Day to special three-month anniversary and so on. He had gifts she'd given him, too, I supposed much later, though I doubted they were worthy of monogamy.

But I didn't know logic. I thought only that my father hated the school system, had no trust whatsoever in public education, and wanted to drive my teacher to a nervous breakdown in order to get her to quit. Or, I thought, it was his way of flirting—that since my mother had "died," he wanted to show a prospective second wife some of the more spectacular possessions he could offer a needful woman.

He said, "I can handle ten dollars a show-and-tell session, for two items. Remind me not to give you an hourglass. I don't want you charging me per grain of sand."

This was all by the first of October. By Christmas break I'd brought in cuff links worn by Louis Quatorze, a fountain pen used by the fifty-six signers of the Declaration of Independence (my father tutored me on stressing "Independence" when I announced my cherished object to the class), a locket once owned by Elmer the glue inventor, thus explaining why the thing couldn't be opened, a pack of stale Viceroys that once belonged to the men who raised the American flag on Iwo Jima. I brought in more famous love letters, all on lined Blue Horse paper: from Ginger Rogers to Fred Astaire, from Anne Hathaway to Shakespeare, from all of Henry VIII's wives to him. One letter, according to my dad, was from Plato to Socrates, though he said it wasn't the original, and that he'd gone to the trouble of learning Greek in order to translate the thing.

Ms. Suber became exasperated with each new disclosure. She moved from picking names at random or in alphabetical order to always choosing me last. My classmates voted me Most Popular, Most Likely to Succeed, and Third Grade

President, essentially because I got us ten more minutes of recess every Friday.

I walked down to the County Bank every Friday after school and deposited the money my father had forked over in a regular savings account. This was a time before IRAs. It was a time before stock portfolios, mutual funds, and the like. They gave me a toaster for starting the account and a dinner plate every time I walked in with ten dollars or more. After a few months I could've hosted a dinner party for twelve.

ON SATURDAY MORNINGS, more often than not, I drove with my father from place to place, looking over land he had bought or planned to buy. He had acquired a few acres of woodland before my birth, and soon thereafter the Army Corps of Engineers came in, flooded the Savannah River, and made my father's property near lakefront. He sold that parcel, took that money, and bought more land in an area that bordered what would become I-95. He couldn't go wrong. My father was not unlike the fool who threw darts at a map and went with his gut instinct. He would buy useless swampland, and someone else would soon insist on buying that land at twice to ten times his cost in order to build a golf course, a subdivision, or a nuclear-power facility. I had no idea what he did between these ventures, outside of reading and wondering. How else would he know about Abelard and Héloïse, or even Socrates and Plato? He hadn't gone to college. He hadn't taken some kind of correspondence course.

We drove, and I stuck my head out the window like the dog I had owned before my mother took him to Nashville. We'd get to some land, pull down a dirt road usually, and my father would stare hard for ten or fifteen minutes. He barely turned his head from side to side, and he never turned off the engine. Sometimes he'd say at the end, "I think I got a fouled spark plug," or "You can tell that that gas additive's working properly."

He never mentioned people from history, or the jewelry of the dead. I took along Hardy Boys mysteries but never opened the covers. Finally, one afternoon, I said, "Ms. Suber wants to know if you're planning on coming to the PTA meeting. I forgot to tell you."

My father turned off the ignition. He reached beneath his seat and pulled out a can of beer and a church key. We sat parked between two gullies, somewhere in Greenwood County. "Hotdamn, boy, you need to tell me these things. When is it?"

I said, "I forgot. I got in so much trouble Friday that I forgot." I'd taken a tortoise to show-and-tell and said his name was John the Baptist. At first Ms. Suber seemed delighted. When she asked why I had named him John the Baptist, I said, "Watch this." I screamed, "John the Baptist!" When he retreated into his shell and lost his head, I nodded. She had me sit back down. None of my classmates got the joke.

"The PTA meeting's on Tuesday. It's Tuesday." I wore a pair of cut-off blue jeans with the bottoms cut into one-inch strips. My mother used to make them for me when I'd grown taller but hadn't gained weight around the middle. I had on my light-blue Little League T-shirt, with Sunken Gardens on the front and 69 for my number on the back. My father had insisted that I get that number, and that I would thank him one day.

"Hell, yes. Do I need to bring anything? I mean, is this one of those meetings where parents need to bring food? I know how to make potato salad. I can make potato salad and cole slaw, you know."

"She just asked me to ask if you'd show up. That's all she said, I swear."

My father looked out at what I understood to be another wasteland. Empty beer cans were scattered in front of us, and the remains of a haphazard bonfire someone had made right in the middle of a path. "Maybe I should call her up and ask if she needs anything."

Although I didn't understand the depth of my father's obsession, I said, "Ms. Suber won't be in town until that night. We have a substitute on Monday, 'cause she has to go to a funeral somewhere."

My father drank from his beer. He handed the can over and told me to take little sips at first. I said, "Mom wouldn't want you to give me beer."

He nodded. "Mom wouldn't want you to do a lot of things, just like she didn't want me to do a lot of things. But she's not here, is she? Your momma's spending all her time praying that she never gets laryngitis, while the rest of us hope she does."

• • •

I DIDN'T KNOW THAT my father had been taking Fridays off in order to see the school secretary, feign needing to leave me a bag lunch, and then stand looking through the vertical window of my classroom door while I expounded on the rarity of a letter sweater once worn by General Custer, or whatever. When the PTA meeting came around, I went with my father, though no other students attended. Pretty much it was only parents, teachers, and a couple of the lunch ladies who had volunteered to serve a punch of ginger ale and grape juice. My father entered Ms. Suber's classroom and approached her as if she were a newspaper boy he'd forgotten to pay. He said, "I thought you'd eventually send a letter home asking for a conference. I thought you'd finally buckle under." To me he said, "Go look at the goldfish, Mendal. You've always liked aquariums. Maybe I'll get you one."

I looked at the corner of the room. My classmates' parents were sitting at tiny desks, their knees bobbing like the shells of surfaced turtles. My third-grade teacher said, "I know you think this is cute, but it's not. I don't know why you think you can recourt me however many years later after what you did to me back then."

My father pushed me in the direction of the aquarium. Ms. Suber waved and smiled at Glenn Flack's parents, who were walking in. I said, "Can I go sit in the car?"

Ms. Suber said, "You stay right here, Mendal."

"I might not have been able to go to college like you did, Lola, but I've done good for myself," my father said. I thought one thing only: *Lola?*

"I know you have, Lee. I know you've done well. And let me be the first to say how proud I am of you, and how I'm sorry if I hurt you, and that I've seen you looking in the window when Mendal does his bogus show-and-tells." She pointed at the window in the door. Mr. and Mrs. Anderson walked in. "I need to start this thing up."

My father said to me, "If you want to go sit in the car, go ahead." He handed me the keys, leaned down, and said, "There's a beer in the glove compartment, son."

Let me say that this was South Carolina in 1968. Although my memory's not perfect, I think that at the time, neither drinking nor driving was against the law for minors, nor was smoking cigarettes before the age of twelve. Five years later I would drive my mini-bike to the Sunken Gardens, meet one of the black boys twirling trays out in the parking lot, order my eight-pack of Miller ponies, and have it delivered to me without conscience or threat of law.

I pretended to go into the parking lot but circled around to the outside of Ms. Suber's classroom. I stood beneath one of the six jalousies, crouched, and listened. Ms. Suber welcomed the parents and said that it was an exciting year. She said something about how all of us would have to take a national test later on to see how we compared with the rest of the nation. She said something about a school play.

Ms. Suber warned parents of a looming head-lice epidemic. She paced back and forth and asked everyone to introduce himself or herself. Someone asked if the school would ever sponsor another cake-and-pie sale in order to buy new recorders. My father said he'd be glad to have a potato-salad-and-cole-slaw sale. I didn't hear the teacher's answer. From where I crouched I could only look up at the sky and notice how some starts twinkled madly while others shone hard and fast like mica afire.

BY THE TIME I reached high school, my mother had moved from Nashville to New Orleans and then from New Orleans to Las Vegas. She never made it as a country singer or a blues singer, but she seemed to thrive as a hostess of sorts. As I crouched there beneath a window jutting out above boxwoods, I thought of my mother and imagined what she might be doing at the moment my father was experiencing his first PTA meeting. Was she crooning to conventioneers? Was she sitting in a back room worrying over panty hose? That's what I thought, I swear to God. Everyone in Ms. Suber's classroom seemed to be talking with cookies in their mouths. I heard my father laugh hard twice —once when Ms. Suber said she knew that her students saw her as a witch, and another time when she said she knew that her students went home complaining that she didn't spank exactly the way their parents spanked.

Again, this was in the middle of the Vietnam War. Spanking made for good soldiers.

My third-grade teacher said that she didn't have anything else to say, and told her students' parents to feel free to call her up should they have questions concerning grades, expectations, or field trips. She said she appreciated anyone who wanted to help chaperon kids or work after school in a tutoring capacity. I stood up and watched my friends' parents leave single file, my father last in line.

Fifteen minutes after I'd gotten back in the car, five

minutes after everyone else had driven out of the parking lot, I climbed out the passenger side and crept back to Ms. Suber's window. I expected my father to have Lola Suber in a headlock, or backed up against the Famous Christians of the World corkboard display. I didn't foresee their having moved desks against the walls in order to make a better dance floor.

My father held my third-grade teacher in a way I'd seen him hold a woman only once before: one Fourth of July he had danced with my mother in the backyard while the neighbors shot bottle rockets straight up. My mother had placed her head on his shoulder and smiled, her eyes raised to the sky. Lola Suber didn't look upward. She didn't smile either. My father seemed to be humming, or talking low. I couldn't hear exactly what went on, but years later he confessed that he had set forth everything he meant to say and do, everything he hoped she taught the other students and me when it came to matters of passion.

I did hear Lola Suber remind him that they had broken up because she had decided to have a serious and exclusive relationship with Jesus Christ.

There amid the boxwoods I hunkered down and thought only about the troubles I might have during future show-and-tells. I stood back up, saw them dancing, and returned to the car. I would let my father open the glove compartment later.

Fossils

It's probably not true that the entire morning-newspaper delivery fleet was made up of KKK members driving country roads in the triangular desolation between Columbia, Greenville, and Augusta in 1970. This was a year filled with nonlocal newswire articles involving desegregation on the front pages daily. We might've learned of school district superintendents who resigned under the pressure, and of biracial committees being formed at every school in South Carolina. And then there were the human interest stories— usually hidden between pot roast coupons and obituaries— about small farm communities where everything went as planned, where blacks and whites worked together all their lives anyway and their children saw no reason not to sit side by side in a linoleum-floored room with mysterious letters of the alphabet strung as crown molding.

We found out later. Each morning the newspaper either came smudged mercilessly with what my father surmised to be a stamp pad, or there were entire items cut out with scissors. On a good integration-in-the-news day about the only things that my father could read clearly were baseball box scores, debutante and death announcements.

A rational man would've gotten in his car—fouled newspapers atop the passenger seat—driven to the newspaper offices in Greenville, and asked some questions. Any sane man might've asked to see one of the newspapers intact, seen that every missing article dealt with desegregation, then deduced that a rogue and bigoted deliverer visited our mailbox each morning between the hours of two and five.

This was before any kind of three-strikes-you're-out mind-set hit the nation. So my father—maybe the only man in town in favor of integration—responded in the only way he knew how. He awoke me at midnight.

"I've got clothes laid out for you. Go ahead and put on this old watch cap of mine."

It was a Sunday night/Monday morning, the last day of August, hot, and I had school in eight hours. As a matter of fact—this was the beginning of the second week of seventh grade—I had to give an oral report about the role and responsibilities of a city's public defender, oddly enough. I sat straight up and said, "Did the firecrackers go off?" My father'd rigged the walls with packs of Black Cats as a sort of poor man's smoke-alarm system.

"We have to get going. We have what's called in many circles a 'window of opportunity.' I'll explain it in the car."

If anyone ever wrote a biography of my family, this

chapter would be titled "Stealing from the Poor and Putting Them in Danger of Fatal Retribution from a Bigot." I got out of bed and said, "Does this have to do with Mom?"

My father turned on the light. "You're going to be in charge of the flyers." That response made me think that, indeed, we were off to find her, even though this was long before any of those HAVE YOU SEEN ME? posters, milk cartons, or weekly cards stuck inside mailboxes deluged us all.

My father had gone to the trouble, somehow, to figure out exactly where our newspaper deliverer—a man named Mr. Dorn—began his nightly route. Halfway through the night I realized that we had to stay one step ahead of Dorn, and that's why we didn't begin at our own house, work backwards, and chance intersecting with a man who probably wore a pointed white hat. On the way out toward Grendel Mill Village I said, "A public defender takes the cases he's given, no matter what. He doesn't get the kind of money a regular lawyer does."

My father drove with his right wrist draped across the steering wheel. "Listen, if we get stopped by anyone, I'll do the talking. You stay quiet. If they ask, say we're sticking these flyers in mailboxes to advertise an auction."

There were flyers between us on the bench seat, but they weren't queries as to my mother's whereabouts. They were handwritten advertisements for an all-out estate auction at what ended up being Mr. Dorn's residence far away on the other end of Deadfall Road.

We pulled up to the first house on the route and I opened the mailbox door. I said, "There's an envelope in here, Dad."

His head jerked up and down, then sideways in a shudder that I'd only seen when he tried to rewire our cement block house the summer before. "Take it out, and put the flyer in, Compton."

As it ended up, Mr. Dorn had three hundred–plus people on his route. More than half of them had envelopes in their mailboxes, filled with either $3.05 or $9.10. It was their monthly or three-month payment for daily delivery. My father had me put the envelopes in our glove compartment. Somehow my father knew that people trusted one another, and that they shoved their dues in their mailboxes at the end of each month. We collected and collected, and advertised Mr. Dorn's upcoming phantom estate sale.

Back home my father said, "I guess I should let you in on what we just did and why. And what we'll do later."

I said, "A public defender must find a way to assume that his client is innocent. Sometimes it's a she, but more often than not a person who needs a public defender is male."

My father opened a beer. I wanted one, too. I wanted my father to call school to say that I had an allergy attack or something, that I wouldn't be able to make it.

"Old man Dorn's part of the Ku Klux Klan. You remember that time they came driving past our house and you and me and Mendal Dawes and his daddy threw rocks at them? Well, Dorn's one of those boys. And he's been behind us not getting the news of the world. We need the news, Compton. The one thing we need is news of the world, son. It ain't right to keep people from knowing what's going on, and that's what some people in Forty-Five are intent on doing. Do you understand?"

I said, "You're talking about Truth."

"That's right." My father finished off his beer. "I have to go help Mendal's daddy take down an old barn. I know for a fact you're going to steal a beer once I'm out of sight. So brush your teeth twice so you don't go in to school smelling of the booze."

MY FATHER BELIEVED that Dorn would go broke. Dorn would call up his clients within the week, and they would all insist that they paid up for the previous month, and then he'd plain give up, maybe after blowing up mailboxes with cherry bombs on his last delivery. My father said that a blown-up mailbox was a federal offense, and that he would lie and say how he happened to be driving around one night and saw Mr. Dorn perform such an act. Then Dorn would go to jail, where the rest of the KKK belonged.

I went to school on that first day of Stealing from the Poor with two rolls of wintergreen LifeSavers in my mouth. This particular Monday was so hot that there was some kind of blackout. We still had school, though without lights. When I gave my report about public defenders in front of class, those green sparks flew out of my mouth as wintergreen mints do, usually in closets while crunched on madly. My seventh-grade civics teacher gave me an A only because she thought I was rabid about the situation. She said, "Compton, it's obvious that you will more than likely become a public defender one day. Are you interested in the rights of citizens?"

Later on this teacher—her name was Miss Johnsey

—would end up having no other choice but to leave the town of Forty-Five after she wouldn't admit that America won in Vietnam. I said, "I want to be an actor," which was kind of true. I'd remembered every word of my lines in a sixth-grade production of a play written by one of the English teachers called *The World is Flat!* and planned on auditioning for every upcoming Forty-Five Little Theater extravaganza, though I couldn't sing or dance.

Miss Johnsey said, "Sometimes an actor and a lawyer aren't all that much different, but don't go tell your parents I said that."

Well, of course, I came home at three o'clock and told my father everything that Miss Johnsey said, so he said he might have to call her up and discuss the situation. Only later did I understand that he'd been looking for a woman who had the same kind of skewed views of the workforce, and that he needed the companionship of a woman who could appreciate his business acumen and knack for irony.

I said, "Did you count up the money?" like any underling might.

My father said, "I put all the envelopes up in the attic. I ain't going to open them. Though from the amounts that people wrote on the outsides, it looks like we kept old racist Dorn from upwards of five hundred dollars."

I didn't say, "We can't keep that man's money, it's not right." I didn't ask, "Are we going to use that money to start up a defense fund for people who need rightful representation?" either. I said, "I wouldn't mind a new bicycle. A ten-speed. There's nobody in Forty-Five with a ten-speed."

My father put his arm around my shoulder. He walked me into the den, and I noticed that he'd spent the day re-arranging furniture and taking down pictures that included my mother in them. He had his stack of clipped or smudged newspapers out on the coffee table. "We can't take people's money, Compton. We'll know when Dorn quits when our paper stops. Now you go on to bed and get some sleep. Some people don't remember the last day of the month."

I know now that this will sound like I was a freak as a beginning teenager, but I'd gotten a book out of the Forty-Five public library called *Plays of the World,* and went back to my room as if to sleep like my dad said. Instead of crawl-ing underneath the sheet, though, I stood in front of a full-length mirror my mother had placed there right before she left us. I stared at myself for a couple of minutes, then re-cited a long, long monologue from *Endgame.* The charac-ter's name was Ham. I'm not proud to say that I saw myself starring in that role later on in life, maybe in Asheville or Charleston.

FOR THE NEXT WEEK my father and I drove around various newspaper routes. I continued to place auction ad-vertisements, then take whatever envelopes stood upright against the side of each mailbox. We strayed from Mr. Dorn's territory. As my father suspected, the other deliver-ers carried a flame, so to speak, for the KKK. Every once in a while there would be a note from a customer saying how he or she kept getting cut-out and/or smudged papers. My father smoked and whistled and drank beer more often as these nights went by. About every ten miles he got out of the car and peed in a pothole. "I read an article that didn't get cut out of the paper about how researchers say there's tar showing up in smokers' urine. I'm just doing my civic duty," he said. "If they ever come up with some statistics saying how water lacks barley, I'll stop on bridges."

I made it to school half-buzzed and sleepy each morning, and learned more than I ever needed to know about city treasurers, mayors pro tem, city managers, school boards, and police chiefs. Libby Belcher's oral report concerned the role of prosecutors—the complete opposite of my study—and how only prosecutors could keep a town like Forty-Five from turning into a regular Sodom and Gomorrah. The whole time she spoke she stared at me, and I almost raised my hand during question-and-answer time to ask what she thought about all of us not getting to know what went on outside our poor town limits. I didn't. I thought, What is my father going to do with all this money? Will he buy up land only to build a park where black and white children can play harmoniously? Will he make me drive around with him at night in order to refund what money we captured?

Libby Belcher pointed at me and said, "I believe that Compton has a question. What do you have to say, Compton?" She was maybe the prettiest and most stupid girl in seventh grade. It didn't amaze me later when she held fundraisers in her home for the Republican party.

Miss Johnsey said, "Compton?"

I said, "I didn't raise my hand."

"I bet you have a question about prosecutorial devices, though." That's what she said. Later on she would use that word during Spelling Bee.

Man, I could only think about how maybe everyone knew about my father's late-night excursions. It wasn't different from being the only non-Christian in Forty-Five—which at the time I thought I was—being asked what church we attended, and how I had to make up some non-church in North Carolina.

I said, "No, ma'am."

Libby Belcher pointed at me as if I'd stolen food from her lunch sack. "Compton Lane is going around sticking things in people's mailboxes at night, Miss Johnsey. My daddy told me so."

I felt my face redden. Miss Johnsey said, "What kinds of things, Libby?"

"Him and his daddy are going around trying to trick people into believing something. And they don't even go to church."

Libby Belcher's father and my daddy were friends. Libby Belcher's father didn't allow his family to go to church either, though I didn't know it at the time. I only knew that my father and Mr. Belcher met at a place called Godfrey's Market for sausage biscuits, usually before most men and women had their first pot of coffee brewing. Years later, as I started college miles away—when there was an energy crunch—they bought mopeds and cruised around Forty-Five getting eighty miles to a gallon or whatever.

I said, "You're nuts, Libby. I never get up before dawn,

just like any good actor won't." I never thought that my fa-ther told anyone, good friend or not, about what we did to keep the Mr. Dorns from our world.

"I just know," Libby said, curling a smile. "My father don't lie none."

Something might've occurred presently between Libby and me and Miss Johnsey, but the black kids who were forced to integrate—and were unhappy with the way they were still treated at a formerly all-white junior high school—stood up in unison and spit on all of us. One boy named R. C. Threatt pulled a chain from his pants and swung it around like a short lasso. Somebody else yelled out, "It's nie-thuddy, it's nie-thuddy!" because they'd all agreed to rebel at 9:30.

Miss Johnsey just stood there, though later on people would say she stuck a black-power fist in the air. The black kids left the school en masse, and the rest of us sat there.

I kind of missed it all. I wondered how Libby Belcher knew what I did at night. I wondered if she knew how I liked her sitting behind and to the right of me in class, how I could feign dropping a pencil in order to look up her dress.

The secretary came over the intercom and yelled out, "Back to class! Everybody go back to class!" like that.

I almost yelled out, "Yeah, I don't go to church ever, so what?" but didn't.

THE AUCTION FLYERS ended up almost killing a man named Mauney. Mr. Dorn wasn't an uncurious man and, upon seeing the first flyer that I'd put in a mailbox, stopped to turn his inside dome light on. He read where there was going to be an estate sale at his own house on September 13. My father, as he explained to me later, only wanted the guy to be bothered, that he wanted people showing up nonstop, knocking on Mr. Dorn's door, asking, "When does the auction start?" and so on. He didn't think about Dorn figuring out the practical joke, then waiting with a shotgun for the first visitor. My father didn't understand how Dorn might have been bred to understand cause and effect a little better than most people.

The ambush certainly hit the newspapers, even though my father had to go out and buy one from the stand on another Monday morning. I came home from school to find my father surrounded by all of the unopened envelopes we'd filched. I should mention that there were mason jars of pennies, too, and that there was a way to understand people who were angry at their newspapers' conditions and those who really couldn't afford three bucks a month in the first place. Those people who needed to pay in change had a slew of wheat pennies.

I said, "Are we going out tonight to put all the money back from where we found it?" We'd kept detailed notes as to who paid how much and the date they paid. I'd kept this information in my civics notebook from the first night, when I thought that my father had only taken me out to look for Mom and I would have time to rehearse my thin notes concerning municipal defenses.

My father pointed to the day's news, in what was the

second section of the paper. MAN SHOT FOR MISTAKING AUCTION, read the headlines. "I might've made a mistake."

I said, "As long as Libby Belcher and her father don't see this, we'll be fine." I hadn't brought up how Libby accused me of what information her father told her via my own father. "From what I can figure out, you might be an accessory, though."

My father walked around the room like any sitcom father might. He paced. He didn't make eye contact. He said, "Goddamn, goddamn."

"Where's Mr. Dorn? Does it say?" I picked up the paper and read how Dorn shot Mr. Mauney, how Mauney's wife sat in the car, how she drove off and called the police, and how a deputy arrived within a half hour to find Mauney "barely unconscious." That's the quote from the paper. I said, "We got what we wanted, Dad."

That ended up not being true. My father had what I later termed "Rube Goldberg Syndrome," and he saw things working out a totally different way: He wanted Dorn to complain to his customers. Then his customers would complain to a district manager. The district manager would meet with all of his carriers and ask them point blank if they noticed papers being smudged or cut up. The newspaper deliverers would either act dumb or confess, but in the end they would see that the jig was up and they could go back to work in cotton mills like their parents did.

Or: Dorn would keep it all to himself, blow up mailboxes like previously mentioned, my father would lie to the police, word would get out why Dorn went to jail, and every scared newspaper deliverer would quit cutting up papers, et cetera.

Or: Dorn would see it as a sign from God that someone accidentally put his address down for an estate sale, that he would use the opportunity to actually sell off whatever near-valuables he kept stored inside, make enough money to quit his job, and everyone would finally learn about the problems and/or successes of desegregation in South Carolina.

"We're going to have to get this money to that Mauney fellow so he can pay his bills," my father said. "Start rolling pennies."

I didn't say anything about how I'd already gone through the jars and extracted each wheat penny, hoping that they'd appreciate enough to get me a couple college textbooks later.

ALTHOUGH I'D EARNED that A on my report about public defenders, I almost felt it necessary to ask Miss Johnsey if I could redo it. My father and I visited the jail to see Mr. Dorn, and I picked up some things I'd never known. Our own public defender happened to be there. The first thing he did was call Dorn "Dunn." Then he went on to explain how he had never defended anyone who was up on assault-and-battery-with-intent-to-kill charges. He closed his briefcase—just like someone on *Perry Mason*—looked at my father, nodded, and left.

We stood there in a common area. I'm not sure why I went along, outside of the fact that I was partly to blame.

My father said, "Mr. Dorn, we were on your route and just wanted to come see how you were doing."

"You always paid on time," he said. "I appreciate that." He wore coveralls with the sleeves rolled up. He sported two tattoos: a Confederate flag on one forearm, and a Confederate flag being held by a corpse's hand on the other.

"This is my son, Compton."

I said, "Hey."

"Stay on the right side of the law, boy. Don't end up in a place like this. Hell, don't answer your door when someone comes a-knocking." Dorn wore enough Vitalis to keep a shotput afloat.

"You know, I was kind of wondering, though, how come our newspapers kept coming all sliced and diced up every morning there for a couple weeks," my father said. He half-circled his neck like a boxer between rounds.

"I don't know nothing about that," Mr. Dorn said. He shifted his glance over toward another prisoner sitting at a foldout table, just like the ones we had in the Forty-Five Junior High cafeteria.

"Word on the street is how you and yours delivering the morning news all had a thing against blacks. Word is, y'all did your best to keep people like my boy from understanding how the world's changing."

It smelled like a gymnasium in there, only stronger. Later on, whenever I hung around my friends who needed heavy-duty chemical-balancing medications, I would think back to Mr. Dorn in jail. The place was stark. Again, this was September of 1970. There were no barbell stations, televisions, library stacks, or computer terminals placed around the room in accordance with feng shui.

Dorn said, "I didn't ask you to come here."

"Maybe you don't recognize me without the hood," my father said. I looked up at him as if he'd stolen from a Salvation Army drop box.

I remember this clearly: Dorn's forehead spanned out, his ears flattened, and he said, "You're a brother?"

And then my father punched him in the nose twice, the jaw once, and only pulled back because he broke his own thumb. Guards moseyed over and pulled my father off. I kind of ran out but yelled, "Stop it, stop it," in the same way I did on the night my mother packed her Rambler and left, more than likely with Mendal Dawes's mother.

I didn't understand at the time how lucky we were to live in South Carolina, that if we lived in California or Vermont my father would've been arrested, stood trial, and gotten convicted of beating an innocent-until-proven-guilty man. My father got escorted out of the county jail by two guards, each grasping an elbow. Me, I sidled along behind them at a distance and then got a free hand-carved electric chair done by one of the inmates who took woodworking classes.

At the local hospital my father got a cast put on his hand, past the wrist. I sat in the waiting room later so he could go visit Mr. Mauney. When he returned he convinced me that Mauney was okay, that we'd done nothing wrong, and that Mauney took it as a sign of God because the woman in the car wasn't really his wife; the flyer had been put in the woman's mailbox. She ran an antiques store outside of town, and he'd been pretending to care about mission furniture when really he only cared about the missionary position.

I found all this out some years later. My father came back down with his hand in a cast and said, "Man's got insurance."

THAT NIGHT I AWOKE at midnight out of habit. I listened for my father and waited for him to take me out to do whatever he needed. We'd taken these trips in the past, too. We drove around looking for taillights more than anything else, for teenagers parking. My father would go tell Mendal Dawes's father about these spots and convince him that where kids parked made for good investments later, that any kind of store built on that spot ten or twenty years in the future brought in people out of nostalgia. And my father insisted on taking down the heart-pine outbuildings. He didn't ask for a finder's fee, only that he could unbuild what he saw as useful wood later.

I waited fifteen minutes beneath my one sheet, then wondered if he was okay. The doctor'd given him pain pills. I tiptoed to what used to be a guest bedroom, where he now slept, and of course didn't find him there.

I walked to the den. All of the envelopes and rolled pennies were gone. He'd left no note. The Buick wasn't parked beneath our carport. I turned on the television to watch the last ten minutes of Johnny Carson. He had on a black comedian who said, "I met a woman the other day in the grocery store who asked me if I knew the difference between a ripe peach and an unripe peach. I said, 'Yeah, in places like Georgia or South Carolina it's about the age of sixteen. Unless they're white. Then it's never.' "

I didn't get it. The station went off the air soon thereafter. I stared at the test screen for about an hour and wondered where my father would be on his route to return people's money.

I stayed awake. I read the dictionary. I pulled out the T-U-V section of our encyclopedia. When I heard a siren off in the distance I worried that my father might be slumped over his steering wheel, drunk and on painkillers, against someone's mailbox over in Grendel Mill Village. I read a fascinating passage about a crablike sea creature called a trilobite that lived some half a billion years earlier in the Paleozoic time. It was an invertebrate, and most species were only an inch long, but some got up to two feet in length. At the time there were more trilobites than any other animals on the planet.

My father returned at dawn and just sat in the carport. I went out, opened the passenger-side door, and got in like any puppy wanting to nipple up. My father held a beer between his legs, and it was apparent that he'd been crying. I said, "Did you take people's money back?"

He said, "I've been with Mr. Belcher. I've been talking to old Belcher." He ripped at his cast with his left hand. "There's a war going on, you know. I don't want you having to go to a war. I was lucky to've been of age between Korea and now. I didn't have to serve. Seeing as your mother might not come back, and seeing as we might end up all goofed up what with people like Dorn wanting to start a race riot, what do you think about Canada?"

Was my father going to save these poor people's subscriptions so we could take off for Montreal? Were we going to slink away like the cowards that we sometimes read about on page 2A? I said, "They speak French up there, Dad."

"Here." He handed me the beer. Later on I would both admire and curse him for my alcoholism: I became a distance runner who needed carbo-loading, then a drunk who didn't.

I said, "The trilobite had long feelers."

My father shook his head. He nodded as if he, too, had read the encyclopedia late at night. I wasn't sure what he said next—I think it had to do with people in the area not being human beings—because he pressed his palm on the horn until I imagined an indentation staying there forever.

This Itches, Y'all

As a child I starred in what I considered the lead role of an educational television-produced documentary on head lice. To this day I can remember my entire monologue: "This itches, y'all." The man playing my father was a veterinarian by profession, but he had several community playhouse credits down at the Aiken Little Theatre. My mom in this affair was a Charleston ex-debutante who might've made it on Broadway had she not developed a loss of feeling in her left foot, which caused her to gimp around, slapping her sole down sporadically. Later on she starred in a documentary involving cockroaches and silverfish, from what I understand. The doctor was a regular pediatrician, or so he said. This was 1970. The entire nation transformed itself. At the time, though, no one talked about anything else outside of the head-lice epidemic that infiltrated our South Carolina schools.

"I don't know why we can't say that there's a direct

reason why these lices showed up on our white children's heads at the same time our schools took in the others," my TV mom said during a break. I sat in makeup; a woman took a red Magic Marker and plowed long furrows on my scalp. She parted my towhead six or eight times sharply, then pulled the felt tip backwards, exactly opposite of how a boy-scout den leader might teach.

I thought, This itches, y'all.

The regular pediatrician—who got a number of lines involving the history of bloodsucking, parasitic arthropods—rolled up and funneled his script. "I don't know how to tell you this, but it's true. Black people don't serve as hosts to the head louse. A louse is white. It needs to camouflage itself. So they don't go to black scalps. I don't know anything about people in between, like Arabs or the Chinese, but this is a white man's problem here in the South, lady." He tapped the top of his head.

I thought, This *itches,* y'all. *This* itches, y'all. This itches, *y'all.* "There's a black girl named Shirley in my class who showed me the bottom of her feet and the palms of her hands. They're white," I said. I kind of liked her. I kind of thought of her as my girlfriend, really, unless she had head lice on those places.

The guy running the little operation said, "That's enough. Okay. Do we have the kid ready? Let's get this thing done. It's not brain surgery. Hell, it ain't even manual labor."

I'd gotten the part because I raised my hand when Mrs. Waymer asked who knew the difference between ticks and tics. She wrote it out on the board, and asked what each one meant. I knew both. My father owned what would be later on known as Tourette's Syndrome. So I raised my hand and explained it all. Mrs. Waymer never said anything like, "Who wants to be considered for a head lice documentary that might be aired over ETV?" or "Who wants to be considered for a movie that might be shown in ninth grade across the state when we teach everyone about sexual intercourse, too?" She only said, "Bennie Frewer wins."

I signed a document, my parents got all excited and signed another document, and the next thing I knew I sat in a room in our state capital, along with a dozen other no-experience actors, ranging from fourth to eighth graders. This was a Saturday morning. Everyone else considered had black hair. They gave us our lines, and I have to admit that almost everyone, except for this boy from Due West with a slight speech impediment, got out, "This itches, y'all" perfectly.

They introduced us to the ex-debutante, who at the time I thought was a hundred years old, seeing as she was at least forty, and they brought out the veterinarian who would be my father. They shook hands with each of us and acted as if we should've asked for autographs. Maybe they'd starred in other state-supported documentaries, outside of their community work in *Guys and Dolls, Oklahoma, The Sound of Music,* I don't know.

The pediatrician playing the doctor came out and pointed at me. "It has to be this boy," he said. At the moment I thought he'd accused me of being the only person available who had a strong chance of having hosted head lice at one time in his life. He looked at me with his head bowed down somewhat, as if he knew I'd later on tell people I grew up so poor that I could only afford ringworms for pets.

My parents drove around Columbia, South Carolina, looking for a warehouse that sold condiments at wholesale prices. My father wanted to get some different barbecue sauce, mayonnaise, and mustard. As he dropped me off he said, "When we come fucking back and you fucking win that head fucking lice part I want to fucking have a fucking big fuck party for all the fucking neighbors, fuck." To this day I can't watch a good Hollywood mafia movie without thinking how my daddy missed his own special roles in life.

I walked into the soundroom. I left my competitors in their sad queue. A couple of them cried when they didn't get the head-lice part; more of them said, "I didn't want it anyway," all crybaby.

I didn't skip my way inside, or point and ha-ha-ha. I shrugged my shoulders and followed the real doctor. I said, "This itches, y'all," that's it.

After my head got liced up realistically I sat in a barber's chair. This story line wasn't even close—somehow it went that I showed up for a haircut with both my parents, a barber saw the head lice, and a doctor happened to be hanging around waiting for his own haircut. Another little theater actor played the barber, a man who taught drama at a college down in Greenwood that eventually should've lost its accreditation. I caught this fake barber guy kissing my documentary father in the wings soon after the shoot, but that's another story.

I'M NOT ONE of those people whose facial features change drastically twice or more in a lifetime. I'm not one of those people who looked one way before puberty, another directly after sprouting hairs and changing voices, then another, say, at ages twenty-one, thirty, and so on. If I lived to be 150 and my classmates did so too, I could go to a high school reunion and look exactly like I did in the yearbook. So the entire time I lived in my hometown of picayune Forty-Five I had people come up to me—my age and older, then way younger as the years went by—and ask about my scalp. They said things like, "You done good getting them lices off," or "Hey, I know you—you the man with what clamps down finally toward the skull bone."

I'm talking that I dealt with these pallet-heads who couldn't understand the difference between movie characters and real life for the rest of my days in Forty-Five. I'd be willing to bet that anybody in my graduating class who ever saw *Night of the Living Dead* or whatever thought that zombies traversed our planet. If one of them ever saw *Forrest Gump* he probably tried to sue the movie company for telling his own life story.

So, needless to say, I didn't get any dates throughout my high school years, seeing as—I'll give my hometown people this—the notion of a willing suspension of disbelief worked too well. Every girl I ever encountered who'd seen the documentary thought that certainly I had head lice as a child and probably would harbor crabs as an adult.

Sometimes I wished that educational television had cast me in a movie concerning aliens, rich kids, dapper horse breeders, and so on. I often wished that I took part in a documentary about voodoo children and the spells they're able to cast. Only now can I understand how I wish my parents would've seen what happened to other real child actors, how their lives turned into horrendous escapades involving drugs, crime, violence, bouts of depression, and severe second-guessing about forsaking public education for the set of a show that revolved around dissimilar characters stuck under one roof.

I had no choice but to study hard, score well on standardized tests, and leave the entire state for college. I took off from my parents and didn't think about what small biannual residual check came their way when my head-lice documentary got shown on ETC-sponsored distance learning channels across the junior highs of South Carolina.

Don't think that I don't know how there's not been a whole lot of dialogue in my story up to this point: most people tell a story and there are all kinds of antagonists— or at least one good one—and they have to have some kind of talk in order to build up what scholars might call "rising action" or "conflict" or whatever it is that scholars talk about. Understand how this is how alone I had been, from the lice documentary on up until I started anew out of state. I went to school, I sat two desks from everyone else, sometimes my almost-friends Mendal Dawes and Compton Lane made eye contact with me, and then I came home. I grew up hearing only, "Ben Frewer's got head lice" from people I spent the day with, and "Fucking fuck-fuck" from my father, and "We're having Hungarian goulash," from my mother. People always talk about dreaming in black and white or color. Me, my dreams never included sound, except when tiny insects closed in on my ear canals to say, "We're having Hungarian goulash for supper tonight, you fuck-fuck-fucking Frewer with head lice," I promise.

IT DOESN'T TAKE a psychologist to understand how I went off to college in Minnesota, far from the South, in order to take a major in anthropology and minor in P.E. Baby, I wanted to understand from which gene pool I hailed, and I wanted to build tri- and biceps so large that should I ever run into a school chum in an airport it wouldn't take much to beat the shit out of him or her. I'd've gone to college in Canada had my high school counselor not told me that there was no university system up there. Anyway, I met and married a woman named Gabrielle who—though self-conscious and unsure of herself—might've understood the stigmas I endured as a child should I have ever told her. It's Gabrielle I blame for the second half of my life.

"I think it'd be rude if you didn't show up to your high school reunion, Bennie," she said the morning after I'd gotten an invitation from Libby Belcher! Who said it'd be major fun! And that we'd have a big old dance! To music we loved in the seventies! "I mean, Christ, they've probably had one every five years and you haven't been to any of them."

I had taken my degrees in anthropology and physical education and put them to good use over a twenty-five-year span. I refinished furniture in Colonial Williamsburg, and some days worked as a town crier when the regular guy—a man with a master's degree in anger management—had to take off work. Gabrielle wrote little skits about frontier life or whatever when she didn't don the costume of a bread-baking woman, waiting for tour groups to watch her shove loaves in a wood-burning oven.

"I have no interest in what my old classmates have done in life, because I already know," I said. "That sounds conceited, I'm aware of that, but it's true. A couple of them maybe ventured off as far away as Clemson to get an education, then scurried back home to take over the one law firm, or the Mr. Quik Fried Chicken, or the bank, or the army-navy store. A couple actually got out of there like I did, and I know they won't be going to any reunion. The boys married the only girls they'd ever had sex with, and the girls never evolved into the kind of women who second-guess their boring lives to the point where they drink alone in the afternoon and down Valium at will. The best a young woman can do in town is marry a dentist. It's sad."

We sat in a house we built ourselves on some land we purchased through luck after one of Gabrielle's skits got bought up by the people who run summer productions near Plymouth Rock, the Lost Colony, and the Cherokee Indian reservation, among other places. She'd found a formula so that John Smith could become Francis Drake could become Chief Skyuka, and so on. She tried to make the skit fit Brigham Young's life, but that never worked out.

Gabrielle took off her apron and bonnet. "It sounds like a good town to bring up children in. You turned out all right. Go back to Forty-Five with a notebook and do some research, Bennie. Go there and figure out why your hometown has turned into an island in and of itself, you know."

My parents had moved to Florida when the local county council banned cursing in public, during my junior year in college. The sentence for anyone blurting out, say, "fucking fuck-fuck," was either thirty days in jail or eight hours picking up trash alongside the railroad track that split Main Street in half. My mother wrote me a letter saying that she and Dad would be leaving in the middle of the night for Tampa, seeing as he had amassed either a year-and-a-half jail time or eighteen straight days with a nail-stick in his hand. My mother wrote to say that all of this had occurred in a two-hour period of time when she and my father had gone to an indoor movie that finally opened in town, had sat in front of a woman who owned the Debs and Brides shop and who kept calling out to everybody how she planned to order "this dress" or "that coat" for the next season. The movie was *Star* fucking *Wars,* and my father couldn't take it.

I reached over Gabrielle to pick up a Swiss Army knife in order to scrape beneath my fingernails the homemade stain I concocted out of plug tobacco and alcohol. Sometimes I used rusted nails and rainwater. I said to Gabrielle, "You know, you might have a point. Maybe I need to go in order to bury some deep-seated animosities or whatever."

"I never wanted to say anything about it, but you do yell in your sleep at night more often than not, and I'm sure it's because you have some wounds that need closure."

I took my knife and scraped a dry patch of skin beneath my wristwatch. "This itches," I said.

This itches, *y'all,* I thought.

NOT THAT I HAVE any advanced degrees in anything, but I would bet that there's something wrong—and telling—about an entire town of adults who still have first names ending in *–y, -i,* or *–ie.* No one of voting age should still call himself Tommy, Jimmy, Wendy, Windy, Windi, Wendi, Wendie, Windie, Jillie, Sammy, Freddie, Bobby, Johnny, or Libby, especially if they've developed stretch marks or been the contributing factor in them. Billy the Kid's all right, but the rest don't work.

Understand that Gabrielle only called me Bennie, I was sure, because that's how I introduced myself back at a freshman get-to-know-you party between a foosball table and Flipper pinball machine in the student center. To everyone else I was plain Ben, the furniture refinisher.

My wife and I took some personal days off in June in order to attend the Forty-Five! High! School! Class of 1977! Reunion! held—get this—at the National Guard Armory. We walked up the walkway between a row of Civil War cannons, and from maybe fifty yards away could hear one of those disco bands singing loudly about roller coasters of love.

Gabrielle, under oath, will attest to the fact that once we stepped through the doors a coagulation of people parted, stepped back, and stared. Wendy Teed said, "I'll be doggone. Bennie Frewer." She seemed surprised at her own voice, as if she'd not spoken with a cheerleader's fervor since seventh grade or thereabouts. "We didn't think you'd show up."

I said, "Wendy. This is my wife, Gabrielle."

Let me make it clear that Gabrielle came from a gene pool unknown to my people—my wife had Scandinavian blood, mixed with one of those other Germanic tribes. She stood tall and lean and naturally blonde, her hair not puffed up as if some kind of nuclear explosion had taken place on her forehead. Gabrielle had not emerged from a cotton mill–owning family who intermingled only with another cotton mill–owning family, or doffers who only married doffers. Her coat of arms showed something other than a cotton boll, a shotgun, and a car engine hung from a tree limb.

Wendy Teed said, "Well. We heard that Bennie got married, but we didn't realize. We just didn't realize. Do you go by Gabby most of the time?"

My wife laughed and laughed. She hit my arm. "Never."

I looked at the Jimmys and Bobbys, the Kennys and Donnies, took my wife's hand, and said, "Y'all got any fucking booze here or fucking-fuck what?"

I led Gabrielle through streamers hung from the armory's I-beamed rafters. We walked toward a wall of blown-up yearbook photographs, of various Jennys, Timmys, and Kathis, all of whom were in attendance, all of whom either played football or waved flags and/or pom-pons.

I noticed not one African-American person in attendance, though our high school must've been split fifty-fifty percentage-wise between blacks and whites. I led my wife toward the bar, thinking about the only people who ever spoke to me back then: Cheryl Puckett, Jacquelyn Sanders, Robert Perlotte, R. C. Threatt, Willie Goode, and Shirley Ebo. I turned and said, "Where are our black comrades, anyway?"

One of the Larrys from the group following at a safe distance behind said, "They have they own reunion, Bubba." Then he asked who'd like to go out in the parking lot and have a foot race.

I looked at my wife and said, "Did you hear that? 'They have their own reunion.' Just like before segregation. I told you. I told you that time's stopped here. I told you that this poor place ain't changed whatsoever."

My wife looked over her right shoulder, away from me. A group of my old classmates started dancing to a Bee Gees song. "At least he called you Bubba. He didn't call you Bubby, or Bubbie, or Bubbi." She didn't need to point out how she meant different spellings.

I looked at the bartender and said, "Bourbon, bourbon, bourbon."

MY WIFE AND I sat alone at a table for four. We sat in the corner of the Forty-Five National Armory, amid pictures of my old classmates sporadically placed between photographs of World War II generals, tanks, and antiaircraft machinery. My ex-nonfriends danced and danced; they formed lines and kicked their legs outward, is what I'm saying. I thought about my blacksmith friend, Amos, back in Williamsburg—he once worked for the Pentagon—and how he'd missed his chance in the mid-seventies to work as a drummer for any disco band that toured America. Gabrielle finally said, "We can leave, if you want," maybe an hour into the situation.

"I want you to see the finale," I said, even though I wasn't sure what would happen.

Libby Belcher got up on the makeshift stage and pointed for the disc jockey to cut it down. "Now, like we've done every year, we're going to give out awards. Our panelists are the 1977 class of senior cheerleaders!" The judges let out a war cry. "Okay. Most Successful again, is Mikey Self! Y'all know him because he runs the Mikey Self Pharmacy!"

Mikey Self stood up and waved. He didn't approach Libby, seeing as there wasn't a trophy, plaque, or certificate for him to pick up.

Libby Belcher went on through Most Changed, Best Preserved, Most Hair Lost, Most Children, Longest Married— which had a forty-seven-way tie, seeing as everyone got married the first weekend out of high school—forever.

I cringed every time she opened her mouth. She said, "Our Traveled the Furthest Award would've gone to Bennie Frewer, who came all the way from Williamsburg up in—" she stopped, and her face let us know that she didn't know the state "—a long way away. But Johnny Russell says he left home and flew around the world to come back. So, for traveling something like a couple hundred thousand miles —the award goes to Johnny Russell!" who lived next door to the armory.

Johnny Russell's father always ran the drive-in movie

theater, right next to his TV and stereo shop, and Johnny
went off to study mechanical engineering for about a year
before returning home and taking over his dad's business.
I hated the little shit from third grade onward, even before
my lice documentary. Johnny Russell had the IQ of an
empty box of popcorn, and made — I imagined — six figures
a year.

"That's not right," my wife said.

"I told you. But that's not the least of it, I bet. You keep
watching, baby doll."

Wendy Teed got up on the stage and listed out Most
Dogs, Most Cats, Most Spectacular Vacation, Best Dressed,
Most Likely to Succeed Late in Life, Best Turnaround,
whatever. Then she said, "Our final category for Most Famous won't be a surprise to anyone who's been in attendance over the last four reunions." I turned around to see
who might've found a cure for cancer or developed a better
penny wrapper. "Well, it might be a surprise to the boy
who'll get the award for the first time in person."

And then this old film clip came on behind Wendy Teed,
of me saying, "This itches, y'all," seated there on a barber's
chair. Gabrielle said, "How did you not win the Least
Changed award? You look the very same then as now."

I said, "I told you. I told you. These people have something against me still, I swear. You saw it."

I didn't imagine a hush over the crowd; my wife later
said that there was that "eerie silence" usually associated
with meteorologists or scholars talking about a writer's response to anything involving symbolism. I whispered over
to Gabrielle, "What's going on?"

She said, "They didn't sit apart from you because they thought you had *lice,* idiot. They thought you were a movie star. They revered you, you hammerhead."

Wendy Teed, I realized later, paused a few times before introducing me. Finally she pointed my way from the podium and said, "I can't believe that Bennie Frewer's here, can y'all?"

There wasn't a spotlight or anything, but the way she pointed my way let me know that I should stick my arm up in the air. I did for a moment, then I brought it down on my scalp and reflexively scratched at the crown of my head.

When Gabrielle and I were asked to lead the next dance—which happened to be "Free Bird"—I could only wonder if I'd made up everything throughout my life regarding these people. I thought, Could it be that I might've been laid every day of my life back then should I have wanted to? Was I just another snot-nosed one-shot child actor?

I dipped my wife during the first guitar solo, naturally.

People clapped and encircled us, but I swear to God by the next song everyone was doing some kind of made-up dance wherein they scratched their scalps as if rubbing flint for spark.

My wife and I moved further south by the end of the summer. We drove from Virginia to Atlanta where I got a job restoring furniture for a number of antebellum plantations within a hundred-mile radius, all of which were on some kind of tour that people could take if they had a couple days to spare. Gabrielle and I drove to North

Carolina, then took a sharp right at the South Carolina border, followed it until we hit Tennessee, then drove down from Chattanooga. I vowed to never pass through my home state again, much less Forty-Five.

"I still think you're overreacting," Gabrielle said when we crossed into Georgia. "It was a coincidence, that dance that they did. And Wendy didn't pause as much as you think. Who were they going to give Most Famous to—the guy who got acquitted for stealing a truckload of carbon paper?"

I said, "Look. Forget about it. It's a new life we're starting. You know, that old guy who wrote Uncle Remus stories was from somewhere in Georgia. You might could take up storytelling, like you used to do. In between writing plays or whatever."

Gabrielle pulled her legs beneath her in the passenger seat. "I'm thinking about going over to CNN and seeing if I could get anything there."

Because we sold our large, open house and acreage in Virginia, we had enough money to either buy a small town house in the city or a twelve-hundred-square-foot house an hour away, next door to a primitive artist named R. A. Miller who made a living selling tin cutouts with "Blow Oskar" printed on the top.

We stayed in the city, and I traveled against rush hour traffic each morning, on my way out to places like LaGrange, Winder, and Jefferson. I stripped down southern dining-room tables only when necessary and spent most of my time finding ways to support legs invisibly.

It wasn't a week into our new lives when Gabrielle announced, "I didn't get the job at CNN, but I got one with Channel Forty-five. It's one of the public-access stations. Something just clicked, and the guy said I had the perfect face and voice to do human interest stories. And public service announcements."

I said, "No more free bread?" and kissed my wife. I could tell immediately that we would never again argue, that maybe we'd have a child in these, our later years, and that I might be able to bury whatever demons I may or may not have conjured up myself.

When the Atlanta area became infested with cooties some month later, Gabrielle was the first on the scene, interviewing elementary-school nurses, nursing home directors, and everyone in between. Me, I picked up head lice for real from a house where Jefferson Davis once slept, all the way over in Athens.

If I'd've known the politics and procedures of public-access stations, how their clips get bought up from bigger stations and so on, I wouldn't have sat down with my wife and her cameraman to talk about how I might've taken a nap on a mattress where Jeff Davis slept, that I didn't know of another place where I could have come in contact with the parasites. I had pet a horse that was from the same bloodline as Davis's horse, but that seemed improbable.

Gabrielle said, "Cut the camera, Gary. Hey, honey, what about you show everyone how to use a nit comb? The station will pick up the tab. I can go into an in-depth report about how to wash clothes and whatnot."

Gabrielle had never liked playing the bread-baking woman back in Colonial Williamsburg, I knew. I said, "Because I love you, and because you finally made it to where you want to be, I'll do it. How many people watch Channel Forty-five anyway, like the six people who don't have cable?"

My wife and her cameraman took close-up shots of me scraping away tiny eggs above our bathroom sink. They showed me stripping our bed and sticking sheets into the washing machine. Gabrielle thought it might be fun if I said, "This itches, y'all," right into the camera.

When my mother called a couple weeks later she said something about how she got all confused, that she didn't know if the nightly news on NBC somehow enhanced my early, early performance in grade school in a way to only make me *look* bigger. Gabrielle's coworkers, of course, took her out that night in celebration of one of the networks picking up her human interest story. Me, I sat at home knowing that I'd never enter another mansion, never be hired to mask any scratches a demilune, drop-leaf, or gate-leg table might suffer through accidental contact. I knew that I would get a telephone call later from my hometown, either to take away my award or give me another.

When Children Count

The only thing Madame Tammy said that may have been overheard went something like, "Oh, hell, it doesn't matter—I'll take paper." She stood in line at a regular check-out aisle in a Winn-Dixie halfway between Charlotte and Atlanta. Fifty customers stood in the 10 Items or Less line. Tammy only bought a roll of paper towels, some finger-nail polish remover, Jewish rye, and pimento cheese, even though she stood between two women with full carts. She held a twenty-dollar bill. It was noon, and Tammy had just read a hundred palms at the Monday/Thursday Chesnee flea market near the North Carolina border, in peach and apple country.

"You sound exactly like my dead sister," this woman said, pushing her full cart into Tammy's backside. "I ain't never heard nothing like that. Say this: 'I will never, ever or-der a club sandwich here with bacon again, what with the ptomaine.' Say it. Say."

Tammy turned around and smiled. She still wore the black turban, the black smock, the golden spangles and half-moons. She stood six feet tall, and raised one eyebrow for emphasis. The woman behind her kept putting groceries on the belt: white bread, frozen dinner rolls, a slew of Vienna sausages, potted meat, Spam, diapers for both kids and adults. "Club sandwich ptomaine," Tammy said.

"Well I'll be damned," the woman said. "It's as if my sister spoke from the grave." The cashier gave Tammy her change. "It's the last thing I ever heard her say. She ate a bad sandwich over at this little place best known for its barbecue, she made herself known how she felt about the food, and then she died later on that afternoon."

The cashier said, "Do you want one of the game pieces in order to see if you can win a million dollars instantly, or save them up for weekly bargains?"

Madame Tammy said, "I don't believe in playing games at the store. I don't like getting my hopes up." She stepped forward and took her one sack.

The woman behind Tammy held out her hand for the little perforated cardboard square. "Listen, I'll pay you to let my little niece call you up and say something. If you'll just talk to her a little bit. She keeps wanting to call up her momma in heaven and all, and me and my husband—we got custody now—we don't know how to handle it. We don't know how to handle it. We just don't know. We don't. It's hard explaining some things." Tammy turned around and nodded, although she just wanted out of there.

The cashier looked back and forth between them. She

slid items across the scanner. Between blips she said, "My mother died when I was twelve. I'd just about forgotten what she sounded like until one day the TV was on and this lady was doing a commercial for getting your credit fixed. It sounded just like my momma. I hope to hell that woman doing commercials don't make it in Hollywood, seeing as I couldn't take hearing that voice oncet a week or nothing. It was just a local commercial, though."

A two-for-a-dollar frozen pizza didn't connect. The cashier kept running a flat box of sausage-topping over the eye. "Well," Tammy said. "I'm not around much. And my brother's coming to stay with me awhile. What would I say?"

The woman said to the cashier, "They're two for a dollar. Just ring the goddamn thing in! It's written on a big orange thing there. Just ring it in."

"Store policy," said the cashier. She had braces, and some boy's high school ring on her index finger. Tammy thought she didn't look more than twelve at the time, and remembered how she felt when her own father left some three decades earlier.

The pizza clicked finally. Tammy said, "Sure. Tell your niece to call me up." She reached in her pocketbook and pulled out a business card. It had an eyeball on an open palm. "Since I'm not there most of the time you might tell your niece that the pay phone's pretty busy up in Heaven, in case she can't get through."

The woman said, "Her name's Edwina, but we call her Eddie. She's a special child. We call her Special Eddie. Listen. You ain't got an answering machine, do you? That might confuse her—why her momma won't pick up and all. Hey, do this if you don't mind: change your message. I'll pay you and all."

Tammy nodded. She didn't ask the woman how they would get together for payments, and so on. "I'll do what I can do. And I can do, I promise." She didn't go into details about how she searched every day for her own father at flea markets across America.

MADAME TAMMY DIDN'T want a roommate, wayward brother or not. She had enough problems, and a list of needs longer than a desert turtle's lifeline. She had to buy rubber-soled boots, seeing as a man selling stolen rebar at the table next to her got hit by lightning last Wednesday down at the Pickens County Flea Market. She needed to hire a new gofer—the school year had started and she no longer had a fifteen-year-old to depend on—to scour the various markets she worked, in search of old men selling used golf balls. Madame Tammy needed to take the only snapshot she owned of her father, Shorty, and get it touched up by one of those photographers who filled in cracks, tears, and fades. Over the years she had felt certain that her father didn't do stunt work in Hollywood like he wrote in those couple letters thirty years earlier; although she wasn't a true psychic she felt certain he still dove into dark, still, nighttime water hazards, retrieved duffers' errant approach shots, and cleaned them up for resale more than likely.

Madame Tammy needed complete silence at night so she could sit in a chair and replenish herself with hope. Her father could've died from cancer, stroke, or heart attack by now.

"I don't have room for anyone, Lamar," she told her brother. "I live in a little place. I'm hardly here, too. Hell, I live in the back of my van more often than not." Right away Tammy thought about how most people might've said, "If you're hardly there, then you'll hardly notice me." It wasn't that she felt embarrassed about her living conditions between flea markets—she owned a vertical, three-story, fifteen-hundred-square-foot house on top of Tryon Peak, never the South Carolina/North Carolina border. Some days she referred to the house as the Tower. After particularly fruitful flea-market days she called it the Steeple, and on bad days the Finger.

Lamar used a phone card to call her. He was already in Opelika, trying to stay off Interstate 85, on his way. He said, "This thing only lasts ten minutes. Look, I just need a few days—a week at most."

Madame Tammy wasn't embarrassed about working flea markets, either. She knew that most people—especially wives—thought she said things like, "For twenty dollars I can tell you that you'll get your next blow job in five minutes." In reality, perhaps it was better than her real modus operandi, namely finding answers about family, commitment, and medical history, among other things. Madame Tammy heard adults walk past her table at various southeastern markets, not able to whisper, "Whore," or "Nutcase," or "Gypsy."

"If you come up here for a week then you better bring

something to sell," Tammy told Lamar. "I'm not going to put up with another free-loading man who wants to spend time in my Tower while I work my tail off holding fat, callused hands in the heat and humidity. All the while I tell goners they got a happy long life ahead of them."

Lamar said, "We haven't seen each other since you moved up there for good, Sis."

Tammy looked out her front window. In the winter, sometimes, she swore she saw the Atlantic Ocean, some four hundred miles away. "Why aren't you teaching? Shouldn't school be starting down there by now? I lost my boy who used to look around for me."

The mechanical operator came on and said, "You have one minute."

Lamar said, "Parents in Montgomery, Alabama, don't have much sense of humor. There aren't any students left in all of America who understand sarcasm or irony, either."

The telephone beeped a series. Tammy said, "Well come on, then. If I'm not here, then I'll leave a note where you can get me. The door'll be unlocked."

She heard no answer from Lamar, realized that she'd spoken to dead air, and hung up. Tammy waited ten minutes for the phone to ring—long enough for Lamar to go buy another phone card from Opelika, Alabama—it didn't, and she went out the door. She carried two pictures with her that needed refurbishing. One photo showed her mother and father together, in front of a DeSoto. Her mother wore a regular cotton dress with some kind of pattern on it. Her father wore suspenders and had his hair slicked back in a way that heightened the receding hairline.

The other photograph was a black-and-white close-up of her father's palm, and the scar that ran from the meat of his thumb to between his index and middle fingers. Initially it was supposed to be used as evidence in some court case involving an inferior and spastic spinning frame in the Forty-Five Cotton Mill where Shorty worked, later as some kind of documentation for workman's comp. Tammy's father left town before he could find a lawyer to help him out. He left after shooting a wealthy man in the groin, at a public golf course, probably on purpose.

The details didn't matter. Tammy and her brother got out of Forty-Five. After college, and after two misguided husbands, Tammy decided to find her father, and not because of every other human being on one of the afternoon talk shows. She would know him by his scars, only. She read a book on the finer points of palmistry, and rented five-dollar flea market tables soon thereafter. When a desperate client had a malformed series of lines, Tammy made up only good news, smiled, and told the person he or she had nothing to worry about whatsoever.

She had made up good news for her brother, too, when he took a job teaching tenth-grade geometry in Montgomery. And though she didn't truly believe in her own fake psychic abilities, Madame Tammy knew she would have to lie to Lamar again. Then there would be the problem of offering the truth, too.

• • •

"Seems to me Jesus of Nazareth could've done better than turning water into wine. Seems He could've done something a little more spectacular, for a miracle. Rock into wine, maybe. Poison ivy into wine. Hell, why didn't He turn Satan into wine?—all your people say that booze is the devil's doing in the first place." These are the words that got Madame Tammy's brother, Lamar, fired from teaching tenth-grade geometry in Alabama.

"I don't understand why you'd bring religion up in a math class," Tammy said to her brother. He'd not had time to even bring in his couple suitcases or the boxes in the back of his car. Lamar didn't arrive until three days after calling from northern Alabama. Because he could't think of anything else, he spent nights diving into country club golf course water hazards and collecting golf balls to have something to sell at the flea markets next to his sister.

"Beats me, too," Lamar said. "I'll tell you this: the parents didn't understand, obviously, and down there no one thinks to ever have a respectable hearing, trial, or closed-door conference. I said that shit about Jesus on a Friday afternoon, and the principal and district superintendent came to oversee me pack up my classroom on Saturday morning."

"Like father, like son, as they say."

Lamar reached in his pocket and pulled out a hip flask. "You can do better than that, Tam," he said. "All that god-damn comparative-lit education you got, you can come up with something better than a cliché." He laughed, took a swig, and handed the flask over.

Tammy shook her head no. "Okay. Where the salmon spawn and die, there the next generation spawn and die. Whatever. Listen, you can either sleep on this couch, or on the floor, or in the hammock outside. You can stay a month. Then you have to go back home. That's the law around here. I read it somewhere. No one can stay with his or her grown sibling for more than a month."

Lamar said, "I didn't come to get lectured. And I have enough money to move, once I get my retirement. They'll hold it somewhere between thirty and ninety days. I don't have to wait until I'm sixty-five or anything like in some of the backwards, unrelenting, selfish states. I don't want to be a burden. I just needed to get out. I'll tell you later."

Madame Tammy said, "I hope this doesn't have anything to do with one of your students, Lamar."

"I thought you were some kind of psychic. Shouldn't you know?" He drank from the flask. "I'm only kidding. It's Fermat's last theorem. Some pinhead figured it out, so there's no more reason to live in mathematics, as far as I'm concerned. Computers, too—there's no need to stand in front of a chalkboard. Some people think the universe is governed by mathematics and whatnot. When I said all that stuff about Jesus in class, it was my way of being mathematical. Just like when I talked about the closest distance between two points, I was being religious. Fuck it."

Lamar brought up his clothes. He took his sister down the mountain to eat at a family-operated pool hall/bar/pizza joint called Shots and Slices. Right after Tammy beat him in their first game of nine-ball Lamar said, "I guess living up here kind of insulates you from undergoing another bad marriage."

Tammy said, "I like these people. It's also a central point for flea markets between mid-Florida and northern Virginia. I made a big mistake going out to New Mexico one time, lost my mind, and came back. Don't give me shit, especially after all you've done."

Lamar reracked the balls while Tammy went to order a large, odd pizza—anchovies and pineapple. Lamar looked at the walls, pictures of people standing in front of wooden tables, everything from milk glass to measuring devices in front of them. When Tammy came back he said, "I know it's your business and all, but instead of reading palms why don't you take some notes and write some kind of scholarly work about it. Why don't you write something with an anthropological slant? I bet it'd sell. I don't know. Give it some kind of racy title. Call it *Hand Jobs in America* or something."

Tammy broke, and the nine ball swerved into a side pocket. "You owe everyone in here a drink. That's the house rules. Listen, I only want to find our daddy one last time. It's not so much that I feel unwhole because he left us early on. I can't explain it."

"What'll you do if you find him?"

"Shoot him twice," Tammy said. "I'll have a scotch and Dr Pepper. Don't make fun of me or I'll tell you the truth about your love line."

• • •

TAMMY'S LOCAL FRIEND Fagen placed two quarters on the table. He said, "Are y'all'ses playing for fun or money or both or neither?" Fagen wore a coonskin hat without the tail. He kept a knife attached to his belt.

Tammy said, "Hey, there, Clarence Fagen. How you doing today?" She slipped up on the pool table and let her legs dangle.

Fagen smiled halfway. "Same old same old. Man's got to do what a man's got to do. Can't complain."

Tammy pointed at Lamar and said, "This here's my brother the mathematician. Or the ex-mathematician. He ain't quite same as us. To him, six hours equals six hours."

Lamar didn't know what that meant. He stuck out his hand to Fagen and said, "I'm Lamar. Good to meet you."

Fagen said, "Fagen." He nodded. "Say. If you're a mathematician then I guess you know that one-hundred-to-one odds is pretty good. I'll bet you a thousand dollars to your ten that you'll have to pee before I do. You think on it." Fagen turned to Madame Tammy and said, "Any luck with your daddy's hand, finding it?"

Lamar didn't like his sister's choice of lifestyle, friends, or secrecy. Tammy said, "Don't bet him, Lamar. Fagen wears a drainage bag and pees down his leg all the time into the thing. He acts like he never has to pee."

Lamar thought this: x times y equals xy. He thought, 3.14159265, but could go no further.

Fagen said, "Damn," and took his two quarters off the table. "If you going to be that way, then I don't want to play no more."

"Fagen sells pelts," Tammy said to Lamar. "He sells pelts and keeps an eye out for his daughter. She'd be about what, now, Fagen—eighteen?"

"Eighteen going on nineteen. Unless she's exactly like her momma. Then she'd be eighteen going on either three or sixty-five, depending on her mood."

"Fagen's wife took off with their daughter ten years ago. The mother had a thing for fur coats, and Fagen here figures, like mother, like daughter. He thinks he'll eventually find her wanting to buy ten or twelve rabbit skins to sew together into something."

Lamar said, "Huh." He rolled the cue ball down to the other end of the table, but not hard enough for it to return. A song came out of the jukebox that sounded like the soundtrack to a foreign wedding—Italian, Jewish, or Greek —which caused a couple boys to pull out their quarters and get the thing back to country music.

Fagen's eyes rolled back somewhat. Lamar figured the guy was pissing into his bag. "The last thing I heard my wife say was that she wanted to find a man who could set her down on a mink couch, drive her around in a car with sheepskin seats."

Lamar said, "Logic's a tricky thing, but I think you're going about it right. My own dad had a love for selling golf balls at the flea market, and I imagine that Tammy here will find him doing the same one day. It makes sense that you'll find either your ex-wife or daughter looking for cheap fur. Shit, I remember when I was a kid, my father would take me out at midnight and we'd dive into golf course lakes. I'd scoop out balls with my forearms, and then later on he'd clean them up in Clorox. Then we'd set up a table at the local flea market on Saturday mornings with some kind of dirty sign, something like 'Look at These Scarless Balls,' or 'Our Balls Still Have Bounce.' It wasn't the best time in my life, but I guess it made me who I am today. Tammy didn't have to put up with all that back then."

Fagen drank his beer. He placed the bottle down on a fold-out wooden chair. "The sign said 'Our Used Balls Still Have Dimples.' I been knowing your sister now six years. She told me. If I was you, I'd get over it. Seems to me your sister has more bruises than you do about your daddy taking off. You want to help her out, take some balls to the tables and sell them a dollar a dozen. Sooner or later your daddy'll come up to buy you out so's he ain't got competition."

"Come on now, Fagen," Tammy said. "We're out having fun." She racked the balls for a regular game of eight-ball.

Lamar said, "I'm not judging anybody, man."

Fagen said, "You right. I'm sorry." He turned around to select a cue stick. The back of his belt was one of that kind with a name branded into it. His said LEONARD.

Lamar chalked his cue and raised his eyebrows to Tammy. "I started a tab up there. If you want another scotch and Dr Pepper just go put one on it."

Fagen turned around and looked down his stick for warp. He said, "What do you think the chances are that someone could break, and then all the balls came right back to where they once were? I'm talking, what are the chances that a man could knock hell out of the balls, have them scatter and ricochet all over the table, then land right back where they were racked, in the same order?"

Lamar said, "Not very good."

Fagen said, "I didn't think so." He broke. The two ball went in. Fagen said, "I guess it wasn't meant for me to do it a third time."

"WHEN WE'RE NOT sitting behind flea market tables looking everybody in the face—or in your sister's case, on the hand—then we're at bars. When we're not in bars, we're at diners—Waffle Houses, Huddle Houses, American Waffles. When we're not eating or drinking, we're watching afternoon shows on TV. The people we're looking for don't go to movie theaters; they go to drive-ins. They don't go down to Atlanta to watch the Braves play; they sit in the front rows of professional wrestling." Fagen kept looking at the side pocket.

Lamar said, "Hey, how come you got 'Leonard' written on the back of your belt?"

"When we're not in bars, diners, drive-ins, or wrestling matches, we tend to drive up and down roads looking for people with car trouble. And I'm not talking about the interstates. The people we're looking for always take back roads, secondary roads. You ever looked at a Rand McNally and seen those little vacant lines where roads are going to be? That's where my daughter is now. That's where your father is. I'd almost bet that your father is with my daughter. I ought to kill you right now, just for mentioning it."

Fagen shot. The cue ball bounced around and knocked in the seven. He hadn't called anything beforehand. "Bought it cheap from a man down on his luck," Fagen said. "Didn't buy it from a man named Leonard, though. Bought it from a man named Eugene. Eugene got it from a man named Horace. Horace got it from Leonard in some kind of bar fight, I don't know. Horace had a lot of belts he sold to Eugene. He had one that said 'Cassius Clay.' Eugene promised that Horace used to be a real contender, in a way."

Lamar thought, Maurice Frechet came up with the idea of metric space in the year 1906. He thought, The tree roots of mathematics are algebra, plane geometry, trig, analytic geometry, and irrational numbers. The capital of Alabama is Montgomery. "I bet that might be worth something. Cassius Clay. I'll be damned."

Tammy came back with a round for everyone. She said, "Y'all didn't wait for me? We could've played cutthroat, the three of us."

With his eyes Lamar said, We are.

"I met a man one time said he fought Rocky Graziano. Not Rocky Marciano. Graziano. Said he fought him when Graziano was finished, after he'd quit fighting professional. They got in some kind of altercation in a bar, like men do. This old boy had a scar on his face shaped like an arrowhead. I believed him. Graziano had a way to twist his boxing glove twice on the skin before anyone knew what hit. He was one of them people who could pull out your heart while it still beat, I bet." Fagen shot hard into the far bank, hitting nothing. "Take over, Tammy. A couple boys just come in thinking they got good kidneys." He handed her his cue.

Fagen stared down Lamar, then winked. Lamar noticed the arrowhead-shaped scar beneath Fagen's left eye. "Is everyone in the flea market business a scam artist? This is like a foreign film. Goddamn, I feel like subtitles might be lined up at the bottom of my frame," Lamar said.

"Your food's ready, Tammy," someone yelled out from the other room.

Tammy placed her stick on the table. She looked at her watch. "We better take this to-go. It's late. We have to get up at four to get good tables next to each other down in Pickens."

Lamar said, "That's no problem. Sometimes I wake up at three and find myself going over square roots."

Lamar slept on the floor. When the telephone rang an hour into his sleep—when there was a pause before some child asked him if he was God—he said, "What's with you people? Tell your mother to find a reason to live, out-side bothering me at all hours of the day and night." He couldn't fathom how they followed his trail all the way from Montgomery.

The child said, "This is Eddie. I'm calling my momma." Lamar sat up and reached for his cigarettes. "This is Eddie. Aunt JoJo said Momma lived here. Are you Jesus?"

Lamar stood up. He said, "This isn't funny anymore, kid," and hung up.

. . .

TAMMY TOOK A bottle of vodka down from the shelf and poured it into three flasks. She shook a half-gallon of orange juice, then poured it into a Coleman camping thermos.

She stretched her fingers back and forth.

Lamar rolled over on the floor, five feet away from the refrigerator. "I had the worst dream of my life. I must've woke up every five minutes. I know where our father is. He's in a telephone booth somewhere fucking with us. That's what I dreamt."

Tammy said, "We need to leave in about twenty minutes. If you want to sell golf balls you might want to take a shower. If you want to mill around with people, don't bother. It's going to be hot today."

"Somebody called up last night and messed with me. You can find anybody's movements on the Internet these days. They found me. All my parents down in Montgomery found me. They called and kept asking if I was God or Jesus. You don't have some kind of weird one-nine-hundred number do you? You don't have some kind of sex number where you talk dirty to women and say you're God, do you?"

Tammy put down the Thermos. "Fuck. Fuck, fuck, fuck. I forgot." Lamar did two sit-ups and got up. "I met this woman at the store." She went to the phone and hit star sixty-nine.

Tammy memorized the number, called back, and got an answering machine. It was four o'clock in the morning. Aunt JoJo's voice said, "Way to go. You better plain find

Special Eddie's momma so she can leave a message for her little girl."

Tammy felt her face redden. She waited after the beep, then said, "Hey, honey. It's been hectic up here. This is Mommy. I'm sorry that I missed your call. Please call me back between five and six o'clock tonight. I'll be here." Tammy spoke as if she tried to lure a stray dog toward her. She looked at Lamar. He shrugged, then took one of the flasks and drank straight from it. "Sometimes the devil is able to tap into our phone lines here, and that's what happened last night. But don't worry about me, and remember that I love you."

Lamar said, "It's okay to drink at the flea market? I don't remember Dad ever drinking behind the table."

"That's the difference between a man who believes in nothing and a man who still has hope, Lamar. Goddamn you, play along with some things every once in a while. The one thing you have to learn at the market is that you have to play along with people."

"What'd I do? What the hell, was that Fagen that called last night?"

"This isn't a good start to the day. I might know that I'm a fake, but I do believe in omens, voodoo, curses, karma, haints, specters, next-lifes, and that what-goes-around-comes-around theory. God's going to come down on me for what you've done, Lamar. I bet you a dollar not one person wants a palm read today."

Lamar put the flask in his hip pocket. "Listen. If you multiply two negatives you get a positive. That's all I have to say. When something goes wrong in life, I just try to find another negative. Then everything's back to normal." He bounced his head up and down like some kind of sideways metronome.

Madame Tammy reached down, squeezed his testicles, and said, "This is what our daddy used to do to me back when I wasn't but six years old. It's okay, understand. I'm not mad about it. I just want you to know."

Lamar placed his rolled fist back down. "Well. I guess that's the kind of negative you can't double." When Tammy showered he hit redial on the phone, got plain Eddie's aunt JoJo's answering machine, and said, "This is Saint Peter. I'm the gatekeeper guy. You can see your mother in person at the flea market this morning. I'm in charge of letting people in or out, and your mom's going to be out."

LAMAR DIDN'T THINK to steal egg cartons from behind Bi-Lo, Winn-Dixie, Food Lion, or Harris Teeter so he could display his unwashed balls to the public. The eight-by-four-foot tables at the Pickens County flea market weren't made up of anything but one-by-four pine strips, with an inch between the boards. Lamar set his balls down in rows and hoped the wind didn't blow them away.

"You don't know me," Tammy said. She shone her flashlight in his face. "No matter what happens, we don't know each other. If I yell out for help, don't come over the boundary, Lamar." She drug her pointy shoe on the red clay.

Tammy kept a fake crystal ball and real tarot cards on her table. Lamar only had his balls. They were across from

Fagen with his pelts, and a guy named Weigel who seemed to specialize in alligator heads and turtle shells. Weigel kept saying, "Snappa, snappa, snappa, snappa," when people walked by shining their own flashlights on his products.

"Golf balls. Golf balls. Balls for golf," Lamar said.

Madame Tammy didn't talk.

"When it's dark, we want light. When it's light, we want cloud coverage," Fagen said. "When the woman comes by wanting table rent we wish we were invisible."

Lamar laughed. He pointed at Fagen and said, "Listen to this one—the summit angles of a Saccheri quadrilateral are equal. Dig: the line joining the midpoints of the equal sides of a Saccheri quadrilateral is perpendicular to the line joining the midpoints of the base and summit."

Fagen held one rabbit pelt in midair before setting it down on his table. "You talk like that to regular people, boy, you won't sell your balls."

Tammy didn't hold her hands together as if in prayer or anything, but she kept her head down and seemed to concentrate. She said, "Lamar, you've turned into an idiot. Please don't tell me that you're an idiot."

Weigel said, "There's a difference between a crocodile and an alligator. I've seen gators. I go down to Florida and kill me alligators every winter. I don't go to Africa for crocodiles. There's where crocodiles live. In Africa. They got different noses and teeth. They're different."

Fagen walked away from his table and said, "This is Tammy's brother. You ain't got to sell him. He knows you ain't ever wrestled a real alligator."

The sun barely labored itself upwards on the horizon. "Twelve balls, one dollar!" Lamar yelled. He'd been to flea markets over the years and knew the going rate was usually four-for-a-dollar, at best. Already people walked the tables, mostly antique dealers looking for cheap yellowware, or stolen service-station signs. Lamar said to everyone who came by, "If you see another guy selling golf balls, tell him I'll sell my entire stock for twenty bucks." It seemed the quickest way to lure his father.

Tammy looked up at the fading stars. Fagen said, "Don't sell off all your stock at once, Lamar. If you do that, you'll just end up sitting in front of an empty table. If you leave, then some asshole wanting to get rid of his pit-bull puppies will show up, and no one can sell with pit bulls in the vicinity, I swear."

Lamar handed Fagen the flask. "Oh, I got more balls in the van. I'm just saying that. I got it under control."

Madame Tammy said, "I'm undergoing a vision wherein you need to go find another job teaching math, far, far away. I'm having a vision that there are geometry-deprived students in Alaska, Lamar."

BY EIGHT O'CLOCK—not two hours into daylight —no other golf ball dealer had taken Lamar's bait. He'd sold a few dozen balls to regular customers, though, and after the woman came by wanting the five dollars for table rent Lamar stood only two dollars in the hole. He didn't respond to Weigel or Fagen when they remarked how it was probably a good thing that he got out of education. Tammy sat in her fold-out metal chair and watched the crowd. When this full-time flea market wheeler-dealer came up to her and said, "I got a proposition—you tell people that their lives will turn around if and only if they go buy a yardstick, slide rule, or micrometer from me, then I'll give you ten percent of the profit," Tammy shook her head no.

"I don't believe in measurements. Measurements cause wars, ultimately. I won't have anything to do with that. To be honest, I've gotten caught up in this game before and it just didn't work out."

Lamar looked over to the man and said, "We use a base-ten method. But there are cultures that go by base three, or base sixty. Look it up. It's in the history of mathematics."

The man selling measuring devices walked away as Lamar tried to arrange his balls on the table to give a specific example. He was engrossed in showing how some cultures have a counting system that goes, "One, two, two and one, two twos, many," when plain little Eddie and her aunt JoJo walked straight up to Madame Tammy's table.

Tammy recognized the woman immediately, and pulled the gossamer veil over her face—not so much to hide herself from the kid as from Aunt JoJo. Aunt JoJo said, "Special Eddie? This woman here can conjure up your momma. She can use your momma's voice, just like in them séance movies we watch Friday nights."

Lamar looked up. Aunt JoJo's normal voice came out as if she spoke to someone a hundred yards away. Even Fagen and Weigel knew something different and decidedly odd was going on at the flea market that morning.

Tammy said, "I'm doing fine, Eddie."

The little girl looked up. Tammy figured out that Eddie wasn't more than ten years old. She wore a pair of overalls and had pigtails. Her blank, flat face pretty much worked as an advertisement for what her future held: a ninth-grade education at most, two children by the age of eighteen, a single-wide mobile home, and a husband who'd beat her whenever possible. Little Eddie said, "I done good on my spelling test, Momma." She spoke to Madame Tammy in the same way a child speaks to big walking stuffed animals at Disney World or Chuck E. Cheese.

Lamar looked up from his balls. He said, "Spelling's important, but math's best." No one looked his way.

Madame Tammy said, "Run for your life, Eddie. That's all I have to tell you. Move to another state. Stick our your thumb and hitchhike to Iowa or Wisconsin as soon as possible. Don't eat any more sausage, white bread, Vienna sausages, baloney, or bacon. Kick in the television set. Never, ever watch afternoon talk shows. And don't let anyone ever, ever take you to the flea market again."

The girl pointed at Tammy and said, "That's my mommy." She turned and looked at Aunt JoJo. Eddie said, "One, two, three, four, five, six. . . ." evenly.

Aunt JoJo lurched across Madame Tammy's table, knocked over the crystal ball, scattered the tarot cards, and grabbed for Tammy's neck. Tammy tried to hold the woman back, tried to use what yoga and tae kwon do knowledge she had to repel the attacker. Aunt JoJo spit, clawed, and yelled, "Don't you talk to your own baby that way. We're doing the best we can do, and not getting no money for it."

Lamar picked up one golf ball and threw it hard. He hit the woman in the left temple and stunned her momentarily. Fagen and Weigel rounded their respective tables and pulled the woman down to the ground. A crowd appeared and circled the area.

Fagen said, "That might run her out of business for good. When a seer can't see trouble right in front of her, she ain't doing her job."

Madame Tammy unraveled her veil. She reached out for Eddie, led her to the van, and drove away.

"I SAW EVERYTHING that happened. I got my table over there, and I saw it all. If you need some kind of witness, I'm the one. I'm Heidi." Heidi stuck out her hand to Lamar. She pointed again toward her table, filled with milk glass. "I've been waiting for something like this to happen here. I'm surprised it hasn't happened sooner."

Fagen said, "Goddamn, Heidi. When did you come back? I heard you moved to California or something. I heard you gone back to teaching college."

Aunt JoJo shook her head twice, looked around confused—kind of like a fainting goat, Lamar thought—and instead of yelling out, "Where's my baby, where's my baby?" like in any ordinary documentary, she only brushed off her pantsuit and walked away. Was she embarrassed? Did she hope that no one saw what happened? Did she think to herself, Well, that's taken care of? When she got about five tables down the row she turned and said, "I was wondering when God was going to let me know what should happen."

Lamar smiled and waved at her. He turned to Heidi and said, "I used to teach. You used to teach? Man, what happened? I was teaching only a week ago."

Heidi said, "That woman attacked that woman."

Lamar said, "No. Not that. I mean, what is it that drove you to work flea markets?"

Fagen walked back across to his table. Aunt JoJo walked out of sight. Heidi smiled and shook her head. Weigel said, "Snappa, snappa, snappa, snappa."

Lamar said, "Somebody's got to give me a ride back. My sister's left me."

Heidi said, "I don't know what happened." Then she said she could take Lamar wherever he wanted to go right after eleven o'clock. She said she'd never sold a piece of milk glass after eleven, that she'd not taken any kind of poll about it or marked down a calendar, but that's the way things worked out. "Plus, that guy selling all of the rulers and whatnot is going to start bothering me pretty soon, if I remember his ways correctly."

LAMAR HAD NO MORE bags, what with his sister gone. He didn't have his full allotment of golf balls. He stood there watching everyone, content with waiting. Lamar watched Heidi across the gravel walkway and a few tables down. He thought, I still don't believe in chance, but things aren't looking so bad.

He thought, *cos a=cos b cos c+ sin b sin c cos A* for no reason in particular. Weigel and Fagen watched him nonstop, and he felt their stares. Lamar nodded at them occasionally, and even told men who came by his table that if they were looking for a deal, they should go buy a pelt, or Davy Crockett hat, or an alligator head.

Now, in the real world Lamar and his new colleagues would've worried about Madame Tammy; they would have packed up and driven up the mountain and found a way for Tammy to either turn herself in or take plain little Special Eddie back to her aunt's house. No one would've put the incident somewhere in the back of his head, only to bring it up later inside a bar where Fagen was conning some frat boy into betting who'd pee first. In the real world this incident of mistaken mother, chance, and loud-mouthed unemployed brother would not end up in the Rolodex of flea market stories on a par with how Frank McNutt and his kid Jacob used to sell Sears Silvertone radios when Jacob crawled into them with his tiny transistor radio, et cetera.

From what everyone understood later, Madame Tammy got the girl home and simply held her for a good twenty-four hours before calling the Department of Social Services and explaining things. On different occasions Tammy would tell people that she told the little girl that there was no God whatsoever, or that God indeed took care of everyone. It's pretty much documented that she made plain Eddie repeat, "The bleak shall inherit some mirth," over and over until she got it right.

In the real world someone would've stayed with Madame

Tammy for more than a week, just to make sure she over-
came the depression that set in, the extended hours of walking back and forth in her small silent house.

Heidi packed up her milk glass in old newspaper and
packed her trunk. She almost skipped over to Lamar and
asked if he was ready to go. They left. Ten minutes later a
tiny man walked up to Fagen and said, "I heard that some
fellow this way sold golf balls cheap. He leave already?"

Fagen pointed at the empty table. "Boy had to go check
on his sister. He was selling twelve for a dollar when he was
here."

"Damn. I get me four bucks a dozen. Course mine are
clean. I scrub mine down with Clorox and all. I use me a
toothbrush. I ain't one them men sticks the cuts and scruffs
downward in the egg carton."

Fagen nodded. "Good for you. You seem like a real
moral man. You should've been here earlier. There were a
bunch of teachers who seemed to have problems. Maybe
you could've helped them out. You could've been named
Mayor of Flea Market."

The man looked at Lamar's empty table again. He said,
"I used to be a stuntman out in Hollywood. I've fallen off
ten-story buildings, and been drug by wild horses."

Fagen smiled. He asked the man if he drank beer much,
if he'd like to see a stunt Fagen could do with his bladder.
The man said he couldn't. He said that he'd had to retire,
and came back south in order to track down his son and
daughter. And although Fagen knew deep down that this
man was Shorty—Madame Tammy and Lamar's father—he

didn't ask, or offer information. Like everyone else in the flea market business, Fagen knew that this man might be faking it, that he might work for some branch of the government, that he might be trying to chum up with everyone in order to make a bust.

Fagen looked at Weigel. They packed their wares simultaneously and drove away while Madame Tammy's father pulled out a ripped and faded photograph of two children.

How to Collect Fishing Lures

1
—

Move off of the family farm, go to a state university that offers a degree in textile management, get a job at a cotton mill that will eventually fail during the Reagan years, marry a woman who will go back to college later on in life then leave you for three states south, have one son named with only initials—like V.O.—and try to get him to understand the importance of moving out of the textile town, get fired so that the company no longer has to pay a pension, and spend too many days sending out résumés to other failing cotton mills that have no need for a forty-seven-year-old midlevel executive. Send your son off to college and wonder what he sees in literature, history, philosophy, art, and Eastern religions.

Try not to think about your lungs looking like kabobs of half-eaten cotton candy. Go to the unemployment office in your small South Carolina town and feel worthless, useless, lost, and emasculated. Spend time watching programs that have more to do with collectible treasures and less with world, domestic, regional, or local news. Watch infomercials into the night. Go to a bookstore where too many young people hang out without touching books, find the section of antique price guides and memorize the names, photographs, and prices of jigs, topwater plugs, spinners, spoons, minnow tubes, and frog harnesses. Decide to take a scuba-diving course that won't cost more than one (1) unemployment check. Learn to cook and eat macaroni and cheese, spaghetti, ziti, rice, and mashed potatoes. Remember the documentary you saw on carbo-loading.

Invest what extra money you don't have into a wet suit, oxygen tank, mask, and flippers. If, for some reason, you did not acquire forced shallow breathing (FSB) from the mill, invest only in goggles and snorkel.

Drive to the nearest man-made lake and walk it. Step off distances. Practice at home using a yardstick so that your steps equal thirty-six (36) inches with each pace. Take extensive notes as to where men older than you fish for largemouth bass. Make a map of the place. Point out points, coves, creek mouths, beaver dams, and where the men in boats—usually the men a level above you at the cotton mill, or their sons—drop anchor or troll.

Realize that just because an antique-price guide claims that a Clothes Pin Minnow goes for two to three hundred dollars ($200–$300) doesn't mean that anyone in Forty-Five, South Carolina, might pay that much money for it at an antique show, flea market, or yard sale. Just because someone in New York, California, or Colorado might be willing to lay down two to three thousand dollars ($2,000–$3,000) for a Flying Helgramite Type II, manufactured by the Harry Comstock Company out of Fulton, New York, in 1883 before being bought out by Pflueger Enterprise Manufacturing Company in Akron, Ohio, doesn't mean that everyone will offer only five bucks ($5) for the thing in Atlanta, Charleston, Charlotte, or Raleigh.

Go to the closest bars, roadhouses, and bait shacks and talk to every human being possible. Pretend to be interested in how they caught their biggest bass. Secretly tally who used live bait, who used rubber worms, and who used lures that you want.

By this time, too, it should become apparent that you should no longer tell friends or relatives about your latest ambitions. They will insist that you go to the local psychologist and take a battery of examinations ranging from the Minnesota Multiphasic Personality Inventory (MMPI) to the Barriers to Employment Success Inventory (BESI), with everything in between—vocational-interest tests, career-interest inventories, the John Holland Self-Directed Search, the Myers-Briggs Type Indicator, and a dexterity test that involves pegs, washers, and caps.

You've already withstood these tests one long afternoon instead of standing in line at the unemployment office.

Buy an underwater flashlight, a mesh cloth bag, and some needle-nosed pliers. Take the first dive somewhere near a cache of sunken Christmas trees. After you find your first Surface Tom, King Bee Wiggle Minnow, or Hell Diver, stick it in your bag and resurface. I don't want to make any broad generalizations or cheap jokes, but you'll be hooked. Go buy a johnboat immediately.

You'll need the boat in order to go out past dusk—using the flashlight—and drop heavy objects into the water where you know men and women fish. Cement blocks work well, as do long bent pieces of rebar, old front fenders, spools of barbed wire, and certain cement statuaries (lawn jockeys). Leave these in place for at least two months before visiting the scene. What I'm saying is, be a patient farmer—harvest, sow, reharvest. If you have searched all of the likely lost, snagged, and badly knotted fishing lure regions of a particular lake, then go to another lake, map it out, talk to locals, and so on. Allow Lake Number One (#1) to repopulate itself with the bait you will find later.

Remember: Scuba diving is not an inexpensive mode of transportation. It's better to take two or three trips down for a hundred lures than a hundred trips for a hundred lures. For those who've retained Pink Lung and chosen simple snorkeling, no one knows for sure about the Bends, really.

Now that you have a good collection of rare vintage fishing lures in various stages of wear, think about presentation. Stick them haphazardly in a shadowbox. Attach them to mesh bags similar to the one you use while on a pilgrimage. Gently stick them into the yardstick you own if that yardstick has some kind of maritime theme, viz., Shady Grady's Bait 'n' Tackle—We'll Give You Worms; or Gene's Marina—All Size Slips. Either clean the lures until they look unused and put them in a fake original box, or dirty them up more so.

There are people out there with large vacation houses who will buy the latter option. It might not be bad to purchase a few bobs, run them over with a car, then reglue them nearly together. The vacation-house people will buy anything to give themselves a sense of doing something dangerous and near-tragic when they grew up.

As did your wife three states away.

If you choose to sell off duplicates—and you will—and if a day comes when you feel a full-lunged breath release from your body for the first time since losing the job, maybe send your ex-wife a cheap Ball Bearing Spinner, plus a note saying that y'all's son is well, and that signs of panic and danger diminish with each new morning. By this time she'll know about your irrational hobby. Write, in detail, complete lies about snapping turtles, gar, water moccasins, a big sale of Wilcox Wigglers and the women who bought them.

Or get in the johnboat, turn off all lights, ride as fast as possible until you hit an exposed stump, and sink.

2
—

Set your alarm clock for 4:00 in the morning on Saturdays and Sundays if you live within a half-hour of a flea market. Otherwise set it accordingly. Make a Thermos of coffee the previous night. Sleep in your clothes if at all possible. In the winter, wear a watch cap. In warmer weather wear a sleeveless shirt and pants with at least one (1) hole in them. Either wear old Converse tennis shoes or comfortable hiking boots. Pick up the morning paper at the end of the driveway.

Be sure to have a pocketful of case quarters only.

Don't wear a goofball cap that reads I COLLECT FISHING LURES on the front. Take along a flashlight and a bag that isn't mesh or plastic. If people selling good old lures at a flea market see you coming with the hat, they'll jack the price about four (4) to ten (10) times what they originally wanted. There's been documentation. If they see a bag that they think contains lures, they'll at least double the original asking price. You have only quarters because if someone's asking, say, two dollars ($2) for a lure, automatically say, "Will you take a quarter for it?"

Let's say y'all dicker until it gets to a dollar, a fair price for a Rhodes Wooden Minnow seeing as it books between fifty ($50) and seventy-five dollars ($75). Then say you forgot to take your quarters, and pull out a twenty-dollar bill. The seller might be likely to either, (A) not sell you the lure; or (B) kill you.

Nevertheless, do not take a loaded pistol with you, especially if someone plans to tag along.

I'll explain this later. Go alone whenever possible, of course.

Now. Get to the flea market and focus on lures. Take out the flashlight—it'll still be dark when you arrive—and shine it on tables. Stray from people who sell figurines, baby clothes, pit bull puppies, rebuilt lawnmowers, action figures, fast-food restaurant toys and giveaways, Pez dispensers, yellowware, silverware, socks and underwear, baseball cards, chickens/rabbits/goats, heart pine furniture, shot glasses, phonographic equipment, Rottweiler puppies, used books, VCRs, computers, advertising yardsticks, and hippie decals.

Look for tables filled with fishing rods, cigar boxes, used tools, guns, and tackle boxes. Look for tables filled with a mixture of everything. Shine your light on wrinkled men who might be selling off their oxygen tanks, flippers, masks, snorkels, needle-nosed pliers, and whatnot, men who've given up altogether on the fishing-lure collectible craze because they didn't map out lakes, talk to old men, plot strategy, sink cement blocks, and everything else detailed in Part One (1) of "How to Collect Fishing Lures."

When you come across a table or display of everything from Gee-Wiz Frogs to Arrowhead Weedless Plugs, keep your beam on them for exactly one nanosecond (one-billionth of a second). Pretend that you have no interest in the fine Celluloid Minnow or the Jersey Expert. Look over at the AK-47 on the table, or the Zebco rod, ball-peen hammer, and socket-wrench sets. Feign disinterest, is what I'm saying. Go, "Oh, man, I ain't seen one them since I grew hair south," or something.

Say a personal mantra that the man doesn't know what he owns. Over and over in your head say, "Quarter-quarter-quarter-quarter," and so on.

Here's the worst scenario: he says, "Yeah, the T.N.T. number six-nine-hundred was real popular. It's going for upwards of seventy-five dollars on the market, but I'm only asking thirty for it."

Do not walk away. Don't nod in agreement. Don't shake your head sideways, either. Slowly direct your flashlight's beam into the man's face and, using all common sense and knowledge of the human condition, measure how desperate he is. Don't blurt out, "Will you take a quarter for it?" Maybe say, "I'll check back with you later," or "Good luck," or "It's supposed to be a nice, sunny day."

After you have picked through all the tables—if this particular flea market has indoor booths and outdoor tables you need only concern yourself with the tables—go back to your pickup truck, turn on the overhead light, and read through the Garage/Yard Sale section of the Classifieds. Circle the ones that'll be near your drive home. Also, look under Antiques and see if anyone sells a large quantity of vintage lures at rock-bottom prices, which won't be there. But you have to look, seeing as you've gotten to the point of obsession.

Drive slowly past the front yards of strangers and make educated guesses as to whether they'll have any lures. The formula is about the same as the flea market—if you see an inordinate amount of baby clothes heaped up on card tables, drive on. If you see a table saw and leaf blower, stop. Yard-sale lures run cheapest, but after factoring in gasoline and wear and tear on the pickup truck it might end up about the same as the sixty-two-and-a-half-cent (62.5¢) average you keep at the flea markets.

It's now seven-thirty or eight o'clock in the morning. Stop and get a six-pack of beer. Carry what lures you nearly stole and catalog them immediately. Write down name, price you paid, and what the particular lure books for.

Open the first can of beer. Change the truck's oil. Cut the

grass. Rearrange all of your lures in alphabetical order, followed by price, followed by oldest to latest model. Watch one of those fishing programs on the same channel that showed infomercials back when you didn't know what to do after becoming unemployed. Give your dogs a bath.

At exactly noon drive back to the flea market and find the man who wanted thirty bucks for the T.N.T. #6900. He'll be sitting on the tailgate, probably staring at the ground. Go ahead and say, "I'll give you five dollars for this lure." He'll get offended but eventually sell it, seeing as it's exactly what it cost him to rent the table. If you want, on the drive back home, tally up what you bought and what you spent— nineteen lures for seven-sixty ($7.60) and one for five bucks ($5). That comes to $12.60 for twenty vintage lures. It comes to sixty-three cents on average, I promise.

Finally, the reason why you're alone and without a pistol is because a friend, son, spouse, or significant other is always apt to walk ahead of you, find a cheap and rare lure, hold it up and yell, "Hey, here's what you've been looking for!"—which will cause the seller to jack the price times fifty. Then you'll have to shoot your passenger.

Prisoners can't keep lure collections in their cells, what with the barbed hooks. So that means more for you. As always, you want more.

3
—

There will be days when you find no lures beneath the surface of natural lakes, man-made lakes, farm ponds, or slow-moving murky rivers. No one at flea markets in a tri-state area will have any on display. A traveling antique roadshow might come through the area and nobody there will have a single common lure, much less overpriced Paw Paw Spoon Belly Wobbler Minnows, Paw Paw Spinnered Plunkers, and Paw Paw Sucker Minnows. You will wonder if your chosen field of expertise has bottomed out. You will think back to the supply-and-demand lecture you heard years earlier in college. If the drought turns into a month, you'll find yourself seeking a palm reader. On a good day she'll tell you all about how long some scientists dedicate themselves to a specific disease, virus, or birth defect without giving up hope. On bad days she'll laugh at you and say, "Fishing lures? You collect fishing lures? Good God, man, get a life —there are three million homeless people in America."

It might cross your mind that idiotic dictum that goes, "Give a man a fish and he'll eat for a day; teach him how to fish and he'll eat for a lifetime." If this occurs as a sooth-sayer tries to make sense out of the lines in your palm, remember this one: "Find yourself a lure and you got the beginning of a collection; *carve* yourself a lure and chances are some moron from New York City will think of you as a primitive artist and want to represent your work."

Okay. It is my belief that you won't find lures for extended periods of time because your body tells you that it needs a rest from either A) staying under water too long; or B) because you're about to lose your temper at a flea market and thus get shot by a seller without a sense of humor or patience. It is at these times that you need to go find an old-fashioned dollar store, a five-and-dime, a Woolworth's if they're still in operation. Buy a bag of wooden clothespins. Buy some plastic eyeballs at a hobby-and-craft shop, and eyelets. Buy red, yellow, and green enamel car-model paint and a thin, cheap brush. Go get some three-pronged trebles at the nearest three-pronged treble outlet.

Because you own a pickup truck and have been in textile management most of your life, you will have a nice folding knife. Thin the midsections of each clothespin, between the head and the two line grippers. Whittle away. Paint the things differently, so it doesn't come across as assembly-line work. Make spirals and polka dots. Paint racing stripes down the legs and think up cool names like JumpaToad, JumpaFrog, JumpaSkink, JumpaMander, JumpaCricket, JumpaHopper, JumpaMinnow, JumpaMouse, JumpaBlowfly, JumpaShiner, JumpaWobbler, and Jumpa-Wigwag-Humdinger-Smacker. Break off some of the legs of every other lure so you can add "Junior" to the title.

With your needle-nosed pliers, open up the treble hooks, insert the free end into an eyelet, close the circle back up, and screw the eyelet into the clothespin's end.

Always screw last.

It is too hard to paint the lure afterwards. To make an authentic homemade primitive lure might cost as much as a dime (10¢). You have two options: either go to the flea market and try to sell them for fifty bucks ($50) each, in hopes of selling one or two to men who also collect fishing lures and haven't been able to find any of late, or for two dollars ($2) apiece, in hopes of selling the entire lot in one sweltering summer day out on the jockey lot.

I've done both. Because you know about men and women with a pocketful of case quarters, it's easier to wait out for wealthy people traveling from elsewhere who think they've found a regular idiot-savant craftsman.

I'm not sure, but I think it's how Bill Gates and every televangelist got started.

No matter what, do not think about your life prior to collecting and selling fishing lures. Forget that your ex-wife gave up on her wrong-headed singing or acting career and is about to marry a cattle-and-citrus tycoon down in Florida. Forget that your son writes folk songs about check dams, culverts, and the silt of humanity when he's not making a hundred grand a year getting hired out as an anti-PR idea man. Don't remind yourself that the neighbors are about to start up some kind of homeowners' association and they'll write a letter about your yard presently, seeing as when you came home from flea markets as outlined in "How to Collect Fishing Lures," Part 2, you never cut the grass.

Remember the hum and drone of the spinning room, before the government lifted sanctions, tariffs, taxes, and whatnot on Southeast Asian countries. Smell the linseed oil barely solid on wooden loom-room floors, and the older doffers, weavers, and spinners who spoke of textile-league summer baseball games as reverently as they spoke of their mothers and friends without fingers.

Think about how you don't want to be remembered merely as a human being who crunched numbers and yelled at workers for not getting yarn and cotton thread perfect.

Understand that there's something magical in a fishing lure—between two-and-a-quarter (2 ¼) inches and five (5) inches long, single, double, or triple-trebled, reversible metal discs and wings, with or without bucktail, propellers, belly weights, joints, week guards, head plates, side hook hangers, and nickel finish. Revel in the mystery of how such a device could, without pheromone or promise, attract descendants of the first living creatures worth noticing.

Admire the notion of symbiosis. Think of how the lost, snagged, sunken lure needs you as much as you need the lost, snagged, sunken lure. On good days, think of yourself as a lure of some type, only half-human.

Answers

Two days after we'd both agreed that the At-Home Marriage Repair kit couldn't possibly work for us, my wife and I went back to those 100 questions. Alexis had cried in her sleep the night before, and I'd had another didactic screaming episode in the deli section of the Winn-Dixie I hadn't seen coming on — and didn't remember happening by the time our groceries were packed inside the trunk of the car.

Back at home Alexis said, "I have a funny feeling that your inner self is crying out for help. I think you're stifling yourself unintentionally by working on the Job book. You don't have that kind of patience. You weren't meant to stand in a line with a number in your hand. Maybe you should be working on an annotated bibliography of the references to someone like Dr. Faustus. I'm not reprimanding you. I'm not laying blame. It's just an observation. It's just constructive criticism."

I wasn't quite sure how Alexis even knew about Faustus. That worried me so much that I actually said, "Let's get back to the questions to figure out what's going wrong." I said, "It's just occurred to me that there might be some things about you I don't know and need to know, if you know what I mean," and did my best at crinkling my forehead, bending my face southward, nodding up and down, and looking like someone who really wanted to know.

My wife said, "Let's do it."

I said, "Let's get to the bottom of all this crying and these supposed outbursts I'm having that upset both cashiers and bag boys so."

We went back to our places in the den. We went back to where we'd answered questions 1 through 11 with little trouble, outside of Alexis finding out about my father jerking my mother and me out of a Baptist church 'cause everyone was racist, and about my biological grandmother handing over the stale chocolate Easter bunny with its head bitten off, and Alexis dreaming about shallow graves all the time. We put the two hardback chairs across from each other and got out our water so that I wouldn't drink. Alexis crossed her legs. We got out the booklet, and the answer sheets, and the Putt-Putt pencils to make our yes or no marks. Outside it rained, and the Saluda River was getting to a point where I didn't trust driving across the wooden bridge to the road, much less into downtown Forty-Five should I need a pound of fatback or advice from any one of its residents on how to hot-wire a car, poison a dog, or make a poultice to cure brown lung. What I'm saying is, I couldn't work, and I couldn't go to the Sunken Gardens Lounge. I said, "I'm all for it."

We stuck to our earlier format: Ardis kept the booklet and asked the question. She said, "Question twelve. 'Have you ever been conned out of something and thought vengeful thoughts afterwards?'"

I said, "What does that mean?"

"It's self-explanatory," she said. "Has anyone ever cheated you and when you found out, you wanted to kill them?"

I thought back. There'd been times when I'd bought something at a convenience store and been short-changed, I was sure, but I didn't get in my car later that night and pistol-whip the clerk. This old boy named Leland lived in my neighborhood growing up, and one time I gave him my bicycle for an arrowhead Geronimo had used to kill a buffalo. I found out later that the arrowhead I kept on my desk probably wasn't what Leland said it was—my father kind of let me know not to ever trade bicycles to anyone again—but I didn't feel like killing Leland or anything. About ten ex-girlfriends in college and graduate school had admitted to fucking either my best friend or someone in the same program in which I studied, but I just said okay and went on.

I've never considered myself the kind of guy who should end up on the nightly news. I said to Alexis, "No. How about you?"

She said, "Are you kidding me?"

I said, "I'm not kidding. It's only fair, goddamn it."

"You don't need to cuss," Alexis said. "In the directions of the booklet it says the husband and wife doing this test should control their emotions." She nodded and touched her eyebrows. I knew that later in the night she'd lock herself in the bathroom and pluck them.

I said, "You didn't tell me that. Sorry. If this test were for Amish couples, it wouldn't end up a problem. If we were Mormons, it'd have to say that the husband and *wives* couldn't cuss. . . ."

Alexis said, "I went on a trip to New York with my theater class back in college and this guy did that shell game with me. I lost all my money, and almost thought about going out to find the guy who took it, but didn't. Randy gave me what I lost and told me not to worry."

I said, of course, "Who was Randy?"

She said, "My drama professor!" like that, all excited. "I've told you about Randy," she said.

I said, "Randy. Randy. *There's* a con game."

I looked over at a cobweb in the corner. Alexis said, "Well, we'd probably be better off if Randy were here. He taught all of us to confront our fears and hostilities and limitations. Randy taught us how to know our inner selves. He taught us how to know our emotions."

"Did you fail that class or something?" I said. I only knew about jealousy, anger, hatred, and envy when it came to knowing emotions.

Alexis said, "No, thank you. I made a B." She said, "I can answer this question with a no also. I never went out for cheerleader, so I don't feel like Carol Haulbrook or anybody back in high school did something to undermine my chances. I've never bought a used car, or gone to an antique auction. I can put down a big no for this answer," and she did.

I watched my wife and thought, This is the dumbest thing I've ever done in my life. I thought, What with a beautiful, intelligent woman under the same roof where I live, why are we lowering ourselves to believing what—more than likely—some adman and some two-bit psychologist have put together for late-night-television infomercials? I thought, Just because I had a grandfather who tried to kidnap me and I got away, why am I relegated to something on the lines of Dear Abby?

I said, "I put down a big no, too." When I put my feet up on the sides of her chair, I noticed that I should clip my toenails.

It was night, like before. It was night, and I had to get up and work on Job in the morning. I'd made a pact with myself—six in the morning until noon, then off to a university library fifty miles away, just in case I'd missed a mention of who I thought was the third most important character in the Bible, behind Jesus and Moses, just ahead of the tie between Noah and Abraham.

It was my theory, and was in the prologue of what I'd written. That's it. There was no real proof, really.

Alexis kicked my legs away from her space.

THEN THERE WERE the easy ones, again: "If you had your druthers, would you rather take a train five hundred miles away from your home, as opposed to an airplane?"

Both of us scored no.

"Do you like felt-point pens better than ball-points?" I said no, and Alexis said she did.

"Crushed ice over cubed?"

I didn't know how to answer. It mattered. I liked crushed ice with plain cola, but cubes with bourbon. Alexis said, "They should mention margaritas here. This is a stupid question. Let's skip it."

I said, "Nope. We can't. It won't spell out what's supposed to be spelled out."

And I wasn't making a joke. Get this: the At-Home Marriage Repair kit said that after we were done we should be able to stack our cards on top of each other—side A of mine and side A of Alexis's facing up, with hers on the bottom—and look through the light to see what it read. It should've read either STAY or STOP, meaning either we should stay together or stop the marriage. My answer card and Alexis's—like every person participating in this stupid experiment—were different in the way the answer blocks were spread out. We both had yes and no answers, but they were spread across the page in different places. What I'm trying to explain, when we answered yes to a question like, "Did you think your father was a great man?" or whatever, my yes/no space for that numbered question might be in the right-hand corner, while my wife's might be in the middle, or left-hand corner. When everything was done we were supposed to place our sheets together and see.

It was scientific. It was psychology at its best, that's all I have to say. STAY or STOP, that's what the advertisement said —there'd be nothing else—that's what we'd see looking up at the light, and there'd be no reason to question anything otherwise.

We went right through question to question, answering things like, "I'd rather eat carrots than corn," or "I'd rather pet a dog than a snake," or "I'd rather wear cotton shirts or blouses compared to human-made substances like polyester or rayon."

We were right on, on those subjects. Alexis and I liked our fathers pretty much, and corn, dogs, and cotton. We just smudged in our answers and then I said, "I like corn dogs, for that matter."

She said, "Be serious, Ronnie."

I said, "Come on. Let's get through with this this time. I don't want to keep this up every two days." I said, "I don't want to seem impatient, seeing as I'm writing an annotated bibliography of Job, but I just don't want to spend all my time taking a test, either."

Alexis said, "The next question is, 'Have you ever feared a musician?' That's a dumb question."

I couldn't believe it. I wanted to get up and track down whoever wrote up this test. I wanted to know how he'd ever come into my inner thoughts and fears, how he obviously knew my history. I said, "I have to put down a yes. Sorry."

• • •

My FATHER ONCE took me down to a juke joint in Macon when I was about ten years old, I'm not sure why. Macon was a good four-hour drive from our house in South Carolina. I remember my father telling my mother that he needed to go see a purchasing agent in some cotton mill, and I remember him telling me, around the time we got out of our own city limits, how there really wasn't a mill in Macon, and that it was our secret. I just said okay. I was getting paid five dollars an hour, even though I knew that when we got home Dad would say we hadn't worked at all, and he'd give me five dollars for only hanging around him.

He did the same thing when I was five years old and living in California, except he told my mother he needed to go down to the union hall, and we ended up in a Tijuana strip joint with a field of burros across the street I found more interesting at the time.

Anyway, we drove down to Macon and my father said, "Where we're going is somewhere around here." He circled the block off the mall. Macon had a split main street with a park running down the middle of it. My father said, "I want you to see how different people live," and he parked the car.

We went through this alley and ended up going into what seemed to be the back door of a club called the Last Note. Some old black gentleman crouched by the slapping screen door, sick to his stomach. My father and I were the only white people in the place, and we sat right down in front. The waitress brought my father a draft beer and me a Shirley Temple. That's what my father ordered us.

This quartet played hard, blasting blues—a stand-up-bass player, a trumpet player, a guy on drums, and a woman on the piano. We weren't there five minutes before the waitress came back and said, "On the house." She wore a skirt like I'd not seen before—a mesh see-through thing that went only about halfway down her thighs. She didn't wear underwear.

My father said, "What do you mean? We have money. Don't give us drinks on the house just because we're the only white people in here."

She said, "Manager says so," and left.

My father called over the manager, who told him that this other guy'd bought the drinks, and my father called that man over—a man who ended up being Otis Redding. I wasn't paying attention, though. I mean, I wasn't paying attention to my father talking to some black man in a red suit. I kept looking at the bass player in the band, and he kept looking at me. He had this shaved head, long thick fingernails, and a goatee. He wore sunglasses, and the ash on his cigarette must've been two inches long but it didn't waver or fall or flake off.

The whole place seemed on fire—smoke wafting, lighters and matches flickering randomly and often, small candles at each table. Every ten seconds the trumpet player pulled his horn down and said into the microphone, "Yeah," or "That's right," or "I'm here," for no apparent reason. The bass player watched me, sitting at the front table.

When the band took a break my father still talked to Otis Redding. My father didn't see the bass player lean his instrument against the back wall and slowly walk toward me. The bass player pulled his sunglasses up and balanced them on his forehead. Later on the drive home my father said I must've misheard the guy say to me, "Little boy like you go for some money."

We pulled off the two-lane road often so I could pee some Shirley Temple out, seeing as I was scared to go in the Last Note. "Little boy like you go for some money," my father yelled out the open passenger-side window.

I said to Alexis, "Yes. I have to put down a yes," and told her the story. She didn't blink.

She said, "No." My wife said, "I guess this isn't the right time for me to suggest us taking a break so I can put some Charlie Parker on." Alexis laughed, and put her feet on my knees.

IF LIFE WERE BOXING, I'd've been a middleweight teacher. I'm a lightweight scholar, and a pudgy, soft, heavyweight husband. I don't cheat on Alexis, and I try not to look at other women when I'm standing in line at the Winn-Dixie or IGA. I'm not quite sure what goes on in my brain that causes me to yell out randomly, but what the hell.

I smoke too much and drink past what people would call "social drinking." Before I met Alexis, I had a girlfriend who went to all the A meetings—Alcoholics Anonymous, Narcotics Anonymous, Victims of Abuse Anonymous, Hit and Run Anonymous—and she'd said to me, "Your friends are all enablers."

I said, "What does that mean?" I said, "Sorry, but I'm not up on pop psychology."

She said, "Your friends know you have a drinking problem, and they let you drink."

I said, "Hey, I buy my own drinks, pal. I'm not a cheapskate."

She said, "You're not getting it, Ronnie. If your friends were true friends they'd not let you drink. They'd say something." Back then I thought to myself, Well you're right about that—I'm not getting any sex off of you. On my way back from the bar I'd even stop by the Quick-Stop for Goody's powders for her to take so she couldn't complain about headaches holding her back from bedroom activities. But it didn't work. We'd ended splitting up because I couldn't take the drapes she wanted—yin-yang things in black and white.

Back then I kept saying that nothing came in black and white, just like the 100 question test Alexis and I took to relieve our marriage. I just kept saying that things weren't working out, seeing as how she wanted me to memorize the complete lyrics of Dan Fogelberg, Jackson Browne, and Todd Rundgren, or whomever.

Alexis said, "So what's your answer?"

I said, "I forgot the question," like an idiot. Outside, a gibbous moon rose. There were kids outside shooting bottle rockets into the Saluda River, because it wasn't illegal. The sky was blue and yellow, except for down the road in poor Forty-Five, where Ned-Ned-the-Cabbage-Head kept a giant searchlight situated in his Chevrolet dealership's parking lot and rotating into the sky.

My wife said, "You've had a girlfriend or boyfriend who meant more to you than your spouse. That's the question."

I said, "No. It seems to me if that were the case we wouldn't have made it to the point of ordering this test off TV. I put down a no," and did.

Alexis said, "I said no, too." She penciled in her mark. That's all I have to say.

"What about that girl you lived with who always made you go to those meetings? You loved her a bunch, didn't you? Before she left you?"

I said, "Not as much as you, honey." I leaned over and kissed my wife. We smiled. "I wouldn't call it love anyway. I'd call it something else."

"Like what?" Alexis said.

"I don't know. Penance. Pain and boredom. Patience—I developed my sense of patience during those years, I'll tell you that."

Alexis said, "Patient men don't start singing 'Chances Are' and 'The Battle Hymn of the Republic' in line at the grocery store, Ronnie. Yesterday I was over in the bakery section and I could hear you start out singing the *Hee-Haw* theme song for no reason."

I still didn't remember doing those things. I trusted my wife—and my cashiers and bag boys, for that matter. Still, I didn't remember. I said, "What's the next question?"

We sat in the dark. We just sat there drinking our glasses of water. Neither of us got up and turned on the overhead or went into the kitchen for those votive candles Alexis bought when she read somewhere that that's the thing to do when it comes to inviting neighbors over for dinner if you don't have time to actually shampoo the carpet. I couldn't even see my answer sheet anymore, to tell the truth. I got up and switched the lamp, and put my miniature-golf pencil in my mouth.

Alexis said, "Thanks." She said, "The next question's not all that hard. It says, 'Do you and your spouse enjoy playing games together—cards, Monopoly, dominoes, and so on?' I like to play games with you, Ronnie."

I said, "I like nothing better. A long time ago I used to enjoy going to bars, but now I like to sit at home and play games. This is a kind of game, as a matter of fact. And I'm having fun, too." I leaned over and kissed my wife again. I nodded up and down like a fool.

We both penciled in a yes. My answer space was about two inches from the bottom of the six-by-eight-inch answer sheet. I looked over and saw Alexis fill in her answer right in the middle of the page.

I said, "We should stay together. I can feel it. I'm sorry that we came to this—and maybe our relationship could be better—but I have a feeling that this is about as good a marriage as two people can have, living under the same roof."

My wife didn't answer me like I thought she should've. She didn't respond. Instead, she looked down at the booklet, got up, and went to the kitchen like she'd done two nights earlier when we started this whole stupid thing. She let out a noise somewhere between crying and laughing and gagging.

I said, "I'll take a bourbon."

She made two. I listened to the ice clinking in the glasses.

Alexis said from in there, "Have you ever cheated on me when we're playing games? Have you ever cheated playing poker, Scrabble, Uno, or dominoes?"

I said, "How does a person cheat at those games?"

She made a noise again. Alexis came back in the den with two glasses filled to the brim. She said she didn't know about how to cheat at Monopoly outside of pulling money when the enemy wasn't looking. She said she didn't know how to cheat at poker or Scrabble, seeing as the opponent was always right there in front of her. Alexis said, "Ronnie, I have something I have to tell you, I guess."

I took from my drink and made a face, more from what I saw coming than from the booze.

MY WIFE AND I play Twenty Questions more often than not. We lay or lie—I forget the right form of the verb and avoid using it whenever possible—in bed afterwards and one of us says simply, "I got one." The challenger always says, "Living?" like that. The first three questions are always the same: "Living?" and "Man?" and "American?" From there it gets technical and honed-in and somewhat tribological.

I don't know what started it. I do know that I used to play with the woman who took me to all of those A meetings. She wasn't that smart, and only knew a few things, and I could figure out the answer by the fourth question usually. After I got it down to a dead American male historical figure I would say, "Ben Franklin!" like that, and always be right, pretty much. If it wasn't Ben Franklin then it was Thomas Edison. If it wasn't Edison, it was one of the Roosevelt presidents. The woman I lived with before I married Alexis had big tits, and I'm not saying there's a correlation—I'm only saying she didn't have much of an imagination. I'm only saying that she wasn't good with Twenty Questions.

Here name was Serene, no lie. There you go. Alexis knows all about her. She gives me shit whenever possible.

I said, "I can put down a no to this one," and looked for the answer spot. I said, "I like playing Scrabble and Twenty Questions with you, and I don't cheat, even if I don't win all that much at Twenty Questions."

Alexis drank her bourbon in one big gulp, just like someone out of the movies. She said, "There's a reason you don't win at Twenty Questions." She recrossed her legs.

I said, "You cheat?" all surprised. I had no idea.

Alexis said, "I can't stand you being smarter than me, Ronnie. And whether you know it or not, you like to show off. You like to let me know that you're smarter than me. You're always quoting people, and telling me how to speak."

I said, "I do not."

She said, "See? You're correcting me now."

"I don't correct you every time. Earlier, for example, you should've said, 'I can't stand you being smarter than I.' But I didn't say anything."

"Fuck you, man."

When we played Twenty Questions Alexis was smart— she'd pick a nineteenth-century male artist from Europe and she could keep lying all the while. When it got down to about question fourteen or fifteen and I had it narrowed down to one of those guys who lived in France I'd say, "Van Gogh!"

She'd say, "Un-uh."

"Monet!" I'd bellow out. Alexis would shake her head.

I'd go through Manet, Toulouse-Lautrec, Gauguin, and Seurat. Alexis would say, "No, no, no, and no," and then say something like, "I was thinking of Théodore Géricault," or Daumier, or Delacroix. There were about a thousand famous French painters in the nineteenth century, by the way. I'd say, "Goddamn, that was a good one," and not even know I'd been hoodwinked.

Alexis would say things like, "I swear that's who I was thinking about," but this night I found out otherwise. She said, "I always picked an artist because I knew all of them, and I knew I could keep lying to you."

I said, "Shame, shame, shame." I drank my bourbon and kept eye contact. "That sounded like Gomer Pyle or somebody, I know, but I mean it, Alexis. Goddamn."

She said, "I shouldn't've told you."

I said, "The instructions say we can't lie. The instructions say we have to sit across from each other and tell the truth. Read the instructions again—you can't lie. There's not room for making things up here."

She said, "Don't yell at me. I hope one of the next questions has to do about how we feel about our spouse yelling. I'm not deaf." My wife held out her arms as if it was some kind of brainstorm announcement.

I said, "And I'm not a cheater," but laughed. I drank the

rest of my drink and got up for more. I took Alexis's glass, too.

"We're supposed to be drinking water this whole time. The directions say we're supposed to sit across from each other and drink water, if indeed we have to drink anything."

There was a squeak in the linoleum, and I knew I needed to take a day off of Job and go under the house to replace a board or whatever people needed to do for a squeak. My dog, Rosonol, didn't piss on the floor, so it wasn't her fault. The people who owned the house before me had a cat, and I doubted it marked its territory right on one spot beside the kitchen table. I stopped and stepped and squeaked and squeaked. I said to Alexis behind my back, "I know about the directions. I know how to play Twenty Questions right, too."

The freezer was out of ice. I stood there with the door open and waited for cubes to fall. They did. I filled the two normal glasses.

When I returned to the den my wife said, "Maybe we should watch the news and see what's going on."

I said, "Why? You think there's going to be some kind of human interest story on some unknown nineteenth-century artist no one's heard about?"

Call me a belligerent drunk.

Alexis said, "Let's drop this right now. I told the truth. I put a yes-I-cheat down on the answer sheet. *I'm* the one trying to figure out why we have problems."

I said, "You're right. I'm sorry. We're trying to figure things out. I appreciate you being honest. And so am I."

It had rained every day or night for two months. These comets collided into Jupiter, according to the scientists. Some kind of astronomer at the university where I used to work opened up his observatory so people could watch. Alexis and I didn't go, although we talked about it.

I couldn't. I worked on Job, the man from Uz. He once said, "The earth is given into the hand of the wicked. . . ."

My wife cheated at Twenty Questions. Job was right, per usual.

RIGHT AWAY I thought, Job chapter 10, verse 22: "A land of darkness, as darkness *itself*; and of the shadow of death, without any order, and *where* the light *is* as darkness." I have no idea what the fuck it means, but it seemed appropriate to say to Alexis there on the outskirts of our sad Forty-Five life. I said, "Hey, you cheating-Twenty-Questions woman, 'A land of darkness, as darkness itself,'" and so on.

She drank her cocktail and said, "Let's do it again."

I said, "Do what?"

She said, "Let's play Twenty Questions again. I won't cheat. We'll take a little break from the marriage-repair kit."

I said, "Abraham Lincoln!" like that. I'd forgotten.

Alexis said, "Be serious. I have a person in mind."

I said, "Man?"

She said, "Nope."

I said, "It's a woman. Is she alive as we speak?"

She said, "Nope." My wife took a little drink from her glass. She didn't grimace.

I said, "Is she from America?"

"Uh-huh," my wife said.

"A dead American woman—the perfect combo," I said. "That was a joke."

Alexis said, "You're going to lose, Ronnie. You're going down on this one."

I said, "Was she in the entertainment field? Was she an actress or artist or singer?"

My wife said, "No."

I said, "Bella Abzug, the politician!"

"You're running out of questions. Nope."

I wasn't sure why we played, seeing as how we still had seventy-something questions left on the test. I said, "Was she from west of the Mississippi River?"

"No. East," Alexis said.

"She wasn't an actress or entertainer or politician east of the Mississippi, right?"

My wife looked down at the floor. "Entertainment's such an odd choice of words."

"She was something like a stripper?" I yelled out. "I can't know every stripper in the world that you know, Alexis. You wouldn't let me."

"She wasn't a stripper. Give up?"

I said, "Connie Chung's still alive."

She said, "Is that twenty questions? I've quit counting."

I said, "One of those NOW women, or anti-NOW women —you can't expect me to know all of their names."

"Un-uh."

I said, "There are plenty of women who you could

categorize in this category. It's not any different from the nineteenth-century artists. You can play the same game."

My wife said, "I'm not."

I said, "Well, hell, you got me. I give up." I said, "It can't be Ruth Gordon, because she's part of the entertainment field."

My wife said, "Yes, she was."

I said, "Who?"

She laughed. She twanged the end of her nose with a finger. "I'm sorry I've been cheating on you for the last half-decade or however long we've been playing."

I said, "I am, too."

Alexis said, "Kudzu," and kept laughing.

I knew kudzu—I'd tried to cut kudzu off of our property, sloping down to the Saluda River. "Kudzu can't be your answer. If that's what you've been thinking, then we can't ever play again."

Alexis said, "No. I'm sorry. I keep thinking of the smell of kudzu, that's all. It's not who I was originally thinking about."

I said, "Right," but nothing else. I thought about how my wife kept cheating, and thought back about the times I'd had nice girlfriends and good ideas concerning Job, both—everything wasn't like it was with Alexis. There was a time when I knew Job said, "How long will ye vex my soul, and break me in pieces with words?" It didn't mean that much to me back then. What it meant was nothing more than whining.

I got up and walked to the window. Below us, down at

the edge of our land, the Saluda overran its banks. I said, "Mother Teresa wasn't an American."

Alexis said, "Forget it. Let's get back to the real test."

I said, "Maybe it's because I'm home all the time. Maybe it's because I'm either stuck here, or over at the library. If you feel the need to win all the time at Twenty Questions, then something's gone awry in your self-esteem, Alexis. I'm sorry you think I try to make you look or feel stupid, or however you feel."

"I was thinking of a dress designer you wouldn't even know. She was born in Italy, lived in the United States, but was a French citizen. Her name was Elsa Schiaparelli. There."

I said, "She was famous?"

"What's famous to you isn't famous to everyone, Ronnie. If you've ever seen a woman on the beach wearing a shocking-pink bathing suit, then Elsa Schiaparelli was famous to you, also. There are different kinds of fame and different kinds of knowledge. I changed the oil in the car last week, by the way."

That was a good dig. Alexis knew I had no knowledge of cars or their maintenance requirements.

I said, "Thanks," and meant it. From afar, those kids kept up with their bottle rockets. I said, "That was a good one. You win."

I didn't pout or call foul. I thought of Job, chapter 19, verses 9 and 10: "He hath stripped me of my glory, and taken the crown *from* my head. He hath destroyed me on every side, and I am gone; and mine hope hath he removed like a tree." If there was a Future Testament to go along with the Old and New, there'd be a Job-like person, and it would be a woman. It would say, "She hath stripped me of my glory."

I wandered back over to sit in front of my wife. She said, "The next question's easy. I bet we can both answer it without thinking." She said, " 'Do voices ever call out to you at night? Do you ever feel that there's a supernatural being saying things to you?' " Alexis said, "Absolutely not, for me."

I sat still and listened to the swollen river below.

Public Relations

I hadn't even ordered from the bar yet when, out of nowhere, I said this: "The women's movement of the late 1960s ruined our educational system." I was with my wife, Ardis, my boss and his wife, and a woman who wanted to hire me to revive her company. This was in an overpriced restaurant in downtown Greenville where BMW executives bring visiting Germans, where Michelin people bring their French. The place could've been called Casablanca's. The woman needing a consultant owned a slight chain of health food/karaoke joints in the Carolinas and needed someone like me to leak out fake news that everybody else's alfalfa sprouts contained hepatitis B. My résumé ran ten pages long in 9-point type with such ruses. I'm the guy behind "brush-rinse-repeat" for a toothpaste company; the water people hired me to come up with that "eight glasses a day" rule. I'm the anti-PR man responsible for claiming grits as the cure-all for fire-ant mounds, thus disabling the insecticide industry while causing the demand for minute-grits to double.

Ardis kicked me. You'd've thought I pulled a bullhorn out of my pocket and started listing off statistics about World War II there in the restaurant. My boss—a pecker-head named Jacob who insisted on a ladder motif in the decor of both home and office—forced a laugh. What didn't bother me whatsoever about sounding harsh, and even irrational, had to do with the the owner of the health food stores, a woman who saw herself as better than every-one else just because she could pronounce a slew of herbs in Latin and list their supposed remedies. She had "found her-self one with the Native Americans" and legally changed her name to Naomi Locust Wind. That bugged me.

"You must be joking," Naomi Locust Wind said. Listen, she was whiter than a pound of Sunbeam bread. *I* had more reason to change my name to that of an Algonquin chief. I'd done some pro bono work on the Cherokee reserva-tion's conversion from bingo outlet to full-fledged land of casinos, and even got to smoke a peace pipe with some kid back behind one of those rubber-tomahawk stores.

The waiter came up and asked if I'd like the usual. I said, "A carafe of Manhattans," because that's what I drank. It had nothing to do with a twenty-four-dollar sale of land. My boss ordered a vodka tonic, like a pussy. His wife or-dered white wine. Ardis said she'd have a carafe of martinis and the telephone number of a cab company. Naomi Locust Wind said this day was her day to go without liquid, which would've pissed off my water-company account.

I said, "When we had good teachers it was because there was nothing else for smart women to look forward to doing. Hell, they became housewives, or secretaries, or teachers."

"I have to disagree with you, V.O.," Jacob's wife said. She never liked me in the first place. Her name was Mimi, no lie.

I said, "Listen. When I was in the fourth grade I had a fifty-year-old woman named Mrs. Flowers for a teacher. She graduated from goddamn Vassar. In the fifth grade I had a woman named Mrs. Breland. She went to Columbia or some place."

"Weren't you lucky," Naomi said flatly. "I went to Smith."

I said, "See? Before the women's movement you couldn't have gone on to run your own business. You would've taught kids at best, and those kids would've gone on to know the English language because of you."

My wife said to Naomi, "Do you know Laurel Hyman-Jones? I took a workshop with her one time up in Raleigh. She was teaching at Smith at the time." Ardis was a painter who could do a realistic portrait if she wanted, but tried her best to make everything look primitive. She spent a lot of time perfecting the value of "flat." I loved my wife, and respected her tenacity.

The waiter brought our drinks. I didn't light a cigarette. Naomi Locust Wind shook her head no. "Here's what I'm saying," I said. "In the old days, women with IQs of one-twenty and above could only become teachers. After about nineteen-seventy all the smart women went on to become lawyers, doctors, and businesswomen. That left the teaching profession with a shelf of nonspectacular scholars to lead kids. Plus, with more women in the workforce outside of teaching, it caused stupid men to go into teaching, seeing as their spots in banking and insurance got taken up. I'm not laying blame on anyone, ma'am."

Does this sound like a faulty cause-and-effect argument? Does this sound like the words of a misogynist? For Christ's sake, I put stupid men into my little theory and maybe even put them behind smart women teachers and second-level women teachers. I poured half a Manhattan into my martini-style glass. I was prepared to go into some kind of reductio ad absurdum argument about how, with the advent of computers, only ditch diggers, asphalt workers, roofers, television talk-show hosts, and evangelists will be around to call roll each morning in the elementary schools of America.

Mimi said, "I always thought I'd be a teacher until I spent a semester practice-teaching my senior year. Luckily I met Jacob."

Ardis shoved her heel into my left toe so I wouldn't make a point. Later on—and this is a totally different story—she took to wearing golf spikes when we went out to dinner or had people over.

Naomi unfolded her menu. I didn't say anything about the steak, pork, lamb, pheasant, alligator tail, or rabbit. Then the goofball waiter came up, looked me straight in the face, and asked, "Do you know the perfect way to prepare quail?"

When I said, "How?" even I understood that it sounded like I was making fun of those extras in any cowboy movie.

AFTER WE HAD ordered and the waiter departed, Jacob said to me, "V.O., I wanted you to meet Naomi because I thought you'd be perfect for finding her a way to separate her chain of health food and karaoke stores from the thousands of others that have sprouted up in the Southeast." He raised his eyebrows, which wrinkled his massive forehead. His upper visage looked like a topographical map of the shifting Sahara.

" 'Sprouted up.' That's precious," Mimi said.

Ardis kept looking at her menu. She had asked the waiter if she could keep hers to look over. I think she was probably looking for a personal sign pointing out whether she should get up and leave or not. My wife liked those search-a-word games, too.

"Lure's an interesting last name," Naomi said to me. "What does the V.O. stand for?"

Jacob sat forward to say what he always said. The table behind us was filled with six men talking in three different languages about grand-prix racing, something no one in South Carolina understood. "It stands for Vice Operator. V.O. can find ways to ruin Fortune Five Hundred businesses in one working day."

My wife touched Naomi's hand. "It doesn't stand for anything. His parents didn't have any imagination. They couldn't have worked in the business world *or* taught school." Her carafe of martinis was dry, dry.

"It stands for V.O., truly. V. O. Lure. Velour. It sounds like 'velour.' My daddy spent some time working in the textile industry."

"Naomi's father was a farmer. That's where she got her basic understanding of pollination, and cross-pollination," my boss said.

Mimi said, "I never understood biology. Osmosis—that's part of biology, isn't it?" Mimi had ordered spaghetti.

Without a twitch of a smirk on her face Naomi Locust Wind said to Ardis, "How did you meet up with this Neanderthal?" I ordered my wife another carafe. Although I didn't know it at the beginning of the evening, evidently I wanted to get fired. And I kind of wanted to see a big cat fight.

"We met right after V.O. invented the White Trash Monopoly game. You probably don't sell it at your stores. I'd just gotten out of graduate school and had a part-time job working for a patent lawyer. V.O. came in. Love at first sight."

In any movie she would've leaned over and kissed me. Ardis would've said, "Ain't that so, honey?" in any Hollywood production. She didn't give me a glance.

"Ginkgo biloba's supposed to help people see clearer in more ways than one," Naomi Locust Wind said. "You might want to take a good ten or twenty drops in a glass of filtered spring water every day."

Okay, so I might go on about doing pro bono work for the Cherokee nation, but I've also turned against clients when they treated me like a rambling dolt with out-of-style glasses. I'm the consultant responsible for putting Beanie Babies where they got to, then back to where they belonged. I don't want to brag, but between slugs of my Manhattan—

before I could even distinguish whether the bartender put one or two cherries in the carafe—I knew that it would only take me one call to NewsChannel 4 and thirty seconds on the Internet to ruin Naomi Locust Wind's Ginseng-Along cafés with news of chemically enhanced paba or whatever. Man, I had the means to hire outright hoodlums who'd infiltrate each store and leave trace evidence of things odd people don't want on their fucking maize.

Jacob leaned back in his chair and said, "Now, now."

Mimi said, "Let's play I Spy with My Little Eye." She didn't look unlike a woman who had worked as a flapper in a previous life.

I'll give Ardis this: she would've stood by me if I'd caught the pope's robe on fire. She said, "I take that Saint-John's-wort stuff that's supposed to cure minor depression. It worked until tonight."

I could've faded away until my mackerel showed up. I said, "Everything didn't come out the way I meant for it to come out. Listen. In the old days, we all got taught by women teachers. They were all right. We trusted them. Nowadays we don't trust teachers, and we shouldn't. Something happened. It happened after Nixon. It happened somewhere along the line. I dare anyone at this table to go look up SAT scores, dropout rates, violence in the schools, and PTA attendance. Fuck, I remember during Science Fair Week there were kids who built rockets. I saw on the news the other day where a boy won regionals with a misspelled poster board explaining cocoons and butterflies. That's too easy."

The waiter brought salads. We all got regular salads—spinach and endive—with the house dressing. There was no choice, like ranch, or Thousand Island. It was some kind of raspberry-vinaigrette shit I didn't like, and I had it in my mind that if the chef was over fifteen years old he or she would've known that there was more than one way to do anything. Unfortunately I said, "I wish the chef wasn't so sure about himself."

"How do you know the chef's a man?" Naomi said. "After everything else you've said, maybe it's a woman, seeing as we've infiltrated every aspect of the workforce that seems to threaten you."

I held a piece of red cabbage on my fork and said, "You know, with a name like Locust Wind, shouldn't you be wearing some fucking beads or something? Give me a break, Pocahontas. At least go get yourself some moccasins, or a feather to put in the back of your hair."

Even the French, Dutch, and German people seated around us shut up on this one. My boss said how I could clean out my desk and computer in the morning, right after I told him how to fix the Ginseng-Alongs. Ardis began humming. She picked up her menu and didn't return my look. Jacob's wife, Mimi, craned her neck backwards toward the bartender for another glass of wine. Naomi slipped off her shoe and touched my leg—accidentally, I'm sure. The band in the corner played a polka.

When the food came Naomi Locust Wind didn't waste time. I'm not sure what she ordered, but it involved shellfish and angel-hair pasta. I'd never seen anyone take care of a plate like she did. Me, I couldn't even figure out what direction to cut my mackerel without it falling apart altogether. By the time I decided what to do with the skin and eyeballs, Naomi was sitting there as if she wanted to order cordials.

"I've been intentionally hard on you people," she said. "I'll be the first to admit that I don't trust anyone, and it's caused me to be hard on everyone with whom I have to deal."

I said, "Perfect English."

My ex-boss said, "Don't think we don't know what you do and don't really want," which I couldn't follow. Jacob held a fork to his mouth and kept his eyebrows raised. He'd ordered a shrimp quesadilla and now wore guacamole on the tip of his nose.

Ardis said to him, "We should start all over. Still, promise me you'll fire V.O. because of this." To me she said, "What in the world made you say that thing about the feminist movement and the education system?"

"Sometimes I just make connections," I said. "Excuse me for thinking. If I'd've been taught in the 1980s we wouldn't have to worry about thinking. We'd all be sitting around talking about how to carry a hollow egg around for a month, pretending it was a baby."

Naomi Locust Wind said, "I have a niece in the third grade. She knows how to put a condom on her finger. Next thing you know, some parent presses charges against her teacher for molestation."

I didn't say, "That's what I'm talking about." I didn't say, "She can put a rubber on her finger, but she doesn't know the capital of her home state." I let it go.

We sat there behind used plates and silverware. The foreign diners lit cigars and laughed as if someone were doing pull-my-finger routines. I poured my drink to the brim, then poured Ardis's. My wife said, "I've heard of people fasting for one day out of the week, but not not drinking liquids. Tell me again what that does for you?"

Naomi Locust Wind accidentally ran her stockinged foot halfway up my thigh. She said, "I don't know." She paused and then said, "Oh, what the hell," taking my glass and slugging down half of it. "I have this theory that the body fills with toxins, and that toxins come even from plain water. I also believe that it's good to shock the system so it becomes adjusted to harsher situations. It's kind of like how plants become frost hardened. But it's a personal theory. There's no medical proof."

The waiter came up and handed us dessert menus. I didn't open mine. Mimi, of all people, said, "It seems to me you should be doing the opposite. If you want your body to adjust to harsh conditions—like maybe you want it to be ready for post–nuclear holocaust life—then you should guzzle down a quart of vodka per day."

I handed the waiter a five-dollar bill and told him to ask the band to play something by Merle Haggard or George Jones.

Naomi Locust Wind stared at my ex-boss's wife for a ten-count, turned to me, and said, "What do stupid women do now, in your opinion? There's always been stupid women who couldn't teach or become secretaries. Do you think that all a stupid woman could do after the women's movement is become a housewife?"

I said, "Women who can't make it in the business world and who can't make it teaching do the same thing that men do who can't handle either job. They sit out front of abortion clinics with vulgar signs. Or they back their stupid husbands, who believe that the Confederate flag needs to fly over the state capitol so everyone can remember his heritage. Listen, I'm Irish, but I don't have to drink whiskey, eat potatoes, and kill Englishmen every day to remember where I come from."

I'd been contacted by the antiabortion front in the past. They wanted me to invent the perfect ad campaign so all young women kept their babies. I told these numbnuts that I'd get right back to them as soon as I completed a twelve-step lobotomy program. In the past I had given other smart-ass answers to PR queries, and that's why Jacob and I worked out of a Butler building fifty miles away in the town of Forty-Five, far from where extremists would be willing to travel in order to shoot ammunition toward us. In Forty-Five, we worked in the midst of a people too worried about their own scams to care much about us. Jacob and I worked on word-of-mouth. We got hired out by big, big companies and people far, far away from South Carolina. And all of this worked, especially after what we did for and against the powdered-aspirin industry. Even one of those mercenary magazines did a spread on us.

Mimi folded and refolded her used napkin. Ardis tried to turn the conversation toward humid weather conditions. My ex-boss clenched a butter knife, and Naomi Locust Wind said, "Very Obnoxious. Vainglory Ontologist. Vortical Operative."

"It's plain V.O., I swear," I said. "You'd think that I'd drink that drink—VO—but it would be too obvious." I'm not exaggerating when I say that Naomi Locust Wind kept staring at me.

Jacob said, "I heard a funny joke today. It's one of those Little Johnny jokes, but I can't remember it. Have y'all heard a new Little Johnny joke?"

Mimi leaned over and said something to her husband. I said I hadn't heard a new Little Johnny joke. Jacob handed me a credit card. He said, "You people can figure out how to smash the competition. Forge my signature. Let's you and me talk at nine o'clock sharp tomorrow." He and his wife left as the house band was playing the end of "White Lightnin'" and right before "Mama Tried."

Naomi Locust Wind ordered a margarita, even though I told her how the French and Germans knew nothing about tequila. She said, "My real name's Naomi Ridgeway. I don't know anything about tequila, either. Maybe I've forgotten my own heritage."

Ardis said, "Another carafe of martinis, extra olives!" like that, even though the waiter stood at our table. He looked at us blankly, then said, "I don't want to cast any aspersions or make any assumptions, but in these litigious days I am required to mention how driving under the influence is against the law, that some fifteen thousand people are killed in accidents per year involving drunks, et cetera, et cetera. The average life span of an umbrella is two years. I like to throw that in, too, whenever I make this speech. I used to work in the resource center of the library." He could've worked for me.

Naomi Locust Wind said, "I could use a man like you managing one of my stores. Hey, what kind of money are you making here? How many Bob Dylan songs do you know? I can give you about twenty-five grand a year plus free insurance and a four-oh-one K plan. Do you know anything about health food?"

"I know that the scallops you just ate were really whitefish."

THE WAITER'S NAME was Duvall. He introduced himself like this: "My name's D-u-v-a-l-l Duvall." He quit his job, evidently, and sat down at the table with us—with me; my wife, Ardis, who tried to make her work look like an idiot painted it; and the woman who had changed her name so it sounded more earthy. I'm not saying that I would've fallen for Naomi Locust Wind, but I knew that no foot would linger on my inseam again once the waiter sat down.

"Are y'all having a good night?" Duvall said.

"I've probably lost a job. Your future boss has a chain of health food stores that won't do as well as they could, and Ardis here," I pointed a thumb at my wife, "probably wants to leave me. Who's our waiter now? I want another round of drinks."

Naomi Locust Wind said, "Maybe you can settle a bet for us, Duvall. How old are you?"

"I'm twenty-two."

"So you came up through the educational system after 1970, right?"

He sat for a minute trying to do math in his head—which proves my point right there, by the way—before saying, "I graduated from high school in 1996."

I said, "What's the capital of North Dakota? Name as many presidents as you can. What were the dates of World War One, World War Two, and Vietnam? Name pi."

Ardis said, "Give it a break, V.O."

Duvall said, "I don't have to be a prawn in your little game." I swear to God. He might've known the difference between whitefish and scallops, but put him at a chessboard and shrimp get taken.

Naomi Locust Wind held up one palm. She said, "He's being an asshole. He's an asshole."

Another waiter showed up with a portable telephone. He handed it to me and said, "It's for you."

I said, "What?"

My ex-boss was on the other end. He said, "Little Johnny goes off to Catholic camp and finds a nun half-naked. She's putting on a new habit and stands next to her old habit on the floor. Little Johnny points to it and says, 'What's that?' The nun says, 'Oh, that old thing—it's my bad habit.' Johnny says, 'Nuns don't keep any of their bad habits?' The nun shakes her head and says, 'No, but the priest still likes altar boys.'"

I said, "That ain't funny."

Jacob said, "It's funny if you're not Catholic. It's funny if you're employed. Listen, V.O., did I miss something tonight? Were we acting out some kind of good-PR-man/bad-PR-man roles that I wasn't in on? I know you think you're being funny and/or shocking, but it doesn't work that way. That's how we lost the NRA account. It's how we lost the tobacco board account. I think you know that I think it's best if we part ways."

Naomi Locust Wind pulled on her margarita with a straw, leaned over to Duvall, stuck the other end of the straw in his mouth, and served him some new kind of shooter. Ardis looked over her menu again. I said loudly, "Well, if you're really bent on leaving Mimi, I'll ask Naomi if she's interested," and hung up.

"What?" Ardis said.

"He remembered that Little Johnny joke." Naomi and Duvall turned my way. "He said he didn't want to tell it at the table for fear of a fork in his leg. It was about Little Johnny going out West, finding a naked Indian maiden in her tepee, pointing at her crotch, and asking her what it was. The Indian princess said. . . ."

"Maiden," my wife said. It didn't bother me that she interrupted, seeing as I was having to make up the joke as I went.

"The Indian maiden said, 'This is Little Beaver.' Little Johnny stared at it a minute and said, 'Now it makes sense. My mom's got one that must be Big Beaver, which explains how my daddy's dick got whittled down to nothing.'"

No one said anything. For the first time, I could feel bourbon high in my alimentary canal. Duvall laughed, which automatically lost him his new job. Naomi Locust Wind said, "I don't know how you people stay in business." She didn't throw out any money on the table. Before she left she said, "I don't need you two palefaces trying to develop Ginseng-Alongs. I can get a number of well-known folksingers to endorse what I have to offer." Palefaces! Our ex-waiter followed her out. I yelled out something about John Denver.

My wife stirred her drink. "You didn't say anything about the thousand other minorities, V.O. Why didn't you say something bad about the Maori?"

"Listen. What I said about women and the educational system was meant to be a compliment toward the entire gender known as female. This all got started because none of us can look past what we're expecting."

Ardis laughed for the first time that evening. She said, "I see myself single, on the beach, surrounded by men offering to buy me drinks with little umbrellas. It'll be Tahiti. They'll call me the female Gauguin.

WHEN ARDIS LEFT the table I thought she'd gone out to hail a cab. I sat there thinking how easy it was to lie about a company's product in order to nudge buyers that way, and how much easier it was to ruin somebody's competition so that consumers had no choice but to choose what's left. Two words: Exxon Valdez.

About thirty minutes after I paid the check with Jacob's

credit card—then burned the thing in the ashtray—I realized that Ardis hadn't gone to look for a cab. She'd either
gotten one for herself or driven home drunk. I thought this:
It seems like I could figure out the right thing to say in every
situation so as not to fuck up continually, seeing that I had
worked with some of President Clinton's advisors, that I
had worked with the agents of NFL players who needed to
explain their recent arrests, and so on.

A new waiter came up and handed me the telephone. He
said nothing. I expected my student-loan cops for some reason, but Ardis said, "I'm at the Hyatt. I'm around the block
at the Hyatt, room two twenty-two. Just like that old TV
show. *Room Two Twenty-Two.*"

I said, "I remember that show. What're you doing?"

"I have the car keys, so you can't drive home. And no
matter how cosmopolitan Greenville tries to get, it's still a
cotton-mill town with only a half-dozen taxis. I paid my
driver twenty bucks to tell his colleagues over the radio not
to pick you up."

I said, "Good trick. Maybe when I have to hang my own
shingle you can be my partner. I've been looking for someone as debonair and conniving as me. As I."

Ardis said, "I've ordered a bottle of champagne from
room service. I want to see how long I can keep you drunk.
I don't want you sobering up and going back to work for
Jacob. He's not a good person. He's not a good person for
you. And the fake Native American's bad for everybody, by
the way."

I thought about saying that judge-not-lest-you-be-judged

thing from the Bible, but knew it sounded judgmental. I said, "Goddamn, I just burned Jacob's credit card. We could've used it."

My wife—who would later change her mind about me altogether—said, "I paid for the room. Don't worry. This is my way of telling you how much I love you, even though you're an asshole. This is my way of saying that I think PR work has turned you into something that, deep down, you're not. Outside of my art, my main project is to change you back into the man I knew who invented White Trash Monopoly."

Listen, I'd wanted to quit my job for ten years. I promised myself that I'd quit once I came up with another game or gag gift that could be sold at every Stuckey's up and down I-95. I said, "Room two twenty-two."

"It was a good, moral TV show about human beings getting along, V.O."

I placed the telephone down. I asked for a to-go cup, didn't stumble around, and left with that high-step walk of drunks worried about level floors growing shin-high barriers. I turned right out of the restaurant-not-called-Casablanca's, and walked uphill toward Main Street. At the first alley I heard near-ululating sobs, and then I saw Naomi Locust Wind on her haunches. D-u-v-a-l-l stroked her head as if shining a bowling ball.

I almost said, "Man, no wonder you don't drink. It must be true what they say about Native Americans' capacity to handle alcohol." I almost said, "Boy, it doesn't matter how much you shake that eight ball, the answer's going to be 'Definitely No.'"

I high-stepped onward, though. I passed an obvious group of magnet high school students playing Go on the steps of the Atlanta Bread Company. I passed a homeless man curled inside a Subway restaurant doorway. I didn't stop until I got to the Hyatt, all the while repeating the room number. Inside the eight-floors-high atrium, a middle-aged bellhop asked me if I had luggage. We stared at each other until the middle elevator door opened. He didn't take any from my drink when I offered it.

"Maybe you can settle this," I said. "Were you in elementary school before the women's movement? I've been in an argument all night long. I just need to figure some things out."

He sniffed hard twice. "I graduated from Sterling High School, right here in Greenville. 1968. This was before integration, sir. I had other things to think about besides the women's movement."

I said, "Man. I agree." He didn't ask what floor I was going to. Neither of us moved to push a button.

"If you're asking me if I can read and write, then I'll tell you that, yes, I can. I know the capitals. I know my continents and most of their countries. I can tell you every Greyhound stop between here and New York, here and New Orleans, and here and Miami. Ask me anything about biology, math, or the poets of the Harlem Renaissance. Don't judge me 'cause I'm standing here with a drunk man inside an elevator. On Sundays I talk truth to the people of Mount Zion AME church. Ask me about the Bible, Old or New Testament. Ask me about how people treat each other these days."

I said, "No. No, I wasn't judging you. Believe me, I wasn't saying anything about your intelligence."

He hit the 2 without me saying anything. When the elevator door opened, my wife stood there wearing a hotel sheet over her head. Later on she told me that she was pretending to be a ghost, nothing else. I believed her. But at the time I could only say, "Wrong floor. Take me back down."

Bank of America

According to Russell, his tenant might've killed one or more members of an Ohio family. The tenant left without paying two months' rent, leaving behind a variety of motorcycle parts, a stack of muscle-car magazines, and a box filled with only letters, repo threats, rehab-clinic notes, and pictures of his two children in front of fake backgrounds. This was in a duplexlike prefab building. Russell kept his workshop in the front of the building, but he had converted the back, framing in walls, laying carpet, putting in a shower stall and kitchenette. "The killer was living behind me the entire time, man. I mean, I'd be on my side, building cabinets or whatever, and this guy Alton was one wall away probably wondering when the cops might show. And those letters I found, they weren't natural."

There were four of us, sitting in a tin-covered tree house eight feet above the swamp, all childhood friends: Russell the carpenter, Dean the banker, Evan the English professor, and me. We'd begun the tree house twenty-five years earlier, when all of us thought we might hunt one day, when all of us thought young women might be enthralled with screwing amid mosquitoes and the persistent sounds of flashing bass, spooked gators, limb-dropping snakes. At dusk the cicadas came out like buzz bombs magnified. Although we missed some of the college years and some soon thereafter, all of us returned to the swamp twice a year, usually Labor and Memorial Day weekends, filled two johnboats, and took Manboy's Creek a quarter mile back into the swamp. Depending on the year's rainfall, we either climbed our makeshift ladder ten or five feet up to our abode, still adorned with 1970s foldouts, a couple dozen largemouth-bass heads, old candle wax, and whatever unknown visitors left us: mostly misspelled graffiti. Over the years we'd brought up a small woodstove, a propane grill, rickety picnic tables, and a gasoline-powered generator. One time we tried to watch the World Series, but it ended up like watching TV while someone ran a jackhammer in the living room.

We never learned to hunt. And we got bored with fishing. Mostly we set turtle traps, played cards, and didn't mention our wives.

I said, "Where'd the guy go?" like an idiot.

Russell wasn't a regular carpenter. He made custom-built cabinets when someone hired him out, but his passion was making furniture so nonfunctional and unusable that only the richest people could afford it. His latest creations involved bottle-cap-covered areas, from fireplace mantels to coffee tables. There's been stories about his work in everything from *Southern Living* to *Architectural Digest*. "I guess to kill off some people. Get this—those love letters?—they weren't from other people. What I'm saying is, the box of letters weren't like how we might keep a box of letters from people. They were letters that *he* wrote but never sent."

"Maybe they were copies of letters. Were they handwritten? Maybe they were carbon copies," said Evan.

We'd not been above the swamp an hour, our ice chests stacked in the corner of the twelve-by-twelve-foot main room. A decade earlier we'd run a twenty-foot catwalk over to the next live oak and built a smaller room, maybe six feet wide and eight feet across. That was the den. Russell said, "Listen. Alton lived alone. Something bad happened long before he moved to South Carolina. He didn't have a wife and kids with him renting out my place, man. But these letters. I wish I brought some of them. Whoever he wrote them to had a second-shift job. She'd come over and they fucked. Then he got up in the morning and wrote things like, 'I loved the way you rubbed the vibrator across your chest and then finally slid it in yourself while I sucked your toes.' I ain't lying. He finished every letter with a P.S., too—something like, 'P.S.—I'm wondering if we can figure out a way where I can see your face and touch your hair.' Bizarro, man."

It made no sense to me. Dean asked, "So how'd you come up with figuring out he's a killer? I don't see where he's a killer. And I'm betting that he never had a wife or girlfriend. He's plain crazy, and writing letters to one of those blow-up inflatable dolls. Hey. I had a man come in wanting a loan one time. He wanted to go into business making inflatable Siamese twins. I hate the world." This was our first tip that Dean might've changed since the last time we had met. He never hated the world before.

I said, "The voice of experience," and Dean threw an empty beer can at my head.

"One letter that he wrote and never sent started off like this: 'Hey, fucker. Listen, I been thinking about Jodi orchestrating that whole kidnapping thing with my kids. I should've killed *everyone* in that family.'"

"That doesn't mean anything, Russell," Dean said. Evan began blowing up his one-man air mattress. "It could've meant that he didn't kill anyone whatsoever, but he should go up there and kill all of them now."

I stood up and looked across the water below at a great blue heron on a stump. Evan held his mattress valve. He said, "I disagree. If he'd not killed any of them, he would've written, 'I should go up and kill the whole family.' If he'd killed one or two of them—or however many—he would've written, 'I should've killed everyone in that family.' That's how that works."

I said, "Is there some kind of grammar law? If there's a grammar law, we need to take into account that this guy probably doesn't know proper English, right?"

Russell pulled out a six-pack of Goody's powders. He unlashed the blue plastic tamper-proof tear-strip and put it in his pocket. "I don't know. All I know is this: that old boy Alton's going to sober up one day and realize that he shouldn't have left motorcycle parts all over the place, and especially his letters. He's going to wonder whatever happened to those bad poems he wrote in his rehab-center notebook. And then he's coming back to find them."

I said, "You didn't give him our address here, did you?" I pulled a chicken neck out of my pack, then fingered my hat for a hook. At the time I meant it to be a joke. It felt like our tree house might've been the safest place I'd ever been, ever.

WE ALL LIVED within fifty miles of each other. Dean went off to college in North Carolina, worked in D.C. early on, then waded through C&S, Bankers Trust, NationsBank, and Bank of America before finally getting the VP job at a main office. Evan got into Vanderbilt, went west to Stanford, then took jobs in Austin, Baton Rouge, and finally Columbia. Russell never left, really. He took over his father's business. Me, I owned a tree farm that sold primarily to subdivision developers. After finally settling down, I traveled between more rows of Japanese plums and dogwoods than I could've done had both my parents been honeybees.

Of all people, it was Dean the banker who wanted to turtle. Although all of us liked eating cooter pie or stew, the rest of us couldn't kill a snapper whatsoever. Dean took an abnormally unhealthy delight in whapping those things on the head, boiling them alive, crowbarring the shells, picking out edible meat. He kept the shells and adorned his office walls as if with medieval shields.

I looked at my buddies and thought, Russell shouldn't have told Dean about how he'd screwed Dean's older sister here, in the tree house, however many years ago.

Russell said, "If I show up dead or missing, y'all can look for a guy named Alton Rogers. He's one of those wiry guys. He's got a tattoo on his front that's supposed to be the back end of a Harley. I don't know for sure, but I'm betting that the muffler got tattooed on his tallywhacker. This old boy had a degree from the Motorcycle Mechanics Institute down in Orlando. He left his diploma among the letters."

Dean held a cat's paw. He waited for me to go down the ladder, get in the johnboat, and check my trotline. Evan said, "Tallywhacker's an interesting word. It's not in the dictionary. I don't know the etymological origin of that term."

Russell stared a six-beat at our friend Evan. He turned toward me and said, "I don't know anything about motorcycles, but I imagine that parts of them are about as expensive as cars. Man, y'all don't know anyone who needs a dozen sissy bars, do you? Listen to this: there was this one letter he didn't send to someone. Wait—actually he wrote this letter three times to three different people and didn't send them. Anyway, it started off, 'Hey, fucker. You won't believe what happened. I was going like sixty-five miles an hour down the road when ka-fucking-*boom!* I threw a rod thirty miles from home. Well, I got the thing back to the house and started working on it in the living room when it caught on *fire!* Shit, man, the landlord ain't gonna like that. Fuck him, though—I could kill him in a second.' I swear to

God that's exactly how he wrote it. Do you understand why I might be a little scared of this guy?"

Dean tapped the cat's paw on his palm. He said, "I work at Bank of America. I fucking work at *Bank* of *America*. If you want, I can get this guy tracked down."

I said, "You can't do that."

"Listen. I can get anything done I want this side of shooting some loan risk into orbit. We got people working for us whose sole job's finding where clients moved. Or where clients' clients' clients moved. They can do anything we can't. Forget the mafia, or even the student-loan corporation. Your worst nightmare's getting on the bad side of Bank of America. I know everything there is to know about all three of y'all. By the way, you've made some mistakes in your life decisions. None of you are in a line of work that works."

"I don't care about the money he owes me. I had enough sense to take security money, so in reality he only owes me one month's rent," Russell said.

Evan stood with his hands on his kidneys, his back turned to all of us. He feigned reading new graffiti but I knew he was listening closely, trying to think of something sarcastic to say. As kids, when we played football in my front yard, Evan would always be the first one to say "Nice catch" whenever Russell dropped the ball. Dean said, "He gave you a security deposit. You just told us that he caught the living room on fire. That's what a security deposit's all about. He owes you two months' rent, he half-burned down the place—hey, Drayton, when're you going down to check the goddamn turtles?—and I'm betting that you fucking don't even know how much money it'll cost you to fix the place up so you can rent it again."

I said, "The snappers won't come in till dusk, earliest. Just like every year. Ease up, man."

Dean raised his eyebrows. He'd taken to shaving his head completely since we'd all last met, six months earlier. "I can find anyone in the world. I have a software package. Listen. Sometimes the FBI calls me up to find one of their most-wanted people. I get calls from that guy on TV with that TV show about missing people."

Evan kept his back turned. He said, "One, you can just say 'I get calls from that guy on TV about missing people.' Two, it's way too hyperbolic to believe, buddy."

"If I were you I wouldn't mess with me," Dean said. "Don't mess with me, Evan."

I said, "I forgot to bring the goddamn poker chips. We're either going to have to play with real money, or I can go down and get three different things to count for chips."

Russell said, "You can really track people down? That's not right. I don't like that idea at all. I mean, I guess it might be good for my situation right now, but that's not good. Overall, I mean." He had thumbs like Ping-Pong paddles. I wondered for the first time how good he was at hammering nails.

Evan turned around. "Nietzsche had some things to say about all this, by the way. Indirectly. Well, hell, I guess about everybody's had something to say about all this shit indirectly. Schopenhauer. Gilles Deleuze. A bunch of people."

Down in the swamp water I heard a plug go down. I heard one of those bubbling bubble noises best known to be made by turtles taking bait or skin divers trying to talk outside of their mouthpieces. I said, "Poker chips don't matter, peckerhead. Acorns are nickels, leaves are dimes, and nails are quarters. There are some nails over in the other room we can split up." It's not like there wasn't high land anywhere—I could find acorns a hundred yards from our tree house.

"Maybe you deserve to die from a blunt object," Dean said to Russell. He spoke slowly. "Anyone who doesn't do an adequate background check on his clients is asking to die from a lead pipe to the cranium."

I wasn't the only man in the tree house to've had an affair with Dean's wife. Her name was Ursula. All of us took to her, before and after she married Dean. Ursula was from Woodfall, too, a year behind us in school. She went to four junior colleges before graduating with a degree in communication, which gave her enough background to either work in a record store or, evidently, marry a banker. I'm not proud of this, even the "before she married Dean" part. It's one of those things. You walk into the house, Dean's not home, and the next thing you know Ursula's either on her knees, stomach, or back, right there on the kitchen floor. I'm no expert on mesmerism, but I've come to believe that somewhere along the line she went to a hypnotist and that guy had told her that whenever she heard the words "Hey, where's your husband?" she would turn horny. To be honest, I'd not fallen victim since marrying my wife. When Dean wasn't around, I just shut their kitchen door and ran like hell back to the car.

But seeing as men will be men, whenever Dean paddled out somewhere for high ground to take a crap, the rest of us would sit in the tree house looking at each other like fools. It took about a nanosecond before one of us would say, "Ursula, Ursula, Ursula" in time with the cicadas, and then go into minor details about the last time he'd seen her.

"I'm sure Dean knows all about it," I said one time. "I can't believe she wouldn't say anything. Maybe they're swingers."

"She keeps sending me pictures of herself naked," Russell said. "I disagree. I think she likes knowing that she's putting one over on Dean. And I think she loves making us scared to be around him a couple times a year. It's a power trip, man."

Dean yelled out from the swamp, "Hey, fuckface, it means something if your cork zigzags down on the bottom of the swamp, doesn't it?"

I looked at Russell and Evan. "It's pretty weird that we've all ended up in these different professions, but I think old Dean's finally seeing himself as something different than us."

Evan said, "Yeah. Yeah. Maybe we should tell him all about how we screw his wife whenever we can. That'll put him back in his place. That'll bring him back down to our level. Hey, maybe one of us should get the clap, you know. Then we can all be part of a losers' club."

I reached in my pack and pulled out a half gallon of

bourbon and four Ninja Turtle shot glasses I found down at South of the Border. I poured three, we lifted them, and all of us said "Ursula" after looking to make sure Dean still squatted far away.

Evan said, "He's going to find out and two things'll happen. First off he'll kill us. Then he'll start robbing his own bank. Mark my words. Write it down somewhere. He'll go nuts long before the rest of us will."

Russell said, "By the way. Those naked pictures she sends me? I keep them in a box in my shop. If I die or something, y'all get in there and get them before the wife. I don't want to end up like crazy Alton."

Dean returned with a fifteen-pound snapping turtle in the front of the boat. It held its ground, a hook stuck deeply in its thick and crooked mouth. The chicken neck hung out like a tampon. I dropped half a broomstick down so he could taunt the turtle, get it to bite, then bring it up tail-first.

In the den we had cut a hole to hold a deep-lipped pot. There we built fires we probably shouldn't have, and placed swamp water to boil atop a grate. At the end of the catwalk we put up a sign to remind ourselves not to step there, not to fall five or ten feet down.

Dean came up and said, "Good job, Drayton. How many hooks did you set down there?"

He handed me the snapper, a round-backed male. "I set six. What'd you do, cut the line?"

"Yes. I cut the line. I took out my handy knife and I cut the line. Y'all understand cutting lines, don't you?"

Later on Russell and Evan would say that Dean had meant he wanted to do some cocaine. Me, I knew that we wouldn't see much of Dean after this particular weekend, that he was talking figuratively, that he spoke in code.

I got up and doused what dry twigs I'd gathered along the way with lighter fluid. I dropped a bucket down swamp-level and got enough water to stick the snapper in. Dean said, "Okay. Somebody light the tiki lamps. I brought back what we need to use for poker chips." He reached in his pocket and pulled out a new pack of Bicycles. We sat down at the makeshift table we'd built when we weren't fifteen years old. "Cut your throat," Dean said.

ACCORDING TO RUSSELL, this Alton tenant of his stayed eighteen months. The only reason Russell knew that the guy left was because he heard the fire alarm beeping over and over, the battery signaling its own demise. He knocked a few times, then pulled out a key he always told his tenants he didn't own. When he entered the place the first thing he noticed was a charred area in the front room, obviously where poor Alton brought his rod-thrown bike in to work on. "The next thing I noticed was that the boy had put fly strips all over the place, hung from the ceiling. I walked right into one."

Evan said, "Do you have flies on your side of the building? Are there flies in the workshop?"

Russell shook his head. He turned his cards over in a game of seven-card stud, low-hole card wild, down and dirty.

Dean said, "Pussy. Pay attention. I'm betting that guy

killed some people and buried them on your property. Thus the flies." He didn't look up. He dealt cards and said nothing.

Russell got up to find the Off! "He wrote letters to God, too. I didn't tell y'all how he wrote letters to God. These were the saddest. Here you go—'Dear God, please, please, please bring Jodi back to me. And if you can't bring back Jodi, then bring back little Tiffini and Jason. If you can't bring back Tiffini and Jason, then go ahead and kill me right now. I can't go on. Hey, Man, see what you can do about either keeping me from wanting to smoke bud every day, or let the plants grow into what I can't stuff into a blunt. P.S. If you can't do any of this, then what good are you?' Man, Alton wrote letters to Dear Abby and Oprah. He never sent them. One went, 'Please don't let things happen to me for what I've done in the past, at least not in this life.'"

Dean turned his cards over to show a pair of threes for his low hole card, and four jacks altogether. He swept a pile of acorns, leaves, and nails his way. "It's okay to write Dear Abby. I don't know about Oprah, but I once wrote one of those shows. They were going to have a program on cheating spouses. Y'all know what I mean. It was the end of a show, and they came on saying, 'Do you suspect that your wife is cheating on you?' Then they gave an address. And an e-mail address. A phone number. I sent an e-mail but never heard anything. Maybe it was for the best." Dean looked up at Evan. He handed him the deck. "Please don't play one of your made-up games with eighteen different wild cards."

I couldn't think of one thing to say in order to change the subject. I couldn't even get up from my chair to check the turtle, surely dead by now, aboil in questionable water. I thought, This weekend should be more about Russell's deadly tenant and less about Dean and Ursula's private problems. "I bet you get a lot of death threats at the bank," I said.

"The tellers catch most of it. People come by and stick dead rats in the pneumatic tubes, you know. One guy one time drove up wearing a beekeeper's outfit. I don't know how he did it, but the next thing you know the drive-through teller opens up what she figures is a transaction and a swarm of yellow jackets fills the entire office. It's a federal offense, you know. If one of my tellers got stung and died, it would've been premeditated murder."

Russell said, "He had notices from one of those finance companies that charge a hundred percent interest. It was like a demand for payment, seven thousand bucks owed. From what I could see he didn't have seven grand in collateral. Sometimes I don't know what anybody's thinking in the business world."

I didn't speak up. I'd often thought about developing a Leland cypress that couldn't last more than three years, thus causing home owners associations to order new ones for the entrances to their gated communities and whatnot.

Dean kept raising everybody. He bluffed better than all of us, so no one knew what to do. He said, "I had an old boy one time realize that we were going to repossess his car. The Saturday before we came to get the thing, he entered his car in a demolition derby. I remember it was an El Camino. He won the derby, and I think back then the winner only got something like five hundred dollars. When we came to steal his car back it wasn't the size of a Yugo, all smashed in."

This might have been the funniest thing I'd ever heard. Of course I was on the El Camino guy's side. I didn't laugh, though, and I didn't call Dean's raise. I stood up and checked on the turtle, which had quit clunking against the pot's side thirty minutes earlier.

Russell said, "That sounds like something my ex-renter might've done. You know, I might take you up on getting inside a computer and tracking this Alton fellow down. What the hell. He owes me." Sometimes when Russell drank bourbon he wanted to get in the johnboat, go back to our cars, drive twenty miles down to Conway, and pick fights with the locals.

Dean pulled the pot his way. "You know, once we get his social security number we have a variety of options to mess him up until he dies. Hell, we can mess up his children, and their children. I'm so goddamned fed up and bored with my job it's all I can do to keep myself showing up at the office daily."

I said, "I believe it's time to crack this shell."

For the most part the good meat on a snapping turtle comes from its legs. The fat, liver, and eggs are edible enough. Most people add tomatoes, some bread crumbs, and bake the thing back in its shell for an hour. We always added whiskey, butter, and cut-up hard-boiled eggs. Much like the yellow isn't supposed to be eaten out of a crab, neither is the turtle's gall. It shouldn't even be used for crawfish bait. If it were up to me, I'd go bury the gall far from our campsite, but Dean always insisted that we boil it up separately and eat a half teaspoon apiece of the thing.

"We can eat this for breakfast, I guess," Dean said. "In the morning someone needs to go check the other lines. I'm betting that we don't need two more to feed us the whole weekend."

Evan said, "I might be going in the morning if y'all don't mind. It was pushing it for me to come even for a day. I'm behind. I'm way behind in things I need to get done."

I nodded. Russell nodded. It was obvious that the three of us foresaw some kind of bad juju imminent. Dean stuck his hand in the still-hot water and pulled the snapper out by its head. He dropped it on the second room's two-by-eight-inch pressure-treated southern yellow-pine planks. He held a machete in his left hand. "I don't know about that."

I said, "I'm supposed to talk to some people at Park Seed Company outside of Forty-Five about some bulbs. That's a ways away."

In a movie Dean would've thrown the machete between the rest of us or stuck it in the live oak next door. Instead, he only shrugged. "More turtle for me," he said. He set aside the shell and went to work cutting up meat. Dean set that meat aside in a frying pan, added bourbon, butter, and a chopped clove of garlic he'd brought along. Off in the swamp a commotion took place that could only mean wild pigs. Dean said, "I guess if we're finished playing poker y'all can just fork over what you owe me. And let me make it clear that y'all *do* owe me. The next time you start talking about that killer tenant of yours, Russell, I'm going to explain how y'all owe me in great detail."

At two o'clock that morning I descended the ladder, got in one of the johnboats, and paddled up-creek to where I set the trotline. I wrapped my anchor around a tree and floated, trying not to think about how Dean could get in the other boat, find me, and whack my head like any other snapper.

AT DAWN I awoke fifty yards from my childhood friends' tree house. The sound I'd heard wasn't unlike a branch struck by lightning, a baseball bat shattering, the sharp separation of a shinbone. I didn't sit up until I heard what followed—namely Dean's voice in *Geronimo!* fashion —the splash of a bag of rocks hitting the water.

Evan said, "I told you, fucker. See what you get?"

I paddled their way before untying the anchor. Dean said, "Right in the hole. I goddamn stepped right in the hole." He swam over to the ladder.

Russell came down to the edge, put out his hand, and never suspected that Dean might pull him in, too. By the time I showed up I didn't think that Dean meant to hold Russell beneath the surface, his feet atop Russell's shoulders. Evan stood at the edge of the tree house floor, looking down. "You like renting this?! You like this landlord you got now?!" Dean yelled out, sputtering swamp water.

I looked up at Evan. He held his arms outward and

shook his shoulders. If I'd had my feet on the swamp floor I could've gotten more power into the swing I took. From the boat it felt like I stood on ice. It was enough to stun him, though. Dean quit pushing down on drowning Russell. Russell emerged from the water swinging, his first punch a nice connection to Dean's nose, the right hook to his temple. Then Evan jumped from above, landing on Dean's head with both feet kicking. When I stood half-crouched in the johnboat Russell held one hand up toward me. "Don't get involved, man. Stay where you are, Drayton."

Evan ricocheted from Dean's head back to one of the live oaks that held our shack above. He stayed under, too. I jumped from the boat like a mad and confused lap dog might, clearing the boat's edge by an inch and belly-flopping in. Here was my first vision: I wondered what the poor hooked turtles nearby thought as they gave up any ideas of surviving, as they quit surfacing for air and remained limbolike, arms and legs splayed outward, hook-mouthed, their plastrons faced our way like stopped wall clocks. I wondered if they understood that what humans fought near them might be one of the apocalyptic signs.

And then I was on Dean, too. I wished to have a hay pick and nothing else. When I got tired of punching I said, "Get him up. Get him out of the goddamn water." I spoke to Russell only.

He held Dean in a loose headlock. "Where were you when all hell broke loose?"

Evan broke the surface alone. He held the back of his head. "He knows," Evan said. He nodded toward Dean, who looked dead to me. "Ursula."

I struggled toward Russell, chest-deep. I took Dean's body and floated him backwards to the johnboat. I might've had more difficulty pulling a sheet of bubble wrap across the dank, pollen-covered skim. For some reason I could only think about how I'd made the right decision a year earlier by closing my two accounts with Bank of America, by finding the smallest local bank possible, where the tellers sent Milkbones through the tubes when I visited the drive-through with my dogs in tow and didn't send checks back when I accidentally overdrew, where no teller inside stuck his or her arms in the air as if a hold-up might occur presently when I chose to walk into the lobby.

I tipped the boat twenty degrees and got Dean inside. He flopped over like a thin waterbed mattress. Russell didn't move, but Evan waded over to help me get the boat tied down. I felt Dean's jugular. His heart beat in rhythm with what cicadas had called out the night before, like stock tickers, like modems revving, like the internal language that keeps America producing whatever it wants but does not need.

"He tried to kill both of us," Evan said. "Right before he fell through the hole he came up to me, kicked my ribs, and said he wanted to make one last deposit. I got up, he went running for the machete, I guess, and he fell into the hole."

"That's the truth. He'd already kicked me upside the head with the back of his boot," Russell said. "It's not like I could sleep or anything. I pretended to be dead, but I heard him say how I had a negative balance. His words, man."

We stood in the water, not thinking about whether

alligators might congregate. We panted without embarrassment. "Y'all didn't hit him hard enough," I said. "That'll make us all feel better, at least one day."

Even I couldn't believe what I'd said.

Listen, Dean didn't come out of his stupor, ever, that we learned. From when we got him out of the swamp to when we arrived at the emergency room that we finally chose, Dean seemed to nod off, sit up, nod off. He breathed. Evan came up with our mantra: There was algae on the deck, a quick thunderstorm passed over, Dean slipped and bang-bang-banged his way right down the ladder. Evan told Dean this same story, just to see if he remembered anything, which he didn't.

"You have to move out of your workshop," I said to Russell on the way to the hospital. "If that Alton guy wasn't going to kill you before, you know he'll come after you now. It's like fate, man."

Evan said, "I'm not going to teach next year. I'm getting out of teaching. It's not the right thing to be doing these days."

I thought to say, "There'll be an opening at Bank of America soon," but didn't. I drove. "None of us paid him for his poker winnings. We either need to fill his pockets, or take all of his money now. I'm not sure which would look better."

Dean sat alone in the backseat, looking out the window. We passed more swamps, some country stores, a slew of shotgun shacks. We passed a Bank of America branch at a crossroads, thought about dumping Dean out there, maybe saying later on how he'd strayed from us all and that we didn't know what had happened to him.

I drove with Dean's turtle shell on my lap and knew that I would row back to our shelter in the evening, that I would cut whatever lines held snared turtles, that I would convince myself that hooks finally rust and disintegrate, that they only leave their prey with scar tissue at most. I banked on this theory.

Deer Gone

When the door to the house burst open, Zink McKinney thought it could only be either his own wife, Alene, or the nearly ex-husband of Cat Byers, the woman straddled atop Zink. When the bedroom door flew open he could do no other thing but grab Cat by both arms and shield his face with her breasts. She, meanwhile, turned around and screamed. Zink McKinney kept his face buried and thought about his uniform draped on a hardback chair over near the closet door. He re-created floor plans in his head: the position of the door, one closed window, the entrance to a bathroom. He thought about the small window in the bathroom and how he could never squeeze through it. Zink thought about the little .22 pistol Cat once said she owned, which she kept, for some reason, in the breadbox, all the way out in the kitchen. The kitchen might as well be a hundred miles away, Zink thought. He imagined pulling himself out of Cat, tossing her to the right, rushing the intruder—either Alene or Cat's nearly ex-husband—and running naked right out of the house to his dump truck.

His keys were in the right-hand pocket of his uniform pants.

He imagined tossing Cat to the left, grabbing his pants and shirt, storming past the intruder, shoving this person toward the bathroom door, and running. Zink thought, Or I could just carry this woman out in front of me like a shield. Later on I can ask if anyone saw my face and they'd have to say that they hadn't.

Zink thought, I shouldn't've left the shotgun with Pete.

Although it seemed as if he'd kept his face clearly hidden between Cat's ample breasts for longer than his own marriage had lasted, longer than he'd been employed with the detention center as a guard and work-detail monitor, all of this took place, of course, within a couple seconds, just like in movies and fairy tales. The person standing in the doorway throughout Cat's scream didn't step forward after viewing the spectacle of a truant man coupled with his mistress.

"Y'all boys stay in the truck and don't leave," was the first real human language that Zink heard, and it was the voice of his brother, Pete. "I got more shells, whether you believe it or not."

Zink leaned Cat to the side. She covered herself beneath the sheets and barely said, "Please don't shoot me, please don't shoot me."

"What the fuck are y'all doing?" Zink said.

The first man to have burst through the front door, then

the bedroom door, had been none other than Vonnie
Ponder, a half-wit man convicted of second-degree man-
slaughter and sentenced to life in the Greenwood County
Detention Center only because the judge knew that Vonnie
probably belonged in a mental institution, that he would
be gang-raped hourly in a high-security correctional facility, and that Vonnie came from a proud, significant, and
otherwise upstanding family of community leaders and
civic-minded pioneers who, three centuries earlier, had
founded Forty-Five, South Carolina, though word was that
the area went by "Sixty-Nine" back then.

The second man to come through was Pete, Zink's un-
employable little brother, a man who secretly subbed for
Zink for ten dollars and a case of beer each Saturday when
inmates needed to walk on litter patrol. Pete pushed Vonnie
aside and said, "I know you're busy. I didn't know that
Vonnie could run like that. I need a favor from you,
brother."

Zink got out of bed and walked to the den. He looked
out the window in time to see one inmate running down the
road, another running through the woods across from
Cat's house, and three others standing in the back of a
dump truck looking down, it appeared, at their own feet.
Zink yelled, "Goddamn it, Pete, they running away, they
running away."

Vonnie stared at the lump Cat made beneath the covers. Vonnie said, "Deer need help. Deer need help." He
smacked his mouth. Vonnie grabbed his crotch. "Deer
need doctor, like me." He might've unzipped his pants and

touched himself had he not worn a one-piece standard-issued jumpsuit.

Cat didn't stick her two-toned blond and brunette curly-permed head out from the sheet. Pete said, "Well *fuck me,* Zink. I told them not to try and escape. I told them I got this gun right here." He held up the shotgun for proof. Pete wore white tennis shorts and a T-shirt that read IMMORTAL, even though his brother had told him to try and wear all khaki or gray while impersonating a prison work-crew monitor.

Zink opened the front door and yelled, "Hey. Hey, y'all stay right where you are," to the men in the dump truck. "No, wait. You—Lester—I'll see to it that you get out immediately if you can round up the boys ran off."

Zink held up his palm to say that he'd be right there. He came back in the bedroom, pushed aside Pete and Vonnie, slipped his pants on, and said to Cat, "I'm sorry, honey. We won't have time to be romantic or nothing."

Cat said, "We can't do this again till you understand how we need a room at the Ramada. I ain't doing this again this way."

Vonnie said, "Deer done gone. Deer gone."

Zink looked at his little brother—a man of thirty—and said, "Do you think you can possibly take care of Vonnie? Do you think you can handle him?"

Pete said, "Hey, quit bitching at me. I got an interview Monday for a real job repo-ing." He held his brother's shotgun upright and safely. He said, "Sorry to bother you, Cat."

She sat up, unashamed of her bare torso. Zink left. She said, "Tuesday and Friday?"

Pete said, "It might be Monday night, if I have reason to celebrate. Come on, Vonnie. Come on, boy." He led Vonnie out of the house and toward the dump truck. "You ain't got to look in the back if it bothers you that much."

PETE WORKED HIS brother's job for three months of consecutive Saturdays while Zink continued the affair with Cat Byers. At first Pete shied from the offer, thinking it was some kind of set-up, that maybe Zink wanted Pete caught for impersonating a prison guard, an officer of the law, or a dump truck driver. Pete distrusted Zink at family gatherings, thought that maybe his brother only wanted to act the big shot at yearly reunions and whatnot.

"You let the boys out at a straightaway in the road. You park off to the side and watch them. They bag up these big orange garbage bags and set them aside. They only got sticks with nails in the end," Zink had said. "At the end of the day you drive back and pick up all the bags. Then you come get me, and you borry my truck to get you home, and I drive the prisoners back. I give them a couple dollars apiece to keep they mouths closed. That's it. This'll work like a pocket watch. What else you got to do, man?"

"What if the warden drives by and sees me instead of you?" Pete had asked. "How come you think you ain't got no asides on this?"

"Warden's off to Greenville fucking some female guard he met at a seminar. The warden tells his wife that he's driving the truck on weekends. Warden's wife's fucking a man named Glenn who still sells fifty-cent-a-week insurance to poor people. Listen, I'll give you ten dollars and a case of beer. That's like twenty bucks for six hours work, no taxes taken." They stood on Pete's front porch, which was littered with various pieces of recyclable metal — from aluminum cans to fenders — Pete picked up to turn in weekly. "The warden's wife might drive by some Saturday, but she wouldn't know you from me. She's never seen me. From what I understand she's kind of a fat woman who spends her other days all the way down in Augusta taking business classes at one of them tech colleges. She wants to open up some kind of calendar store she read about. A place that only sells calendars."

Pete said, "That's stupid. There's a gun inside in case one them prisoners tries to run for it?"

At the time Zink had only thought about Cat Byers, how she'd treat him differently than his wife, and how no prisoner picking up litter on the roadside had ever thought about running. He said, "Shotgun."

Pete stood in front of the two-room shack he rented off Bad Joe Road, not far from where Vonnie Ponder's parents' run-down antebellum mansion stood off Deadfall Road. He said, "I'll do it if I can listen to the radio. I'll do it if you get me a bag of aluminum cans from the jail, too." But he only thought about the shotgun stretched behind his head as he sat on the berm, watching men pick up tossed Hardee's and Dixie Drive-In wax cups, brown Tall Boy beer bottles, cigarette butts, empty ten-pound ice bags, and the sheetrock, molding, shingles, and pink insulation that flew out of the back of contractor's pickup trucks. "I know those boys in jail get a Coke a day or more. I want a bag of aluminum every day."

"I'll get you a bag of cans, too," Zink said. "This'll be a lot easier than you think. You can sit in the truck and zone out. The only thing you have to worry about is when you get to a curve in the road. Don't let them get to a curve in the road. Drive up behind them then."

Zink said he'd give an example, that he'd drive his little brother around to curvy roads and show him how to act. He never did, though. And it wouldn't have mattered, had not a herd of deer crossed every late morning at a curve in the road between Old Laurens Road and Old Coronaca Road, off of 72. Pete's prisoners walked ahead, picking up trash and thinking about the two dollars they'd later get from Zink for keeping quiet.

Pete saw the first doe lead the way. He pulled a shotgun from behind his head and opened the door as if it were a wasp that needed swatting. He stood in the road, on a double yellow line, and leveled his aim, waiting.

A bouncing, dumb, majestic eight-point buck followed.

Pete pulled the trigger slowly—five years later Zink would tell this story at a family reunion, noting that the moment Pete pulled the trigger might've been the same time that Zink "busted my second nut inside Cat Byers"—and the buck fell hard not twenty yards from the prison truck. Twenty yards ahead of the kill moseyed the crouched inmates, picking up litter.

A series of yearlings followed, but Pete had the shotgun pointed at his own right foot at this point.

He checked the deer, ran back to his dump truck, and drove it forward. The prisoners—including Lester—pretty much said, "Goddamn, boy, you could've hit us, motherfucker."

Pete said, "I know what I'm doing here. Help me get this bad boy in the back. I got to get it dressed out. Meat goes bad fast."

It was Vonnie who said first, "We don't do this." Vonnie jumped up and down and bit his own hand. Vonnie shook his head sideways. "Not dead, not dead!"

"Y'all get in the truck." Pete shoved the buck above the high tailgate himself. "I got to get Zink to take over here so I can get this thing dressed over at Ray Coker's Processing. Y'all like venison jerky, don't y'all? Y'all like venison jerky? Hey, I'll be making some jerky out of this and bring some to the jail." Pete shoved the buck, with the help of D-man, into the back. "Y'all like jerky, right?"

"Yeah," said D-man. "We like jerky, dog. We going to see Zink? Take us to see Zink." He crossed and recrossed his arms, held his chin toward the uncaring, even, autumnal sky.

The convict who went by Meltdaddy, a white boy caught for driving his El Camino into a bank's front door, said, "Zink might be the man to help us out in this situation, if you ask me."

When the prison dump truck reached Cat Byers's house, Meltdaddy and D-man jumped out and ran. So did Vonnie, though Vonnie went in the direction of a perfect centipede lawn, an unlocked front door.

MELTDADDY AND D-MAN were whiter than freezer-burned slices of Sunbeam bread, which is why they were jailed. They took on ghetto monikers, pretended to be the first gangsters of tiny Forty-Five, and got thrown in jail simultaneously for what the sheriff's department considered obstructing justice. And drunk and disorderly—though the boys weren't inebriated, just hemming and hawing around in front of the Dixie Drive-In, crossing and recrossing their arms in a way that might've looked as if they were practicing semaphore to bring an F-16 safely atop a battleship.

They didn't get but thirty days, and on their first roadside pickup stint they took off together.

Zink was the first one to say, "Goddamn it. Those boys will get a couple years apiece for escaping. They shouldn't've done what they did." He left the prison truck in front of Cat Byers's house and said to his brother, "You go that way and I'll go this way," just like in some kind of horror movie.

Lester—a black man—took Vonnie and sat him inside the truck. Behind them, down the asphalt, they had a good sixty bags of roadside detritus. Lester said, "I know you worried up and sad."

Vonnie said, "Deer in back. Sad deer in back."

Lester said, "Listen, you can't worry about that none, boy. This ain't one them stories about no Indian from eastern India where some boy named Nareesh tries to figure out his family's woes. That's all I been reading about in the prison li-bary. It ain't like that none down here."

Vonnie said, "Fall down. Deer fall down and bleed," and then started crying. He looked at the house and its closed Venetian blinds. "I want me some that woman."

Lester pulled Vonnie into his own chest and said, "We all do, Bubba. We got to get out first, though." He said, "We living here in Greenwood County Jail / No one here to make our little bail / Little Opie Taylor gotta daddy goin' fishing / We got us shampoo, but where's the hair condition?"

No dogs bayed in the background. There were no police sirens, or people cursing when they stepped in hidden holes, or helicopters overhead, or armed patrolmen afoot.

"Me. Me. Me," Vonnie said. And then he escaped from Lester's grasp.

Two other black prisoners still stood in the back of the truck, straddling the kill. One said, "They goes Vonnie," and pointed. "White boy. They go Vonnie running again."

But Vonnie veered from the front door and went around to the back of the house. He ran through the backyard that hadn't been tended since Cat's nearly ex-husband took to a Weed Eater some year before. There were brown October briars and intricate webs of dormant honeysuckle vines.

There was the old, inoperable, open well barely hidden by it all.

Vonnie ran, and in his head he thought about returning to his brother, a man who still operated the family business as best he could, a man named Mead who had strayed from owning land and letting other people work it, to the junk business. Vonnie thought, I get home, I give jumpsuit to Mead. He thought, Na na na na na na, la la la la la la, one, eight, seven, grits for breakfast, my momma love me, two times two, egg runny, quit drinking that beer D-man, ha ha ha ha ha ha, me Vonnie, me Vonnie, me Vonnie.

Vonnie stomped as if he was killing fire ants. He ran past Cat Byers's white-faced lawn jockey. He trudged by a fallen gutter pulled sideways, a dead azalea, a haphazard circle of cigarette butts where Cat flicked them lit from her cement front porch after ten P.M. Vonnie looked straight ahead, but he couldn't get the deer out of his mind. Sweat ran down the sides of his massive head and into his eyes. He saw the buck stumble, and fall, and turn its head until only one eye stared upward at the cloudless sky.

Vonnie turned the corner of the house, on his way home, thinking, Baa baa black sheep—have you any wooooo?, three times three, George Washington chopped cherry tree, Abe Lincoln, I saw titties, I saw titties, I saw titties, Coca-Cola, don't drop the soap says Mead, my momma wanted a girl, bird in spring, bird in spring. He thought, I got my picture took at the capitol of United States.

He turned the corner into what was once a luxurious backyard, and right before he tripped on vines and fell headfirst into the abandoned well he thought, *Barometric pressure*. He even thought, Why am I thinking about barometric pressure? And on his way down the hole got out "Bare!"

Lester heard "Bear!" and shut his door. The two remaining prisoners in the back of the truck heard it, too. One man said, "I knowed they'd be a bear in country with these deers."

Inside the house, Cat Byers heard nothing. She took a shower, put on some blue jeans that required her lying down on the bed to get them on, and called her sister. As Vonnie fell in her well hole, unknowingly Cat said, "You want to drive on out to Wal-Mart or something? I ain't got nothing to do."

Cat's sister said, "They's a tractor pull up in Ware Shoals. You want to go? They's going to be catfish stew and bands playing."

Cat said, "That sounds boring. And it's boring here. We got to find something to do."

Her sister said, "I ain't sure but I think the weatherman said there'd be a meteor shower tonight. You want to go get some beer sit on the hood down at Lake Between? It's dark out there."

ZINK MCKINNEY WENT *that* way. His brother Pete ran the other, west, through some brambles. Pete high-stepped his way into the woods, then zigzagged between pine trees, thinking that he was following either D-man or Meltdown. He saw one of them veer off on a deer run, maybe a quarter-mile from Cat's house.

Pete ran the mile in five minutes flat in high school track, and figured that he could take on a man wearing boots and a baggy jumpsuit. He said, "You might as well stop now, you might as well stop," out loud. But while he ran, his right arm stuck up like a carpenter's square in order to rip through spiderwebs, he could only think, This wouldn't've happened if Zink stayed true to his wife. He thought, I wished I'd saved his ten dollars a weekend.

He yelled out, "I see you. I see you," though he saw nothing. He ran until he had to pull up beside a patch of flattened morning glory. Pete held his side. He panted. He looked up and realized that he followed nobody. Pete said, "This ain't right," to himself.

Zink wasn't any more successful: he ran a hundred yards into the woods and yelled out, "This can get you boys some time in the *hole*," as if there were a hole in the Greenwood County Detention Center. He yelled, "Hey, if y'all come back I won't say anything, I swear."

There was no answer emanating from the woods. There weren't pitter-patter sounds of a jailbird running through a land where he didn't belong.

D-man and Meltdaddy crouched low in a deer stand they found a half-mile from the road. This particular stand served as a campsite, too, for it had a three-foot-high wall around it and a trapdoor that locked from the inside. Old, bloated magazines lay scattered around. D-man said, "I can't believe I remembered this place. I used to come here as a kid."

Meltdaddy held his side. He looked at the homemade tattoo he'd started on his left knuckles the night before, which read M-E. "We ought to turn ourselves in. We'd get caught anyway. And they'd lock us up forever. If we turn ourselves in they ain't no way Zink will tell on us, what we know on him."

They panted and peered over the edge, listening. They heard Pete yelling, "I ran a five-minute mile."

"You right," said D-man. He cupped his hands around his mouth and screamed, "You don't turn us in, we'll give up."

Pete stopped running. He tried to pull a briar from his leg. He yelled back, "We ain't gone tell." Pete released himself from the briar and ran toward D-man's voice. He thought about his upcoming job interview as a mobile-home repo man, and wondered if it would be best to show up perfectly groomed or with the half-healed scratches that would cover his face and arms. He thought about getting the job and reporting to Cat Byers that night, and about them laughing over Zink not figuring out their own history. Pete ran, slipped on pine straw, and didn't have time to an-nounce his arms backwards to the ground. If someone stood in a deer stand above the situation he might've no-ticed that Pete went down in much the same way as the buck he'd shot earlier—that his limbs buckled and splayed, that his eyes rolled back.

When D-man and Meltdaddy ambled up to him five minutes later Pete could only say, "I think I broke my ass bone."

D-man said, "Your head's bleeding."

"Y'all go get Zink. Go get Zink and tell him to bring me a stretcher out here. I'm scared to move and get paralyzed."

Meltdaddy said, "It ain't too cold yet for snakes to go a-hiding. You sure you want us to leave you here on the ground?" He said, "That deer meat's going bad the longer you wait, dog."

"Goddamn it, go get Zink and tell him I'm dying."

D-man and Meltdaddy walked away, following the path that Pete had taken into the woods. One of them said something about maybe breaking into Cat Byers's house and seeing what it was that Zink saw in her. The other said he wanted to take a class at the technical college in how to become a locksmith.

When they got to the road they looked down toward the prison dump truck. They waved to the men in back, who still straddled the deer. Lester wasn't visible, nor was Vonnie. They heard, faintly, a radio playing gospel music. They walked back on the center line, but never called out for help.

"Set into the woods right there between the sixth and seventh bag of trash," D-man said when Zink returned to the truck an hour later. "Your brother's straight into the woods. I counted our trash bags. Go down between the sixth and seventh bag, take a right, and follow the little path. You'll hear him."

Meltdaddy said, "He's moaning and groaning like a dog that's locked while boning." His hands were stuck in some kind of cryptic gang-sign petrification, fingers all E's and W's.

"Where's Vonnie? Lester! Get out of the truck and go find Vonnie," Zink said. "Damn it to hell. This whole day is burning my balls up."

Lester cracked open the passenger door. "I ain't going looking for him. Last I heard he run acrost a bear."

Zink asked the ex-escapees, "Y'all sure he can't walk none? Did you look at him good?"

"He broke his butt bone, he said," said D-man. "I ain't no doctor, but I seen one one time where they moved a man broke his butt bone and the next thing you know that guy's stuck in a wheelchair the rest of his life, getting people to hold his pecker when he aimed."

Cat Byers came out of the front door and said, "What're y'all still doing here? Go on. I don't want my neighbors down the road driving by and thinking I got so much trash in my yard that the prison's got to stay here."

Zink said, "Hey. Hey, you got a big board or anything inside? Can we use your coffee table?" He explained his brother's predicament.

"No." Cat put her hands on her hips. She wore the blue jeans that might as well have been slathered on with a cheap paintbrush, and a halter top that exposed her navel. "I got a hammock out back you can go get. It ain't rotted out much."

VONNIE WASN'T DEAD. When Zink, Meltdaddy, and D-man went to the backyard looking for Cat's hammock they heard, "Water wet, water wet, water wet. Hole dark, hole dark, hole dark. Seven! Lucky number seven!"

"There's your Vonnie," Meltdaddy said. "He's lying in the grass over yonder."

They walked until they came to the well. Zink looked down and saw Vonnie eight feet down, standing up. Vonnie said, "I didn't run away. I didn't run away."

"Goddamn, Vonnie, what're you doing in this hole?"

"I didn't run away. Fall down like deer."

Zink looked down and said, "Y'all boys find the hammock. We can use it as a rope to pull this old boy up." To Vonnie he said, "If we slide something down there can you hold onto it tight?"

Vonnie nodded.

In the front of the house Lester turned up the radio. One of the two men in back said, "Here come the flies." They stood away from the deer. Cat Byers started up her Camaro and backed out of the driveway.

Zink twisted the thin twine hammock like an expertly rolled joint and handed it down to Vonnie. There was about a foot to spare. Vonnie grabbed the end and said, "Elevator."

It took Zink and his two ex-escapees to pull Vonnie from the well, but the hammock ripped apart just as they saw his head emerge. Like in a cartoon, Vonnie kept his claws out and raked his way back down until a slight splash occurred. Vonnie said, "Oops."

I just don't know what to do, thought Zink. Should I go get Pete in the woods first? What if he's dead?

"We get Vonnie out of here and we got one more man to help get your brother out of the woods," D-man said. "Vonnie's big enough to carry that boy hisself."

Zink stood up and stretched his back. He said, "Screw Pete. That boy ain't been right since the day he came out of my momma. We in this trouble 'cause of Pete."

They pulled the deer out of the dump truck. They shoved it down to Vonnie headfirst. "Hold on to its antlers, Vonnie," Zink said. D-man took one hind leg and Meltdaddy took the other. In the background Lester sang along to "I'll Fly Away."

"It looking at me, it looking at me," Vonnie yelled from the hole.

"Turn your head, Vonnie," Zink said. "Don't make eye contact. Just grab his antlers and hold on." D-man and Meltdaddy pulled the buck's legs straight out, and Zink grabbed its torso. They pulled up, and Vonnie held on. "We get you out of this hole right, we'll mount this head and give it to you for your cell."

Vonnie didn't answer. He emerged and remained holding the deer's antlers after D-man and Meltdaddy continued to pull him halfway across the yard.

"There's a man upstairs," Zink said. "Thank you, Jesus, for getting us through this." He looked at his watch. "I don't know what I'm gone say when we get back and ain't cleaned up half the highway scheduled."

Vonnie kissed the dead deer's snout.

"We can borry one them fake shutters off'n the window to carry your brother out," D-man said. "The girl's gone. We can get it back on before she comes back."

Except for Vonnie, everyone looked at the back of the house. Vonnie stayed on the ground, holding on to the deer's antlers. His jumpsuit was wet from crotch on down, and his elbows bled. Five years later, as Zink and Pete told the story at the family reunion about how Pete had only bruised his tailbone and twisted an ankle, Vonnie would sit in his cell with a new roommate and say, "My best friend pulled me out the well. My best friend pulled me out one day. Eight feet down. Eight feet down. Water."

The two men in back of the dump truck would forget about this particular day. Lester would get out of jail, label himself a minister, and talk to people beneath a makeshift tent. He would tell a story involving mysterious ways, and sin, and redemption—about signs, betrayal, and resistance. The warden's wife would speak likewise.

Duke Power

This vice president from the home office—my boss's boss, really—wants to come down and see what we're doing right down South, and out of everything we can offer for entertainment the man wants to go bowling. Bowling! Of course somehow my own boss has a family reunion scheduled, as always, and I get stuck in charge. In the past I've taken both men and women out to play golf, pool, or darts. We've eaten entire barbecued pigs. I've found clandestine strip joints, poker games, moonshine festivals, dope dens, and cock fights. I've set up dates for bad husbands who had no business being in the company of clients or management. I've gotten good race tickets for Darlington, Charlotte, Bristol, and North Wilkesboro that my boss found excuses to miss, also—I'm not sure if he's Mormon or Catholic, but he has a family reunion about twice a month—but bowling is a new one.

I come in one Friday and get this note that goes,

"Johnny Capozzi's arriving Monday P.M. from New York. He wants us to take him down to the bowling alley. I'll be gone until next Wednesday. If you don't know how to bowl, take today off and learn. If you do know, make sure you lose to him." About eighteen Capozzis have come visiting since I've been here. I'm not sure what's done with the wire and cable we make. Every time someone from the home office shows up he only talks about "connections" and "capacitance" and "power transfer," all of which could have double meanings, at least.

I go to my boss's secretary and say, "Is Mr. Gobert in yet?" In four years she's never said my name. Hers is Olene, which she's not, exactly.

She doesn't look up. Olene wears this inch-wide piece of elastic tight to the back of her head, attached to her eyeglasses, as if she might go compete in an Ironman competition at any moment. "In Florida," she says. "Read the note. Family reunion. Be back Wednesday morning."

I think to myself, Fuck, I better go practice salvaging a six-ten spare, and I leave.

On my way out I run down the alleys I know. Fifty miles away in Greenville there's some kind of reconstructed place in the basement of a boutique mall that used to be a cotton mill, a place where pin boys actually work and a bottle of beer costs four bucks. I think, Is Capozzi out for that kind of atmosphere? Is he some kind of strike shark looking for bets?

The local alley, Forty-Five Lanes—which isn't really but thirty-eight—is in the middle of two mill villages and run by a guy named Bobby since the 1940s. The locals call the place Bobby Lanes for when some guy played quarterback for Detroit. I drive directly through the center of Forty-Five, take a left over the railroad tracks about three seconds before the hourly freight train limps through, and make my way to the alley. I walk in right in the middle of league play—understand, again, this still isn't ten o'clock on a Friday morning—and walk up to the woman who rents shoes and pours draft. She wears a name tag with yellow bowling balls on both ends like smiley faces, and in between them MARY!—not Loretta, Norma, Luann, or Glenice, like most bowling alley workers across this great country. I say, "Man, I didn't think it'd be so crowded this early."

Mary says, "It's the Four-Ten League. Everybody here pretty much works some kind of four-day week. You know, ten hours a day Monday to Thursday. Mostly construction. Roofers. Bricklayers. Electricians. Some them spinners over at Forty-Five Textile."

I said, "That's cool," and wonder why these guys would get up early on Friday to bowl. I wonder if maybe I've missed something over the years, spending all my time trying to learn how to par more than two holes in a row at the course I play. "When'll they be done? I can come back when it's slower."

Mary gets on a microphone and says, "Hey, Felmet, you want a partner?"

I say, "No, no. I don't want to be in the league or anything. I don't even know how to play," and start to go into detail about my situation with the boss's boss's boss, but before I know it the woman hands me a pair of 10 ½ shoes without even looking down at my feet.

She says, "Felmet's not in league play. He got kicked out and just comes here out of meanness." Mary says, "Last lane. Thirty-eight."

Let me say here that Bobby made money off all the mill workers over the years, and upgraded his bowling alley when necessary. First off, it's called a "Bowling Centre," like that—British spelling and all. There are those electronic scoreboards so no one has to remember simple math. There are even disengageable bumper rails for kids. I walk to the last lane and find this little wiry guy standing there all smiles, as if we'd known each other back in junior high or something. Felmet nods twice fast, turns to the console, and says, "What's your handle?" so he can enter my name.

I don't know why I can't ever realize when it's necessary to use an alias. I say, "Chuck." I don't know why I can't tell Felmet it's not "Chick" when he makes a typo.

Felmet says, "My name's Felmet. It rhymes with 'helmet.' That makes it easier to remember. Hey, there's some good balls on the back row over there. Me, I always use a sixteen. A lot of people think that's too heavy, but not for me, man. What I lack in speed with a sixteen I gain in pure-tee power." One of his eyes goes off funny. "I used to have my own sixteen but I got mad drunk one time and threw it out the window of my truck. You'd think a bowling ball would crack in half or splatter apart at seventy miles an hour, wouldn't you? It don't. It just bounces, at least down highway seventy-two it does."

I think, If this guy hyperventilates and passes out, I'm going to pretend I need to use the bathroom. I say, "I ain't played in a while so I'm going to use a little twelve."

"Blue ball," Felmet says. "If anyone comes over and makes fun of you having blue balls, I'll stick up for you, Chuck." He runs over to the shelves of balls, brings back three, and sets them in the trough. "One of these will feel right for you. Feel of them—one will have finger holes you want, I'm betting."

The first one does. I say, "This one's good."

"I'm up!" says Felmet, and already I'm thinking about taking Capozzi to the place where yuppies bowl to save the whale or whatever.

FELMET WALKS HALFWAY down the lane and puts a hard nonspin on the ball in such a manner that it looks like the way Phil Niekro would bowl. I start to say something about the foul line but after Felmet scores a strike he says, "Next ball I'll throw from a few feet behind the line."

I'm not sure why it matters to me whatsoever. I get my ball and try to remember watching Sunday bowling on TV when the football teams on other stations didn't concern me, like when I didn't have a parlay card penciled in. In my mind I can't figure out if it's four steps or five, et cetera, but I pretty much get it down seeing as it's not that much different from going into the production area at work and unsnagging spools of wire. I bowl the first ball with no English whatsoever, it hits the first pin straight on, and somehow I'm left with only the seven pin standing.

"That's nice," Felmet says. "That's not bad at all. There's worse things in life that can happen to you, Chuck." I look up at the screen above the trough and an arrow directs me to hit the remaining pin on the right side for some reason. Because I remember some geometry, I stand to the far left side of my lane and plan to roll the ball right down the edge. I do, but it's leaning into the gutter. Felmet jumps off his perch, pulls the end of the kiddie bumper out, and helps ricochet my ball straight into a spare. He says, "That'll make up for me going down the lane on my first strike. We're even now."

To my left all the way down to the other end of the bowling center I hear league bowlers talking and laughing. I think to myself, How can I get out of the situation?, and wish my boss provided me with a beeper I could pretend to answer. Felmet stands right on the line with his ball held down by his right knee. This time he takes no steps and uses a spin that weaves twice, I swear. Unfortunately he ends up with a weird 2-10 split, and I say, "Tough."

Felmet says, "Not in the Land of Felmet." He says, "I'll need to use one of your balls for my left hand. I ain't as strong with my left hand, but I'm working on it." Before I say anything he walks to the line, bowls the light ball toward the 2 and his ball toward the 10. They fall simultaneously. From somewhere between three and twenty lanes away I hear more than two people yelling "Felmet!" as if cursing a dog.

I say, "So you're not in the league anymore, huh?"

Felmet points at me as if I don't know it's my turn. He

doesn't smile. He says, "Duke Power. Let's you and me split a pitcher of beer."

I don't want beer. I'm not allowed to drink beer for a variety of reasons that range from blacking out to paranoia—at least that's what I think people at work have been saying since the previous year when two Capozzis came down together on St. Patrick's Day. I say, "Well." Felmet gets on our console speaker and orders to Mary.

Felmet says to me, "I used to work for Lightning Fast Electric. We done nothing but residential work. Well, let me say that there's some kind of collusion between Duke Power and the city's building inspector. I'm not sure that's the right word. Somehow Duke Power and a building inspector split up some money. Maybe there's a politician in there somewhere, too."

Felmet reaches in his pocket for a cigarette. He's wearing a bowling shirt with a tiny pocket down at the bottom of the shirttail. He says, "I'm not taken care of by the government. I pay my bills by what I make out at the flea market on weekends now."

Mary shows up with a pitcher and says, "You know I ain't supposed to be doing this, Felmet. Hide it over there on the floor."

I say, "Is it my go? I don't want to tie up the lane or anything."

Mary looks up at the scoreboard and says, "Chick. I like that." She says, "You don't start acting crazy after a couple beers, I hope, Chick."

Felmet pours two plastic glasses without regard to head

and says, "Go on and bowl. In the Land of Felmet you get to do whatever I got to do. It's kind of like playing H-O-R-S-E in basketball."

I grab my ball and think, Somehow this is going to end up a day to remember. Somehow this has either been set up to get me fired or will cause me to do something that'll end up in the newspaper. I approach the line and let the ball roll slowly until somehow it hits just to the right of center and all the pins fall as if imploded. This big X shows up on the monitor with *Chick!* underneath.

Felmet says, "Here's what they do. Sit down and I'll tell you what they do." He seems to be in no hurry to finish the game. Felmet appears to be the kind of man who focuses only on one thing at a time, and for now it's his beer. "Duke Power won't admit it, but they let out these big power surges that end up blowing people's heat pumps out. A surge ain't good for your power box, either—it'll melt the wires fast, and make this scorch mark that looks like the house caught on fire the night before or something."

I say, "I think collusion's the right word." Mary leaves, saying she's heard this one too many times.

"Okay, then, you know, you notice it, and call up Duke Power to come take a look. They come out, switch off your electricity, and say you need to call someone like me because you got yourself a fire hazard. You don't want a fire hazard, so you do it almost immediately, you know, and because it's dark inside your house. Hey, go talk to anyone— they always wait until like right before five o'clock to come turn off your electricity."

I take a drink. I take one small sip and remind myself not to forget that I have to drive later on, and maybe even go back to work. I say, "I bet they get some kind of psychological training for that."

Felmet pulls up his short sleeve further and for the first time I notice a handmade tattoo that reads BORN TO LOOSE. He says, "So then you call up Lightning Fast Electric, say, and then I come out there already knowing what's going to happen. It's going to always cost you $350. I fix you up. Then—and this is where it gets real dirty—Duke Power wants you to either have me go get a building permit after I've done the work, which will cost you another seventy-five bucks—or you can go stand in line two hours and say you're doing it yourself and it'll cost only twenty-five. The bottom line is this—they say they got service technicians who can spot a fire hazard, but they ain't got service techs who know when your goddamn power box is in good working order."

I say, of course, "Motherfuckers."

"Right," says Felmet. He finishes his first beer and pours another. I follow suit, seeing as it's like H-O-R-S-E.

As IT ENDS UP, Felmet's been blackballed from the league for a number of reasons, one of which happens to be telling some people at Duke Power that every construction worker in the area knows how to rig wires to get free electricity without a kilowatt meter, and that most of these boys bowling to my left have at one time or another figured out ways to run kilowatt hours backwards. "In the old days,"

Felmet says, "we just pulled the meter straight out, turned it upside down, and shoved the prongs back in. Do you get my drift? Let's say the Duke Power meter reader comes by on the tenth of the month to your house. He reads your meter. Let it run for ten or twelve days regular-like. Then go out and clip the little wire lock, pull the meter out, and turn it over. Let it run for ten or twelve days the same. Don't go using a whole bunch more electricity, or less either. Just go about your daily life, you know. Then go pull the thing out and right it. You should be about where you started. Bend that little metal lock thing back so it looks like you ain't tampered with it. When the meter reader comes back to write down your monthly usage, you won't really be paying but for six to ten days of electricity."

Mary says over our intercom, "Y'all need to start playing faster. We got people waiting."

I stand up even though it's Felmet's turn. I say, "That's a good one. I like to go over to this church near where I live and rearrange the magnetic letters on their sign so it spells something else," for I feel like I need to be on the wrong side of the law.

Felmet says, "It ain't as easy as all that nowadays, but it can be done. I ain't ever had a personal problem with any Duke Power meter readers, but it might be because they know my reputation. Any worker at a utility company has a little black book with a list of troublemakers. They trade names and stories all the time, and take notes." He nonchalantly walks crabwise down our lane, tosses his ball without looking, takes his foot out and pulls on the bumper. The ball ricochets and only the 9 pin's left standing.

I say, "Damn."

Felmet reaches in the back of his pants and pulls out a pistol. He says, "I could shoot it down from here if I wanted."

I look over to the lane next to us. I stand close to the intercom button and want to hit it in Morse code somehow. I say, "Man, you're going to get us in trouble."

Felmet laughs and rolls his head funny. He says, "I've learned not to fire this thing anymore. I had a little problem with my sewer one time and the guy who come out to tell me the back-up was all my fault got all mean about it. He kept asking me if I knew anything about my wife's Kotexes, you know. When we got outside I lost it and shot him straight in the head. Get this—the water and sewer authority hired a bunch of people with plates in their heads on purpose. I fired my pistol, and that bullet ended up coming right back at me. I ducked, but it took out my windshield out in the driveway."

I say, "Bullshit." I say, "Knock that pin down so I can go."

Felmet walks straight down our lane and kicks the 9 over. "You ever seen hockey?" he yells back to me. There's a din he has to keep his voice raised over. "Go ahead and roll your ball down here and let me see if I can stop it."

I look back for Mary. I look over at the four bricklayers next to me. Mary's not in sight. One of the bricklayers says, "I'll help you, Cuz." We get four balls and roll them hard, one after the other, and I hate to admit that I kind of want to take Felmet out. I don't think about how he only has to retrieve his pistol. I don't think about how my company makes cable probably used by Duke Power in some capacity.

Felmet's wearing those slick-bottomed bowling shoes, and the only thing that can logically happen happens—the first ball hits Felmet right on that hard bone sticking off the inside of his ankle. He pulls that leg up, and the second ball upends him altogether. Balls three and four push him right into the pins, and before he can get up the sweeper gate comes down on top of him, gets wedged, and neither continues down, breaks off, or returns to its high position. I'm not sure if everyone stops bowling at that point on purpose, but there are no sounds of pins clattering and we can only hear what sounds like gears grinding on top of Felmet. I'm not sure if it's cause and effect or pure coincidence, but all the power goes out at the bowling centre about a nanosecond later.

MARY'S AT MY ear saying, "Most men would've taken this opportunity to have high-tailed it out of here, Chick. There're two men down in the middle who were bowling perfect games, and they ain't gonna be happy about this none whatsoever."

I can barely make her out by sight. What gray light comes through the double glass doors in the middle of the alley makes a halo around Mary's entire torso. From the end of lane 38 Felmet yells, "Goddamn it to hell someone get this bar off me," and I can sense that the construction worker who helped me roll balls that way has sneaked back toward his own team's lane. Felmet screams, "Duke Power! Duke Power! I shoulda knowed they got this place wired," which I take him to mean in an espionage kind of way.

I say to Mary, "I'll go down there and get him, but I want to go on record as saying he's nuts. I'm not nuts, but he is. Go check the breaker first." Halfway down the lane I turn and say, "We might need to get some oil or Crisco to slide him out," because I saw this documentary one time about someone stuck in a crevice or something.

There's total silence in the place outside of what I figure is one of the perfect bowlers kicking his console. I get down the lane and say to Felmet, "There's got to be a reset button somewhere for this thing," meaning the sweeper. Sure enough he's stuck, from shoulder to right hip.

Felmet says, "You goddamn right there's a reset button. But it only works if there's electricity, you idiot." He says, "I'll tell you what's worse, and that's there's a reset button in my brain about to click on for Duke Power. Once I get out of here, watch out. You're gonna read about me, Chuck."

I pull on one end of the sweeper as if I'm working out on a curl bar at the local gym. I think, I need to bring Capozzi down here if he wants to see what we're doing right in the South.

I jerk hard once and one bolt bends enough for Felmet to move his hips. I grab his legs, disregard his claims of a broken ankle, and pull him out hard. I say in a whisper, "You can probably get out of here if you crouch around the wall. That's what I'd do, man."

Felmet doesn't whisper when he says, "I think that bar scraped off one of my nipples. I'm going to sue this place for all it's worth."

I help him to his feet. The lights come on as if a Hollywood director's in control of the entire scene. Every league bowler in the place looks our way. It doesn't appear unlike the stands at a stock car race after the leader drives by the grandstand into turn three or whatever, the way each man stands there with his body straight and his head turned at the proper angle.

Everyone holds a can of beer, too, which makes me think someone snuck into the cooler with the lights out and handed them down the line.

I start to say something, but every sweeper in the place comes down simultaneously and takes every standing pin down. Mary gets on the loudspeaker and says, "Y'all all get a free game 'cause of the problem. We apologize for the inconvenience and hope y'all understand." I can hear everyone yelling out what he'd bowled so far, or what he could've bowled with six strikes in a row, and so on. "Motherfucker" seems to be the expression of the day. Mary says, "Lane thirty-eight's open. Felmet and Chick—I got no choice but to ban y'all from here ninety days."

I walk down the lane alone, not wanting to be associated with Felmet anymore. I do not plead my case or make excuses about the draft beer. I don't dare add my accomplice bowling next to us to the list of why things happened the way they did.

I pass Mary on my way out. She carries a socket wrench and says, "Just don't come back on Friday mornings. You ain't really banned for ninety days. If you come any other day chances are these old boys won't be here. It just makes us look like we're doing what we got to do to keep this place clean, fun, and respectable, you know."

I say, "I understand."

"Maybe wear a hat, or grow a moustache next time you come in," she says. "I like you, Chick. I got a way of knowing who's good people down deep."

I nod, then shake my head back and forth and point my thumb to Felmet. He's walking down the lane and dragging one leg as if he needs a fife and drum corps at his side and a roll of gauze around his head.

Halfway home I realize that I'm wearing rented bowling shoes and no longer own a pair of shiny wing tips to impress my boss's boss's boss.

THE NEXT MORNING, Saturday, I get up early and drive to the flea market because where I work still doesn't pay enough for me to buy dress shoes willy-nilly, and I know a man who sells good used wing tips for ten bucks a pair. Plus I want to find Felmet and make sure he's alive, that he's not wearing a cast, that he doesn't have a grudge against me in such a way that means a lawsuit. I park in the middle of about sixty thousand cars and start down the rows knowing I'll hear Felmet's voice long before I see him.

I'm wearing bowling shoes and am careful not to step in mud puddles, seeing as they don't need to slick up moreso.

I wade through the people of Forty-Five bartering over building supplies, tube socks, chalkware, used tools, dolls, tin advertising signs, whirligigs, shotguns, chickens, plates, birdhouses, rebuilt bicycles, and pitbull puppies. I pass a tent evangelist trying to sell a cassette of himself singing old gospel tunes. I find some guy selling large cable spools I'm pretty sure came from my plant, and wonder if he works there somewhere in back. Fifteen minutes into the trek I buy a half-and-half bag of scuppernongs and muscadines from some guy with a white trash vineyard, thinking it'd be a good gift for Capozzi, seeing as he's Italian and probably appreciates anything from the grape family.

It's not much past dawn and a thick fog lifts from a creek behind the flea market that feeds the Saluda River. For some reason I look in that direction and wonder if I can find any cheap bait in order to go fishing later on when I hear, of course, "Mr. Strike! Hey, there's the man who saved me from getting cut in half!"

I turn around and see Felmet two tables down, propped on crutches. He's next to a turban-wearing woman who proclaims to know past, present, and future. Felmet's wrapped an Ace bandage around his waist, on the outside of his clothes. I walk over and say, "Are you okay? I came over here to see if you got out of there alive yesterday."

Felmet looks both ways and jerks his head for me to come closer. I lean across his table. He's only selling wire cutters and thick rubber-soled work boots, the exact kind I've seen Duke Power men wear up on telephone poles. Felmet says, "I ain't hurt. People buy from those they pity. It's one of the laws. There's a trick to it, though—you can't dress up so pitiful that it scares people off. I've already sold twice what I sold last week when I only wore a patch on my eye." He points to his left eye, shakes his head, then points to the other. "One eye or the other, I forget which, now."

I say, "Where you get all the cutters?" like I don't know.

Felmet says, "Duke Power's gonna pay. Duke Power's got to learn not to mess around in the Land of Felmet. Duke Power embarrassed me in front of all those league bowlers, and they got to get more than a little slap on the wrist for spending all their time following me around."

A man approaches the table and picks up a pair of boots. He says, "What size?"

Felmet says, "What size you wear?"

"Eleven and a half," says the man.

"Them's the ones," says Felmet. "Ten bucks."

The man takes one boot and sets it on the ground next to his foot. "Will you take eight?"

Felmet says, "I'll take nine. I'll take nine dollars." I pick up a pair of wire cutters and read where Felmet tried to erase LIGHTNING FAST ELECTRIC written on the handle. The man counts out nine one-dollar bills and hands them over. Felmet says, "Now remember, those are good enough to wear while working with major wattage."

I say, "Felmet, I don't think Duke Power's following you around trying to embarrass you. Hotdamn, man, they got enough problems without having to worry about every person pissed off with their performance record."

Felmet cocks his head and holds his mouth in a way that reminds me of a man fighting with a dentist's suction tube. He picks up a tool I've never seen — part monkey wrench, part cutter, part ball-peen hammer. He says, "I should've knowed. You're one with Duke Power, ain't you? Now it all makes sense. They sent you down to bowl with me on purpose so's to learn more about me and my ways."

I know there's not enough time for me to pull out my wallet and find my employee ID. I know that Felmet would only think that it was part of my undercover attire.

So I take off running in a way that might remind some of the flea market comic-book vendors of their favorite characters caught in midair, twenty feet from the edge of a cliff, a hundred yards from the bottom of a gorge. I'm only hit once in the middle of the back with a pair of wire cutters, but I'm pretty sure that innocent bystanders get nailed upside their heads. I hear people screaming, even as I reach my car. I'm hoping no one sees my face, that later on there aren't sketches of me handed out at flea markets across the Southeast for suspicion of shoplifting. I don't know why it seems important that no one sees me siding with every enemy out there—utility companies—that preys on regular men and women who only try to get away with what they might or might not deserve in terms of light, power, and general comfort.

CAPOZZI ARRIVES IN total darkness Monday night. Something's gone wrong, and the entire town's out of electricity. In the car driving forty miles to the airport I get a radio station saying how someone's tampered with the substations, that police and firemen are on the scenes, that no one knows what could've happened, though foul play is suspected.

Capozzi's a frightening man, like all of his brothers and cousins—six-six, three hundred pounds, a nose smashed down, I'm sure, from giving head butts instead of from being some fool's target. I say, "I don't know that we can go bowling. There's some kind of power failure going on throughout half of South Carolina." I tell him about the radio, how it's a mystery, how terrorists may have missed their targets altogether and hit my home state instead of, say, Nevada.

Capozzi has one bag that he carried with him on the plane. We walk past the baggage claim horseshoe. He says, "No electricity. Sometimes that's a good sign for the company." He stops and looks down at me. He says, "Sometimes it's a bad sign. Matters if we get tabbed making a faulty product. Or if we can talk our way out of it."

My bowling shoes clap loudly on marble. I say, "I was ready to go, sir. I tell you what—there's something about bowling that's like nothing else in the world. A perfect strike imploding on itself. It's physics."

We walk out of the airport. I'm parked illegally on the curb. Capozzi says, "I like the noise. There's two places I'm comfortable doing business: a bowling alley, and a firing range." I open his door, but Capozzi's staring straight ahead. He says, "Goddamn. Are those stars?" Call me paranoid, but I think it's a trick. I'm thinking it's some kind of test. I don't answer.

I say, "I'm sure your hotel has some kind of emergency generator. There's probably some bellhop out on the sidewalk cranking a Coleman Powermate 4000 right now."

I walk around and get in the car. Capozzi keeps standing. From outside he says, "I don't remember the last time I saw stars. When I was a kid sometimes I'd take drives with my father out in the country at night. I remember seeing stars then. But nowadays, Jesus. There's too many lights in the city."

I say, "I don't remember a night without stars, really," which isn't all that true, seeing as I'm one to watch the ground always, in fear of holes and dog shit.

Capozzi gets in and says, "I forget the laws down here. We ain't in a dry county, are we?"

I say, "No. We can get beer anywhere except on Sundays. Liquor stores close at sundown, though."

Capozzi nods. He doesn't know my name. He says, "If we can't bowl, let's go get us a couple twelve-packs and take the car out in the country somewhere. I want to burn these stars in my memory."

I nod once. I turn the key and think, I need to find a place out in the country that I know well enough to escape, just in case my boss hasn't been pleased with my job performance and has sent a hitman down to take me out. I think, Goddamn you, Felmet—if there was light, I could think better.

We drive back toward Forty-Five and I'm careful at non-working stoplights and railroad crossings. We find a Drop-In store run by cashiers with flashlights, and I'm surprised that Capozzi doesn't want some imported beer, or at least beer from a bottle.

Not five miles outside of town there are dirt roads I knew as a kid driving around smoking dope. On weekends these roads stay four feet deep in unfurled dust, what with high school kids parking, roaming, and racing. As I head toward a bluff between the Saluda River and Lake Between, Capozzi has his head out the open window. He looks skyward. He says, "This is good. Pull over here," which I do.

I try to think of the Hail Mary. I try to think of one of those mantras I memorized one time. I say, "The cops come by here about every two minutes. You want to keep that beer hidden mostly," which is nowhere close to the truth.

Capozzi gets out and sits on the hood. He opens his second beer and says, "Big Dipper," as if he's been trying to think of it for ten years. He says, "Little Dipper. Son-of-a-bitch." He points up to Pollux and Castor, two stars I know for some reason. Then he looks to the horizon where a distant glow pops, then goes dark.

"That's Forty-Five going out, I think." Then I turn around and look straight up at the Southern Cross. I say, "It gets even better near dawn."

Capozzi looks at me as if I've insulted his family. He asks if I stay up that late, or get up that early. I tell him the truth, that there's no reason to stay up late around here. He stares, looking in the direction where another glow had gone dark, probably Ware Shoals, or Due West. "I have the power to give you a raise," he says. "A promotion, even."

I start laughing and pull the bag of muscadines and scuppernongs from the backseat. I hold the bag his way.

A final glow on the horizon goes dark, but I can still see Capozzi's hand against the stars. He points. "Ursa major," he says, chewing on one of the thick-skinned grapes. "Ursa minor. I'll be fucked. It's logically possible that the stars will all go out one night, just like what's going on around us. We need to invent a cable that'll reach outer space. Plug it in. Give us back what we need most."

I'm wondering if he doesn't hold his booze well, if maybe he had a couple pops on the flight down. I say, "Well, I know a man named Felmet who'd probably be willing to volunteer working the spaceship that far out." What else could I say? We were supposed to be bowling.

"Back in New Jersey," Capozzi says, "my father used to point up and say he could see my outline in the stars. To this day I look for it. Like a chalk outline of a dead body, only made from stars, like connect-the-dots. Maybe it doesn't show down here in this part of the hemisphere."

I think about how I need to type up a résumé and look for another job. I wonder about wire and cable manufacturers elsewhere, if power and light companies are detested worldwide. I wonder if madmen live among us all, either armed with wire, or wire cutters.

My boss's boss's boss doesn't even know that I'm standing next to him. He takes his index finger and appears to count. I walk ten paces away later on, relieve myself, and notice that I'm spelling Felmet's name in cursive.

Impurities

It took three or four seconds before I realized that the glaze-eyed man on my front stoop used to corner me in college and recite, I assumed, damn near all of the Gospel according to St. John, in order. He hung out in the laundry room in the basement of my dorm. Back then, I took my still-soapy clothes out of the washer half the time so I wouldn't have to hear him rant during the spin cycle.

I looked through the side transom I'd put in myself. Carl Gerver still looked nineteen—which pissed me off—and wore the expression of a man who'd been struck by lightning twice in one day or beaned with hail the size of New York cornerstones while stuck two miles from basic cover. But he didn't wear a suit. Carl didn't have that godawful cross around his neck, so broad it looked like he got affixed to it backwards. Instead of one Bible in each hand he held a shagreened box with a worn grip. It looked like maybe he sold microscopes. It looked as though he had finally accepted Darwin.

The moment that I opened my front door I began computing the times and hours he'd kept me from whatever nonspiritual nonactivities I'd managed to discover. Listen, I got along with everyone back when I attended college unless they were members of the Young Republicans, Campus Crusade for Christ, or one of the four pathetic fraternities that weren't allowed to live in houses but took up entire dorm halls. I hated rich kids with low SAT scores, the northern prep-school graduates who complained about slow and stupid Southerners, and any woman with a poster on her wall. I couldn't stand anyone in the drama department, naturally, and tired of precious artists moaning about how no one understood their works. I basically went to class and spent the rest of my hours hiding at the opposite end of campus from the chapel and music building. I stayed in the library, where no Reagan Youth speak-in-tonguer, SAE/TKE/KA/PiKap or member of the Stonewall Jackson Fan Club ever visited. I hung out daily amid anthropology shelves as further camouflage. No one bothered me, ever, outside of blanch-eyed Carl Gerver, who held membership cards to every organization that I feared or abhorred.

"How could I help you?" I chose not to reintroduce myself. Over the years I'd run into other college classmates and liked to watch their tiny Rolodex memories shuffle backwards, trying to glimpse me in our college yearbook.

"Well, sir, you can't help me in any way other than to live a long and nontoxic life." Carl Gerver hadn't changed, I thought. I wondered what biblical oddity he kept stuffed inside the sample box. "Would you be interested in having ninety-nine percent of the lead out of your drinking water?"

I don't want to brag or anything—but sometimes I have the ability to look into the near future and understand exactly what will happen. This phenomenon began in college, when I decided to double-major in philosophy and geography. Right away I knew that South Carolina wouldn't be a place to think up decent ideas. "Man, I was just thinking about my water. Come on in. I've been so scared of lead, mercury, and sediment that I've been drinking beer only."

I stood back to let Carl Gerver walk in. He didn't recognize me whatsoever. "Don't forget copper. And there's bad taste, odor, and hardness."

"Come in the kitchen, mister," I said. "My name's Briggs."

I held out my hand. Gerver put his case in the foyer, shook, and said, "Carlisle Gerver. Are your wife and children around? I like to demonstrate my product to the entire family."

My wife, Vonica, still stayed in Lily, Kentucky, for her job working for Project Welcome!, some kind of education foundation wherein poor South Carolinians get to intermingle with poor Appalachian children, and vice versa. There was talk of coal mines and cotton mills, from what I could understand. I thought about telling Carl Gerver that maybe my wife met people up there who needed cleaner water, but didn't. I said, "She's visiting her aunt." I opened the refrigerator and pulled out six beers. "Let's you and me turn this into cocktail hour while you demonstrate your little device."

Carl opened his sample case on the counter. "I don't drink," he said, pulling out a plastic one-gallon pitcher. "This is the Walk on Water filtration pitcher. For our Spanish friends it's the Walk on Water *Jarra Con Filtro Para Agua*. You'd think that Mexicans would be happy enough without their parasites and amoebas, wouldn't you?"

I downed one beer and started another. It was part of my mean plan. Carlisle Gerver, indeed, still walked around preaching at people about fire, brimstone, blood, flesh, and forgiveness. My wife seemed to prefer the treacherous, thick-dust countryside of eastern Kentucky over the state of South Carolina where every original, abstruse philosophical tract begins with "I think, therefore I think you're wrong."

Carlisle pulled out jelly jars filled with various dirty-water samples. One looked clear already; the worst looked like Yoo-hoo soda. I said, "We went to the same college, man. I thought you went on to the seminary or something."

Carlisle Gerver held a bottle marked POND WATER. "I don't remember you at all. Forgive me." He cocked his head twenty degrees in that you-poor-soul kind of way, I swear.

"I bet you would remember if I started up the washing machine, fucker."

WHAT I'M ABOUT to explain, I know, will come off as irrational, petty, vicious, hard-hearted, vengeful, and sophomoric. I don't care. It's true that I didn't believe that Jesus walked on water, or that Moses parted the Red Sea, and so on. I thought that if Lazarus had really died and returned to this planet then he'd've gotten a bigger speaking role. But that doesn't mean that I deserved—as an eighteen-year-old first-year student—Carl Gerver always bringing up my name when he stood to offer his personal testimonials at Wednesday night chapel services.

"Each night I pray for the aborigines of Australia who don't know Jesus in their hearts. I pray for the Chinese who believe that their Buddha—*not* the son of God—is the true way. And I pray for lost souls here on this campus like Briggs Burgess, a young nonbeliever who does his laundry on Monday nights in the basement of E Dorm East."

This is true. Don't ask me why I was in attendance twice. The service wasn't mandatory. Suffice it to say that a hundred near-Pentecostals surrounded me on the following Monday night as I tried to relay whites from washer to dryer. From that night on I was careful not to smudge my clothes—to wear pants three or four times before taking them into town, or home over holidays.

"I'm Briggs Burgess, bullethead. You goddamn brought my name up so many times praying that I would've been voted Most Likely to Fry in Hell had we done that sort of thing in the stupid yearbook."

"Briggs Burgess. I pray for many people, Briggs." Carl pulled out baby-food-sized jars marked POOL WATER, MUD PUDDLE, and VINEGAR. "It's good to remeet another good scholar."

I said, "Right," and pulled two more beers out of the refrigerator.

"What have you been doing over the last—golly, how long's it been now?—fifteen years."

I wasn't sure if Carl Gerver spoke or I heard only that little voice in my mind, seeing as I woke up daily and asked the same question. "I went to law school and only stayed a semester when I figured out that I didn't want to work with such people. I got a job selling paper products for a company that didn't care about trees. I got another job working for an environmental group screwing with companies like the one I used to work for. Got married." Carl didn't listen. He unscrewed various caps. He pulled out the replaceable filter from the Walk on Water pitcher and inspected it against the kitchen light. "I took a night class in how to kill people using only my bare hands."

"That's super. I can honestly say that the Lord has blessed me a hundred times daily. He's led me into a line of work that makes His children healthy. Man has polluted the Earth in numerous ways, but this little gadget might be the godsend we've all been needing in order to live to be a hundred."

I felt my bladder lift. The telephone rang, I answered, and a student volunteer asked if I would be interested in donating money to the college where Carl and I met. I said I wasn't. She said that they were trying to get fifty percent of the alumni to make a donation, and that I would receive a sticker for my back window.

Carl Gerver poured pond water into the plastic pitcher. It came out clear in the bottom section.

Over the phone I said, "Well, I'd be glad to kill myself about right now. That would serve the same purpose, wouldn't it?" and hung up.

"We can't officially advertise it, but the Walk on Water pitcher also traps deadly microscopic microbes." He poured out the filtered pond water into a six-ounce juice glass he'd brought along. Carl downed it in two gulps. "One filter lasts for a hundred U.S. gallons—twice as long as the filtration systems sold at Wal-Mart. What do you say, Mr. Burgess? Thirty dollars isn't much of a sacrifice for a pure body, and the Walk on Water people donate a dollar out of every sale to the poor nonbelievers of east Africa. We got a mission group over there right now, showing the light."

I said, "You're telling me that this thing can take the taste of vinegar out? You'd be willing to pour vinegar in the top and drink what percolates out?" A belch escaped my lips. "Excuse me. Pond water's good, I'll admit that."

Carl picked up the vinegar and had me smell it. "Jesus drank vinegar up on the cross."

I actually remembered his telling me the same thing in the laundry room. My mother taught me to plash some vinegar in the rinse cycle, which had brought up the anecdote back then. "You must be desperate, Carl. I wonder how desperate you are now."

I tried not to think about how my father once sold hammocks part-time, and how little the commission was that he received for each sale. I unzipped my pants and picked up the pitcher. "I remember you from college now," Carl said.

Then I peed in the top of the Walk on Water pitcher and said, "You drink what seeps out directly and I'll buy it." I waggled my pecker once, zipped my pants back up, and put the lid back on. Carl Gerver stared at what slowly dripped into the bottom.

I watched him. When he placed the juice glass down—when he poured what was once inside me into his glass—I didn't balk. "I'm a firm believer. I'm a firm believer," he said, more to himself—or God—than to me.

I let him drink it. When he turned to the kitchen sink sick, I opened the refrigerator. What cold air exited didn't make me think about any safety I'd seek later once I stood in Hell.

I HAD NO CHOICE but to order another pitcher, plus the one I had peed in. Carlisle Gerver's company would send the untarnished Walk on Water filtration system via Federal Express. My bad conscience catalog got filled years before—about the same time my paper company got me to come up with how Blue Horse filler paper was laced with LSD, just so we would benefit.

"I'll admit that maybe I judged back when I preached judge not," Carl Gerver said. He wrote out my name and address in his order book. "I've done my best to change. I'm not judging you for making me drink of the bodily functions in order to prove myself and my product."

I thought of my dwindling mutual funds and wondered if I could buy more than two Walk on Water filtered pitchers. "I have an extra toothbrush. I have an unopened toothbrush the dentist gave me."

"Listen, I'm used to getting treated like a door-to-door leper."

"There's more than beer in the fridge. I can make some iced tea. I have coffee. Hey, Carl, you're not Mormon, are you?" I needed to pee again already and didn't want to bring it up.

Carl held up his palm. "I've been diagnosed with Not-Drafted-Not-Registered syndrome. That might be part of my personality flaw."

This stopped me. If I had not been exposed to every New Age symptom discovered and lit up by the daily-talk-show circuit, then I had made them up for my own purposes in regards to paper and antipaper products. I said, "What?"

Carl Gerver closed his empty square valise. "I turned eighteen after the military draft ended. By the time Congress voted in the Selective Service Act I was too old. They've finally acknowledged that men in this particular age group have a tendency to irritate others, or act in ways not socially acceptable. I can get disability if I so choose."

He handed me a receipt. "I'm the same age as you are, man. You're just making it up. It's all in your mind. I'm so tired of people inventing excuses for their failures in life. Listen, men our age don't deserve fake symptoms."

Carl Gerver held his head toward eleven o'clock. He didn't blink. "Do you think that men who served our country came home and forced salesmen to drink urine?"

If it had taken Carl Gerver forty days and forty nights to gather his belongings and leave my house I still wouldn't have had time to offer a logical explanation or defense. When he left I'm almost certain it wasn't the voice in my head that mumbled out, "You're going to pay for this one, Briggs."

Listen, I had no conventional weapons. It's not so much that I don't believe that human beings in America should be denied the right to own pistols that seem only good for maiming other humans. Whenever people start preaching to me about inalienable rights and the Second Amendment I normally nod in agreement and hope that someone shoots them. I'm of the belief that no one should be kept from owning guns unless they—like I—might be prone and tempted to stick the barrel templewards.

And here was my arsenal two minutes after Carl Gerver left my property: a cloth jumprope that could be fashioned into an instrument of strangulation. I kept it in the attic, though, afraid that I might accidentally hang myself on bad crick-neck days. Or when Vonica finally called up from Kentucky to say that she had other plans outside of being married to a mean and focused man named after half of an engine. By the end of the night I had gone to Big Lots, bought three ax handles and six trailer hitches, cut the handles in half, drilled holes in one end of each, stuck in the metal tow balls, and constructed a half-dozen mean handheld clubs that resembled medieval maces without the spikes. I put them behind doors, beneath the bed, and in the oven.

I bought a peck of questionable M-80s, a gross of Roman candles, and some plain old smoke bombs from a man who kept a fireworks stand open year-round in his front yard off Powerhouse Road on the way into the town of

Forty-Five. I thought to call my wife, just in case I turned up dead before she showed up home. I thought to call a real estate agent.

VONICA CALLED AND SAID, "I met a neat woman today. She owns a diner in this little town and wants me to take some pictures of her food, then see if I can get a muralist of some kind to paint something on the side of her building, like breakfast-related. I'm here now. I'm thinking maybe I can get Ardis Lure up here to do some work, you know. She and her husband are still living in Forty-Five, aren't they?"

I said, "What does that mean?"

My wife said, "Are you drunk? It means like, they haven't moved, have they? We used to see them all the time."

I looked out the den window. It sounded like some chariots rode by. "I'm sorry. I didn't mean, 'What does that mean?' What I meant was, what do you mean by 'breakfast-related'—like bacon and eggs on a plate?"

Vonica said, "Did I get any mail? Have you cut the grass? Have you watered the garden? Are you picking the tomatoes before they get overripe on the vine? Are you putting food out for that stray dog that's coming by? Go turn off the burner right now 'cause I know you've left it on. Have you sent off the bills?"

I said, "Hey, how much does ninety-nine-percent clean water mean to you? I want to know. Tell me this answer."

"Why? Has there been some kind of problem with the water? I knew we should've dug a well, Briggs. I told you.

We should've dug our own well instead of getting city water."

"I'm just saying," I said. "This old boy came by earlier and I bought a couple of those pitchers that infiltrate the water, you know."

My wife said nothing. I could hear people in the background complain that their orders weren't right. She said, "Infiltrate? That's like some kind of military operation. What's wrong with home?"

I closed the blinds. I walked around the den and looked at the ceiling. I said, "There's some kind of new symptom going around called Not-Drafted-Not-Registered syndrome. I'm in that age group, if it matters. I met this guy and he told me that there's something like ten million men suffering from feeling that they didn't matter, or they couldn't matter, or that they felt inadequate. I forget exactly how he put it, but I'm thinking that I might be showing some of the symptoms."

My wife said, "Who?"

I didn't have time to think about any of this. Maybe I'd kind of fallen asleep between the time I fashioned my implements of head trauma and my wife Vonica called. I said, "This guy. This guy I ran into. At the store, buying some dog food for the stray dog that comes by."

There are some kinds of telephonic communication devices wherein people can talk and see each other at the same time. I thought about this marvel and was glad that we didn't have one of those things between Lily, Kentucky, and Forty-Five, South Carolina. My wife said, "How red are your eyes, Briggs?"

Listen, I didn't even have time to think; I said, "You have to come back as soon as possible. I don't know what I did to make you take off for forever in Kentucky, but I'll take it back. Finish up your job there, come back, and I promise I won't make fun of the fact that South Carolinians probably don't have much to offer people who smoke burley tobacco. I'll be the best husband ever, ever. What's past is past. I won't ever do anything wrong again that might hurt us in one way or another. These crazy Christians are coming to kill me, I swear to God."

A man in the background said, "I ordered grits. These is hash browns."

I knew immediately that I would only think *These is hash browns* for two days straight.

My wife said, "Let me guess. You've been watching one of the seven religious channels, haven't you? You can come up with ideas without watching cable TV, believe me."

I tried to tell my wife it wasn't like that. I meant to build myself up and say how, if anything, I'd been only watching world news and cooking programs since she left two weeks earlier. I said, "Did I ever tell you that I used to have a horrendous addiction to hard candy, Tootsie Pops, and chewing gum? The doctor told me to take up smoking, that whenever I wanted a piece of peppermint I should pop a cigarette in my mouth. It's worked so far."

I heard someone say, "Hey, this milk's gone bad!" and then my wife hung up the phone.

I hit *69. I took down the number. I called, and this waitress said, "Dixie Meat Diner," as if she was ordering shoes from a catalog.

IT WASN'T HARD to find Carlisle Gerver, compared to what I deserved to go through. First off I called local information and subsequently talked to a couple C. Gervers over in Ninety-Six and Due West. Then I made my way through a C. A. Gerver, a C. B. Gerver, a C. L. Gerver, and so on. I talked to a woman named Callie, thinking maybe Carl went by some kind of pet name or pseudonym. Finally I called the college and promised some pinhead I'd donate a hundred dollars if he'd only tell me Carl's number. I said we were old fraternity/Baptists Student Union buddies.

It was ten o'clock at night. Carl answered with, "Walk on Water."

I said, "Man, do you ever stop? Give me a break."

He said, "I know this voice."

I poured some bourbon, added water, and made a point not to stick ice cubes in the glass. I didn't want any clinking going on while I talked to Carl. I had enough trouble when Vonica stood at the other end of the line. "This is Briggs. You sold me a pitcher today. Two pitchers." There's probably some kind of study out there that would explain why he dry-heaved at the moment I introduced myself. I said, "Do you know who you're talking to?"

Carl cleared his throat. He said, "I've already sent in your order. Please don't tell me that you've changed your mind. It would take forever to turn things around."

I looked out the window. I swore I saw a cross on fire, off in the distance. I said, "I've been drinking out of the pitcher I peed in. You're right. This water tastes so much better."

"It's the charcoal filtration," Carl said.

"Well I just know that I want another dozen of these things, man. I want to send them to some people I care about. I'm serious. Dixie Meat Diner. I want to send some to the Dixie Meat Diner up somewhere near Lily, Kentucky."

I could hear Carl slap a pad down on the table. It sounded exactly like when he hit palm to forehead back when I shook my head no down at the laundry room when he asked if I'd been saved, if I wanted to be saved, if I came from a family of saved souls, if I understood what the blood of Christ meant, if Job's sores meant anything to me, and so on. He said, "I need your Visa or MasterCard number. We don't take American Express."

I said, "No. No, you'll have to come over again tomorrow. I don't give those numbers out, buddy."

Outside I heard our stray dog howl. This freckled, white bird dog barked and barked, as if he wanted me to spoon-feed him. I had put out some chili earlier. I'd put out some white-bread crusts. Any dog that didn't understand such a menu, I figured, wasn't good enough to hang out in my driveway.

Carl Gerver said, "Is that your wife I hear in the background?"

I didn't pause. I said, "Yeah." I said, "Come on over here tomorrow, and don't bring anybody with you, Slick."

I heard Carl tap either a pen or pencil on his writing pad. He clucked his tongue five times. "I don't know what that means. What does that mean, don't bring anybody?"

I said, "Oh goddamn don't bring anybody who's going

to try to introduce me to Jesus. That's all I'm saying. I have
enough problems with my wife taking off and wanting me
to become a man of all men. That's all I'm saying."

Carl said nothing. He sat on the other end, much like
anyone I'd seen on one of the seven religious channels during Pledge Week.

Presently I let the dog inside and named him Dooley. I
found a stack of newspapers by the fireplace and scattered
them throughout the house. Understand that I'd already
looked under the kitchen sink to make sure we had some
spot remover, carpet deodorizer, Lysol spray, and carpet
shampoo. "Tell me your life story," I said to the stray.

Dooley didn't look uncomfortable with the situation. As
a matter of fact he didn't even look my way when he
jumped up on the couch and stretched out, long and skinny,
like having a crack whore visit. I sat in a wingback chair
with the channel changer. "You thirsty or anything?" I said
to my new dog, then got up and poured some tap into the
Walk on Water pitcher. When the thing finished dripping I
poured it into a Tupperware bowl in the kitchen and set it
down. Dooley flopped off the couch, sniffed at my feet,
looked me in the face for the first time, and walked away.

His hair stood up along the ridge of backbone he held
high naturally. This is not a story: Dooley looked back at
me as if I'd just pulled snippers out to perform a homemade
castration. Then he walked back, gave the bowl one more
sniff, and lifted his leg.

CARL GERVER SHOWED up at eight o'clock. He
wore seersucker and carried his sample case. I looked past

him, toward the Chevy he drove, in order to make sure he hadn't brought reinforcements. "If you don't mind I'll just keep my pitcher inside its case this time. You know what it looks like and how it performs."

I had a checkbook in my back pocket. Dooley came outside but didn't bark. "Come on in, brother. I just made some coffee. I used regular water, though. You want some?"

Carl looked at his watch. "I don't have to be in Walhalla until ten o'clock. Yeah, I'll have some coffee."

The dog sat at his feet. I said, "This old stray showed up a month ago. I let him inside for the first time last night. I believe he's house-trained." Carl stuck out his right hand and Dooley stuck up his paw to shake. I said, "I'll be damned."

Carl took the coffee black and said, "Now how many of these things you say you want?"

"I'd say a dozen. I'd say twelve. I don't know why, but my wife called last night from a little diner in Kentucky where she's doing her work, and the only thing I could hear in the background was people coughing up what I assumed was coal dust. Maybe this'll make their lives better."

Carl pulled out his order forms and said, "Do you want me to send them here, or there?" Dooley whined. He stuck his other paw up and set it on Carl Gerver's leg.

"I want them sent there anonymously, but I don't exactly know the address. I'm thinking there can't be but one Dixie Meat Diner in a place called Lily, Kentucky. The mailman can figure it out. He'll know. He's got to be the smartest man in town."

"You could call and ask," Carl said. "That might be the easiest and best thing to do." He looked down at Dooley and said, "You're a good little buddy, aren't you?" The dog barked once.

I held up a finger. I figured I could call, say I was someone other than Vonica's husband, and talk to the woman who answered the telephone and say I needed the address to send some information about a special corned beef hash I peddled.

My wife answered. She said, "Dixie Meat Diner," all upbeat.

I said, "What the hell, Vonica? Are you leaving everything we have here in Forty-Five so you can trade your life in to be a waitress?"

She laughed. Vonica laughed, and in my mind I saw her shake her head much like she had on the night I'd proposed, way back before the end of our senior year in college. "The place is closed down this morning so the dance troupe can practice. Tonight they're opening up for the public. Our South Carolina people will show them South Carolina clogging, and then the Kentucky people will show off Kentucky clogging. There's a big difference, shithead. Then the Kentucky people are coming down to Myrtle Beach later in the year. What do you want?"

I handed the phone over to Carl Gerver. He said, "Hello. I'm Carl Gerver with the Walk on Water water-filtration-system company. Y'all are about to get a gift of our product, but we need to know where to send it. Could I get y'all'ses address?"

Dooley started hunching Carl's leg. I pulled him off, then walked around the house picking up unused filleted *Greenville News*es.

When Carl hung up the telephone I said to him, "I forgot to give you any paper and pen. To write down the address."

He smiled. His eyes frosted over like they did when we stood together in the dorm's laundry room. "Your wife said a dozen won't do. She asked that you send a hundred. She said she'll only come back home if you order a hundred. That's what she said, I swear on my father's sepulcher." Carl's eyes didn't waver one way or the other. He kept eye contact in a way I didn't know, seeing as I lied almost non-stop in my line of paper business. Carl Gerver kept his hand on the telephone. "One hundred water systems."

My first thought was to call his bluff. I thought about taking the phone, calling Vonica, and checking on both of them. But then I started thinking about signs. I thought of what Carl Gerver once told me as I sorted my corduroy pants from my underwear, how in that last chapter of the New Testament there were all kinds of signs, from angels to plagues to vials of wrath. My new dog, Dooley, sat at attention beside Carl Gerver. I said, "Y'all don't have some kind of installment plan, by any chance, do you?"

Carl sat at my kitchen table, unwavering. He said something about how, in other religions, there were worse things than snakes of temptation, that I should be glad not to live in a land that believed in half-goats, half-men, or women whose nether parts hold teeth.

The Half-Mammals of Dixie

I took a folding chair in the back of the Ramada Inn's Azalea Room without looking for any of my coworkers. I'd parked next to the guest speaker's car, I figured—the vanity tag read MOTIV8R—but restrained myself from slicing the goddamn evolved Lincoln Continental, headlight to atrophied fin, with my own car key. My boss had paid to have his entire six-person southeastern sales force attend, in hopes that we would pick up pointers on how to talk more seafood restaurants into setting up giant aquariums in their dining areas, stocked with everything from horseshoe crabs to sand sharks, cleaned and maintained by trained and licensed aquatic technicians who spent most hours thinking up ways to kill salesmen like me so *they* could travel from Virginia to Mississippi, lolling around places like Whitey's Crab Shack, the Splashing Mermaid, and Grouper Therapy. I sat down and stripped the back of my name tag. I placed it askew over the Salty's Showfish logo on my left breast pocket. Then I looked over at the woman seated next to me, a thirty-year-old wearing a black-and-silver skirt that provided her lap with only a cocktail-napkin-sized piece of cloth. She crossed her right leg over toward me in such a way that created a tunnel to look into. I thought, This ain't going to be bad at all.

Then I looked up to see that her face had a giant tic-tac-toe pattern carved into it.

A man from the Jacksonville Chamber of Commerce went to the podium and said, "We want to welcome all of you to this workshop. As you can see from the agenda, af-ter Mooney Gray speaks we'll break for lunch, then recon-vene in smaller groups to brainstorm. Also, as you can see in your packet, we have more than thirty businesses repre-sented, and y'all know that it only takes two companies to get a little networking done, so there's no telling what can happen here. Especially—" this guy held up his hand as if holding a champagne glass shaking with plutonium "—once y'all discover the two complimentary drink tickets stapled to the room-service menu."

I didn't notice how everyone in the audience clapped or hooted, really. I focused on the podium but peripherally saw the woman's scars. Her nose was in the center space, her eyes to the top left and right corners. The woman's mouth took up the entire bottom middle space but spilled over to the lower corners of the game.

When I dropped my pen by accident, I pretended it hadn't happened. But the woman bent down, tapped my knee, and said, "Here you go."

"I'm sorry. Thanks. I'm truly sorry," I said.

"My name's Lorene." She swiveled her torso a quarter turn and touched her name tag. I could only look at her face and wonder what had happened. The scars were deep, wide, and only a touch off being purple. It looked as though she had been placed belly down on a table saw set to cut grooves a half-inch deep. I tried not to think of those old silent movies wherein the hog-tied heroine barely gets saved at the sawmill.

I took off my name tag completely and said, "I'm Drew Gaston." I couldn't get the tag to stick on my shirt again. "I work for Salty's Showfish."

Mooney Gray came out wearing a blue suit. He took off his coat. He made a big point of ripping off the necktie, as if he didn't trust it. He ripped off his pinstriped blue dress shirt in a way that made buttons fly off onto people seated in the front row. Mooney Gray now stood before the crowd of salespeople in need of motivation wearing his pants and a T-shirt that—from his right to left—had a picture of Moe Howard's face, then a lowercase letter *t* that looked like a cross, and finally Darth Vader's helmeted head.

Lorene said, "I've seen this guy before. It gets worse."

I tried to remember if most children started in a corner box or right in the middle when they played tic-tac-toe.

"I want to start off this morning by telling y'all a little story about two brothers. One was the ultimate optimist, and the other would take bets with complete strangers that the sun wouldn't rise the next morning. You know this second old boy, I'm sure. They had the same mother and father, who fed them the same food, and enrolled them in the same schools, and provided for them the best they could. One turned out eternally optimistic, and the other damned toward pessimism."

I thought, This is easy. Cain and Abel. If he asks us if we know who he's talking about, and if I were the kind of man who yelled out answers, I'd yell out Cain and Abel.

Lorene bent over with her pound-sign face and whispered, "If he asks who he's talking about, don't yell out Cain and Abel."

I nodded. I tried to stick my goddamn name tag to my pants leg and wished that I'd gotten coffee so that I'd have an excuse to throw away a Styrofoam cup, or get a refill, or feign scalding myself.

Mooney Gray held one hand up to quiet the crowd of salespeople, all ready to yell out Cain and Abel. "One an optimist, and one a pessimist. Well, these old boys liked to go fishing together, you see. The pessimist would just throw his hook in the water without any bait or anything. He'd say to his brother, 'I ain't gone catch nothing noways.' And then he'd stand there on the bank watching his brother bring in fish after fish off his wormy barb, you know. Bream. Shellcrackers. Sunfish. Cats. Crappies."

Lorene scratched her chin. She said to me, "You're in the fish business. Which one would you hire?"

I said, "Look at my leg," and pulled my pants up to the knee. I showed Lorene a birthmark the size of a small pancake. A woman on the other side of her leaned over and looked, too. I said, "Sometimes this itches, y'all, really bad. I don't know why."

Mooney Gray walked from one side of the foot-high stage to the other. He looked at the ceiling. "The pessimist brother never said a word until, one day, the optimist caught a fish so big that it doubled his rod in half. He pulled and reeled, and pulled some more. He'd snagged a grass carp somehow. Finally the fish freed itself, causing the hook to fly back out of the water at a speed so fast not even Superman could've detected what flew toward the optimist brother's face. That hook ended up embedding itself into this old boy's right eyeball, and it blinded him completely. Soon thereafter it got a serious infection, and the doctor had to take his eyeball out with a spoon."

I put my pants leg back down. I didn't look at my seat-mate but thought about how the perfect nine squares on her face resembled the shell of a box turtle. Then I could only think about how cruel this motivational speaker was to tell a story with such a maimed woman in the audience. I knew for certain that Mooney Gray saw Lorene in the audience —that's what motivational speakers did best, wasn't it? They noticed faces and memorized names. I said out loud, "I think I'm in the wrong place." I leaned to stand up, but Lorene turned my way, uncrossed her legs, and kept them apart as if she practiced holding a kickball between her thighs.

Mooney Gray said, "The pessimist brother said one thing. He looked at his brother in the hospital room and said, 'You can buy fish in a market these days, buddy.' So there you go."

Some people clapped. Once they began clapping, every-one else outside of Lorene and me nodded or laughed.

I looked at Lorene and said, "I didn't get that story. Did I miss something?" I figured my mind had wandered up her dress or whatever.

Lorene said, "You don't have to show me all of your inadequacies. Don't think you have to show all of your scars and blemishes. There's no way you'll catch up, dearie."

I picked one eye and focused. I said, "I'm sorry. I'm trying not to look up your dress. I'm that way."

Mooney Gray yelled out, "I see all of y'all nodding your heads and acting like you know what I'm talking about, and that's what I'm trying to tell you is the worst thing about your salesmanship. That story I just told made no sense. But y'all didn't want to look stupid. Here's rule number one: If you're lost while listening to a client, ask for a road map as soon as possible."

I was about to continue my apology for staring at Lorene's disfigurement, but she raised her hand and said, "Mr. Gray, this man here didn't have a clue as to what you were talking about. He didn't get it." She held her left hand up, her index finger down toward my scalp. When the rest of the seminar-goers turned around, though, I saw how they could only stare at mangled Lorene.

I KNEW THE rudiments of a filtration system better than anyone in America. I talked to prospective clients about how fish defecated in their own environment and couldn't live long if no one came around to clean out the tank. That's not what sold the product and services, of course. I had statistics concerning restaurants and bars

without aquariums and the same establishments' grosses after installing walls of glass, water, and sea bass. I provided
legitimate telephone numbers for people to call in case they
didn't believe my claims. More often than not I dealt with
ex-surfers, ex-Northeners, ex-husbands. I didn't see many
switchblade victims.

And I dealt with local oceanfront women who hung out
at places like Blowfish Aft up in Murrell's Inlet, sat with elbows propped on a foot-wide bar staring at miniature toy
scuba divers, said things like, "I picked out that hammerhead all by myself." I wasn't prepared for the remainder of
the world that lived and thrived on dry land.

Mooney Gray stalked the tongue-and-groove boards
bending beneath his penny loafers. He jutted his chest and
wagged one finger left and right as if to a James Brown
song. "You've learned to make eye contact. You've learned
to shake hands with a firm grip. You've learned to shake
hands and make eye contact before giving your spiel. So
what? So what?! I have a dog that shakes hands and makes
eye contact."

Lorene wore no underwear. I let my right hand fall to the
side.

It wasn't ten o'clock in the morning yet.

"Listen," Mooney Gray said. "Listen, I got a story for
y'all. This'll mean something. This ain't no trick."

Lorene said to me, "He's going to start this whole thing,
and then he'll call for a break. Don't get too wrapped up
in it."

"What happened?" I asked, pointing to her face. "I don't

want to be rude, but I have this problem with needing to know things."

"Listen up," Lorene said. She took my hand and set it on her small lap. "Even a man more worried about fish than anything else might want to know what this is all about."

I wasn't sure if I then underwent my first petit-mal seizure or what, but my middle finger twitched uncontrollably for the first time ever. It went in X's and O's, as if I were playing tic-tac-toe on Lorene's face. I felt the same warmth on my hand that I might have felt if petting a black poodle in the sun.

Mooney Gray continued. "My daughter joined a gang when she was fifteen years old. We lived in Anaheim, California—you know, right next to Mickey Mouse and Goofy. Gangs don't emerge out of Never-Never Land. That's what me and the missus thought. Well, my daughter didn't take much stock in all that. She joined a gang, and as in all good gangs there was an initiation. She didn't have to go out and kill anybody, thank God. No sir. Don't get me wrong, but sometimes I think what she had to undergo was even worse. She had to self-mutilate herself."

I put my hand back on my own lap. I crossed and re-crossed my legs and pretended to cough. Looking back on it all, I kind of figured things out at about this point.

Mooney Gray shook his head over and over, then turned his back to the audience. "Living so close to Hollywood, these gang members thought that they should scar up their faces as a protest to—" he turned around and made quotation marks in the air " '—the beautiful people.' They got box cutters and sliced open their faces. One girl made an *X* right across her face. She could've been a model before her decision. One girl make like Frankenstein and just put incisions every whichaway."

I turned toward Lorene. "This is your father?"

Mooney Gray pointed at Lorene and said, "My daughter in the back of the room decided that she wanted to stay young forever, and to do so she needed to slice a children's game on her face."

This was Lorene's cue. She stood up, walked past me, and joined her father on stage. Lorene said, "You would think that I would have no sales ability whatsoever because of my face. Let me tell you that last year I cleared almost a half million. And you know that if I can get clients to buy my product without looking at my face, then you can sell whatever it is you sell."

For the first time in my life I thought about how I wished I'd married a woman who taught first grade. I didn't want to sit around motivational speeches ever again. Somehow I knew that whatever Lorene would say, it would end up with me either buying her product out of pity or feeling a guilt known only to biblical characters.

Mooney Gray said, "We're going to take a break for those of y'all who smoke and/or drink coffee. When we reconvene my daughter will tell you everything she knows about selling audiotapes and Braille books to the blind."

I KEYED MOONEY GRAY'S Lincoln down the driver's side, from front wheel well to mid–back door. I rounded my own car, got in, and drove straight to a place called the Halibut Inn near Neptune Beach, thirty minutes away, where I'd once sold a wall aquarium to a joint that served mostly bikers. The aquarium kept clown fish only, seeing as they held the same colors as the Harley-Davidson logo.

Inside, I ordered a draft and said to the barmaid, "I'm the guy who sold y'all the aquarium." I pointed behind her.

"That's not enough to get drinks on the house." The barmaid had her hair pulled back in a French twist. She wore leggings and a T-shirt that read, IF YOU CAN'T LAUGH AT YOURSELF, THEN MAKE FUN OF EVERYONE ELSE.

"I wasn't looking for free beer. I got money. I was just saying."

She said, "I remember when you came in here a couple years ago."

I said, "Drew Gaston," but didn't shake her hand or offer her a business card.

This biker sat down next to me at the bar and said, "Gaston. Gassed on. Son, you must come from a people who got farted on. That's how last names come about. People named Baker come from people who ran bread shops. Smiths are from horseshoers."

"We don't need no more aquariums," the barmaid said. "I can't say that this one does us much good. The owner's gone crazy and talks to the fish most nights."

I looked behind the woman at their hundred-gallon tank—a small one compared with what I'd sold to places like Dale Ray's Delray Bar and Grill, which only held skates and mantas, or what the locals grouped as devilfish. "I been to some kind of motivational-speaker thing I had to go to. I'm not selling today."

I looked at the barmaid's perfect face and thought, There's something missing. She placed a glass of beer in front of me. "I've seen those people on TV when I get home at three o'clock. In the middle of the night. That what you're talking?"

I watched the clown fish, which seemed to be healthy. "I don't know what I'm talking," I said. I looked at the biker, who wore an upside-down tattoo on his left arm that looked like a woman's privates but ended up being the devil's goateed face.

He said, "My daddy was a motivational speaker of sorts. He ran the local KKK. Oh, he talked and talked and talked. Then somebody shot him in the eye and killed him. Up in a South Carolina prison."

I looked at the barmaid. Her jaw didn't drop.

"This man I went to see brought along his goofball daughter as a sidekick. She had scars from here to there." I zigzagged my hand like Zorro across my face. "I don't get what people are saying about anything anymore, man. I have no idea what anything has to do with selling what I have to sell. I'm thinking about moving to South Dakota or someplace."

Six clown fish wavered toward the biker and me in such a way that made me think of synchronized swimmers. The barmaid stood before us. She said, "My best friend in high school got cut up while diving down in some of those underground caves over near there." She pointed west. "She was lucky it didn't snag her oxygen. She got cut up on coral or limestone. She got scraped like she got throwed from a motorbike onto pavement. To this day she looks like she had a bunch of skin grafts that didn't quite take."

The biker waved at one of the clown fish, a tiny wave, as if to a newborn human baby. I looked at the barmaid, stood up, and dropped my pants. I showed her the scaly patches of psoriasis on my upper thighs. "Did it look like this?" I asked her. "Look at me. I'm a goddamn skink, mother-fucker."

The biker left his beer unfinished and said he needed to rough up someone for money. The barmaid said to me, "Maybe you should lay off beer and drink pure water only. I read something about dehydration one time. And about water that's ninety-nine percent free of lead and other toxins."

I ordered a bourbon and water.

I CALLED MY voice mail from the car. My boss had left one message for me to get in touch with a woman up in Savannah who owned a basement bar called Carpal Tunnel, which was supposed to be geared toward after-five-o'clock secretaries. "Seeing as 'carp' is part of the name, Drew, well, you can figure out how to talk them into an aquarium." Salty left another message that went, "I didn't pay all this money for y'all to get motivated properly only to have you drive around town listening to your messages." That was it.

I drove back into Jacksonville. I parked at the far end of

Mooney Gray's scarred sedan. Somewhere between the bar and the Ramada I had decided to ask Lorene out for a date that night, maybe take her back to the Halibut Inn. Maybe I'd ask the rest of my sales-force colleagues to go there, too, seeing as the Brunswick-to–Fort Pierce section of the Atlantic coast wasn't their territory.

I opened the trunk and pulled out an unopened pint of bourbon from beneath some Salty's Showfish brochures, stuck it in my back pocket, and entered the Azalea Room meeting space just as Mooney Gray said, "I hope y'all had a good lunch. Before we break up into groups I want to tell y'all a little story, seeing as that's what I get paid to do."

I sat in my original chair. Lorene wasn't around, but there was a piece of folded-over paper on her seat. She'd written "Fish Guy" on the top. I took it and read, "I hope you don't think I tricked you or anything. I didn't intend to trick you. After my father got me to an antigang intervention expert one of the first things I had to learn how to do was quit tricking people." She signed it "Sincerely."

While Mooney Gray went into a long story involving people who die to plan and those who plan to die, I shoved the note in my pocket. I got up and went to the reservation desk and said, "I know there's a bar in here open somewhere."

"Yes sir. Second floor." The clerk pointed up. "You can either take the elevator and then a right to the end of the hallway or climb those stairs at the end of this hall and it'll spill you out where you want to be. Which ever's easiest."

I found Lorene at the bar, drinking something that

involved a paper umbrella. Most of the Salty's Showfish sales force sat at a round table at the other end of the room. "Mind if I join you here, lady?" I said, pulling a leather-backed stool out.

"You get my note?" In the near-dark Lorene's scars blended into her face naturally. I wanted to run my hand over her visage, either for security or to make sure Mooney and Lorene hadn't pulled some kind of makeup job to gain sympathy.

"Nothing against you and yours, but I can't take these motivational seminars. The last one I went to involved everybody holding hands and singing, 'If you're happy and you know it, clap your hands,' which wasn't easy, seeing as we were told not to let go of our partners on either side." I pointed at the draft-beer dispenser. The bartender poured a pint and slid it over. From behind me I heard Mike Cobb bragging about an aquarium he'd sold to Dollywood when he was on his vacation, far from his Wilmington-to-Norfolk territory.

Lorene tipped her glass in a toast. "I don't travel around with Daddy often. We just happened to be in the same area. There are more than a few blind people in Florida, let me tell you. They want books on tape. They want Braille. I know he's my father and all, but let me say that Mooney Gray is a moral person. He's not like us. He genuinely wants people to succeed in what they do, and he believes in what he espouses."

I thought, *Espouses*. I would use that word from then on out. "That's a true story about the gang? What were you people thinking?"

Lorene ran her index finger down the alluvial chutes of her face. "I wanted to be queen of the gang, pretty much. Hell, any kind of self-etched disfigurement allowed a girl to join in. Some of my friends only scratched an inch-long crease into their forehead or wherever." She took the umbrella and straw from her drink. Lorene set them aside on a clean paper napkin. She slugged down the mixture like a shooter. "It's not easy living in such close proximity to women who can afford perfection long after their looks decline."

I turned to my friends. Danny Clement was in the middle of a story about how he went through some picayune town called Forty-Five somewhere in the Carolinas, how he sold two hundred-gallon aquariums to a man who owned the local cotton mill, how the man only stocked them with fishing lures he'd bought over the years at estate sales when his spinners, doffers, and weavers died. Mike Cobb caught my eye and gave a thumbs-up.

I RETURNED TO THE seminar alone. I got in a group of five other men and a woman. Mooney Gray told us to close our eyes and envision anything that might make the world better that didn't involve money. Mooney Gray said, "You can't think about turning slums into condos, seeing as that would take too much money. You can't think about feeding kids in Appalachia or Rwanda, seeing as rice, flour, and wheat cost money. You can't even think about cleaning up the environment, seeing as it'd cost money to filter out what toxins we pour into the Mississippi and places."

I closed my eyes and thought of Lorene's scars. I tried my best not to think, A world without low self-esteem, a world without women who know that they can't compete with what advertisers put in magazines and on television so that said women feel as though they need to lose anywhere from ten to a hundred pounds in order to look like an airbrushed woman midway through a two-hundred-page magazine with ten pages of actual text. I tried not to think, If people still had gills.

"Okay. Now I want everybody to tell their secrets. Y'all vote on which one you think's best in your group, and then I'll vote on which one's best overall. I believe I got another—" Mooney Gray reached into his waistband "—set of complimentary drink tickets for upstairs."

My group members stared at each another. One man said, "Well, seeing as you're in the club, why don't you start off," to me.

"I ain't in the club. I don't even know what the club is. I sell fucking aquariums."

"I'm in golf balls," another man said.

The woman in the group said, "My boss sent me here because I couldn't talk people into two months' worth of suntan sessions. We live in St. Augustine, by God! Who needs suntan sessions?"

I said, "Eeny-meeny-miney-moe," and went around until it ended with the guy next to me. "You start."

It was worthless. Every salesperson said something that would've cost money—free cars for every American, free groceries, obligatory armed service. One guy said, "To make the world a better place I'm thinking maybe we could all move to space stations and live above it all." He sold air purifiers door-to-door.

I wrote down every suggestion on the lined memo pad provided in each participant's packet. When it got to my turn I said, "The world would be a different and better place without mandatory motivational speeches to attend." My team members stared as if I'd piped up about how Jesus was a gay man who couldn't decide which of the twelve disciples to date seriously.

"That's just plain mean-spirited," said a man who sold a cleansing agent called Scour Power. "Go with the flow, man. Do you know how lucky you are to be able to spend a day not knocking on doors?"

I stood up and looked at Lorene's father onstage. I yelled out, "It would be a better world if we wouldn't have to go to motivational speeches, man. It would be a better world if parents could understand that their children cry out for help in ways unknown to the live-bearing population." It just came to me. I nodded twice hard, turned, and walked out of the room all slumpy and boneless, as if I wore a pimp's costume.

LORENE SAID, "I'm not ragging on your car or anything, but it would be nice to have a convertible right now." I'd gone back up to the Ramada bar, taken the scarred woman by the hand, and led her outside. We drove to the Halibut Inn.

"When you first sat down next to me at nine o'clock this

morning, did you intentionally show me your crotch? I want to know. It doesn't matter if you did or didn't. What I'm thinking is, a person with a, well, blemish of some sort might subconsciously redirect another person's line of sight. I'm trying to figure some things out about the human condition."

Lorene adjusted the passenger-side mirror in a way that allowed me to see only the roadside ditch clearly. "We couldn't rob banks when I was in the gang. It was too easy for a witness to give clear descriptions. What we did, though, was hang out down in Beverly Hills and find ways to fuck movie stars. Men or women. I can give you a list of leading men to character actors to sitcom women who will never forget me. I'm etched in their minds, so to speak."

I got behind a slow-moving truck with WORLD'S LARGEST ALLIGATOR printed on the tailgate. I didn't switch lanes and pass it. "What?"

Lorene studied strip malls. She kept her face turned away from me. "Listen. I met a man who opened a New Age bookstore. He had this big gay-and-lesbian section. He had an entire wall of books on holistic healing, and another on how to garden without using any pesticides or insecticides. This was in New Mexico. You'd think that he'd've made a killing. This was in Santa Fe, where all those rich people come buy bad artwork to fill the walls of their new vacation homes up in Taos or wherever."

I listened to Lorene, but what I really wanted to know was if the world's largest alligator was in the back of the pickup truck. It was one of those wide-bed trucks with four tires on

back. I wanted the alligator—which certainly had to curl itself in half if it was the world's largest—to raise its head.

"He had a slew of those self-help books, from finding
your inner child to finding your soul to finding your perfect
mate. He had books on how to read tarot cards. You could
even buy books on how to read crystal balls. There were
books on discovering souls you didn't even know that you
had, like from past lives and whatnot. In the philosophy
section he had everything from Plato to Shirley MacLaine."

The world's-largest-alligator truck turned off Highway
10 toward the Regency Square Mall. I fucking followed it.
"I want to see this thing," I said. The truck pulled into a
Citgo gas station.

"Well, this guy who owned the bookstore went out of
business completely. As a matter of fact, he didn't average
selling more than a book a day over a six-month period."

I put my car in park. The driver of the pickup truck
pulled to the pumps and got out. I yelled, "You got the
world's largest alligator in back?"

Lorene pulled me by the arm. "Listen. This is important
to me, man. You need to listen to what I have to say."

The guy pumping gas said, "I *did*. You ain't seen her,
have you?"

Lorene pulled and pulled. I said, "Goddamn. I wonder if
that thing escaped."

"It ended up that this man with the bookstore had all of
his feng shui books in the wrong spot. He had them in
the wrong corner of the room, and pointed in the wrong direction. Faced the wrong way."

I looked at Lorene and imagined what her tears would do should she cry. She needed a gutter hanging off of her chin, I thought.

"She's loose? Wait a minute. You lost the world's largest alligator?" Lorene asked.

I stared straight ahead. "That guy lost her." I put the car in drive and took off. "Now that's bad feng shui. He won't be able to espouse his find anymore."

Lorene said something about how she appreciated how I listened to what she had to say. "My father never listened until he had no other option, and then he only used what I said in his speeches across the country."

I turned back onto Highway 10. I turned up the radio. There was a local talk show going on. The guest and the disc jockey spoke of changing weather conditions. The guest was some kind of avant-garde meteorologist. He said it wasn't impossible to imagine the earth reverting to another Ice Age. Likewise, it wasn't far-fetched to envision total water. I thought about saying how my business would probably go downhill if the world went all water. I stuck my tongue out and said nothing. Lorene turned toward me. She closed her legs intentionally and said something about how she got tired sometimes of dragging from one spot to the next.

What Slide Rules Can't Measure

Fagen wears a drainage bag and never breaks from be-hind the flea market table where he sells rabbit pelts, rac-coon tails, and Davy Crockett hats. At night he goes to the nearest college bar and wins money off frat boys after feigning only a large and weathered bladder. Weigel tells his customers stories of alligator-wrestling each Florida winter, but we all know he orders gator heads and turtle shells from a discount house down near the Everglades. Hassett only seems to be there for sport—more often than not he pulls a one dollar bill out of his wallet and tapes it on the table next to a sign that reads "50 cents" to see how many people will dicker with him, or ask if it's counterfeit, or say that they'd buy it if it were either older or newer. Hassett only sells levels otherwise. Joe Ray specializes in sledge hammers and turn plows. Heidi sells milk- and carnival glass. Me, I only deal with old-fashioned measuring de-vices: Ames micrometers, starch refractors, slide rules,

Shore hardness indicators, Pitney-Bowes postal scales, pro-tractors, compasses, antique yardsticks, special-ordered Stanley tape measures with company logos, cotton scales, and anything in between. My customers come in extremes, and out of proportion. Average-height-and-weight people have no use for my products for some reason. Mostly I sell to men who want to remember working hard, men who scatter tools throughout their homes as if to remind friends and relatives what bought cars, appliances, and educa-tions over the years. I could write a scientific paper in the psychology/sociology/anthropology field if I cared whatso-ever anymore.

I wait for Father's Day all year.

On good days I set up a table across from Hassett or Heidi. Hassett attracts the misfits, the idle, and the geeks, too. Heidi flirts, brings in both men and women, and when she's sold a few vases and candy dishes always drinks wine with me in the back of the van. Once a week we splurge on a motel room with an ice machine and cable TV. We go out together to yard sales, auctions, and estate sales when it looks like rain past a mist. Heidi talks about settling down again, maybe getting an indoor booth in Fletcher or Asheville, Anderson or Greenville. I let her talk it out until she seems almost determined, then ask her again about grading a hundred essays a week for working-poor wages. Heidi shakes her head and laughs, and mentions how only now can she afford a steak each Sunday night.

On bad days Hassett, Fagen, Joe Ray, and Weigel get up late, or decide against unloading, and I set up across from or beside a local gun dealer. There are no laws in the Carolinas against selling firearms off a wooden or cement table, against handing a loaded rifle to a stranger so he can look in a scope and fire toward overhead clouds, against gaining some kind of trust and pulling that stranger into the back of a van to check out banned automatic weapons. There's a law against selling bottle rockets and firecrackers without a license. There's a law against wooden pipes, ceramic pipes, hookahs, roach clips, and rolling papers. There's a law against booze on Sundays in most counties, but any man with at least one whisker can throw down cash for a .410 thirty-ought-six or Beretta.

On bad days some local lawn mower repairman might set up across from me and feel it necessary to crank his fucking Sears Craftsman, Toro, John Deere, Snapper, Murray, Troy-Bilt, or Husqvarna over and over to prove that it works. On worse days some slopehead opens his trunk and sets a litter of pit bull/rottweiler–mix puppies out so that the only thing I hear is, "Oh, they good dogs now, but they'll grow up mean. I had a cousin who got her face bit off by a rottweiler," from customers too scared to linger near my wares. On the very worst days some traveling tent evangelist sets up to sell cast-off stringed instruments, and insists on playing his guitar six hours straight while singing some song about Jesus being a road map, until I finally reach inside my van, roll up the Rand McNally atlas, and beat the guy senseless.

All of us have tetanus shots. We own no insurance policies. We pay no taxes outside of what's added for gasoline, groceries, cigarettes, and booze. We remember every KOA campground in the southeast and every fallow field behind a copse of pines between.

There are no rule-makers.

EACH AVERAGE MORNING Hassett reaches for a Magic Marker and blackens out the name EVELYN tattooed to his left forearm. On bad days he borrows sandpaper from one of us and attempts to eradicate the ink altogether. On good days he only draws a moustache and goatee on the picture of Evelyn above her name. "She was the perfect mate for me until she got caught up in Amway," Hassett says at night by the campfire, or lounging in front of a motel pool, or sitting at a table inside the Sunken Gardens Lounge in Forty-Five, South Carolina, waiting for a college kid to either wet his pants or run for the men's room after accepting Fagen's twenty-dollar challenge.

"I would move to Minnesota or someplace if I thought people there bought levels," Hassett says. "It's cold near year-round and I'd have to wear long sleeves all the time. It'd save me Magic Marker costs. But I have a feeling the outdoor-flea-market trade might not be all that thriving like it is down here. Plus, it's a little too flat for level demands."

I say, "They got that laser surgery down now so you can get the tattoo lifted, Hassett. I don't know what it costs, but I'd bet the price lessens almost every day."

"Maybe Madame Tammy can look into your future and let you know when the time's right," Heidi says.

Madame Tammy sets up a crystal ball on a card table, always at the end of the flea market. For five dollars she'll point out your life line and explain all of its nuances. For ten dollars, we all believe, she'll sit you down in the front seat of her Dodge Dart and give you a hand-job.

JOHNNY MARONI ONLY sits in his tiny new used Geo until noon on Saturdays and Sundays. During the week he works at a comic book store his dad bought him. Johnny Maroni doesn't need the money. He waits, for his entire stock is made up of action figures. His area's professional wrestling. Odd teenagers who collect action-figure wrestlers don't get out of bed and drive down to the flea markets until eleven at the earliest. Sometimes Johnny Maroni turns his car stereo off and walks the market, hoping to find some poor mother selling off her kid's entire collection of toys, or an angry and hurt teenager who never got a response after writing fan letters to Hulk Hogan, Nature Boy Ric Flair, Randy Savage, and all of the ones wearing masks, especially Mankind.

Weigel thinks Johnny Maroni sells drugs on the side. He feels certain that those six-inch plastic dolls are stuffed with cocaine. Hassett, Fagen, and Joe Ray don't like Maroni because his father bought him the car and job. Heidi says she's got too much to worry about with other women ready to sell off their milk glass than to think about prepubescent boys playing with dolls.

Me, I put up with Johnny when he shows up. Every morning and afternoon he weighs his stock on my scales, then subtracts to see how much lighter he'll drive home. On good Saturdays it's in the three-to-four-pound range. Weigel says the only people concerned about the weight of their stock happen to be drug dealers, and that he should know, seeing as he comes in contact with them when he's hunting alligators down in Florida each winter.

I say, "One ounce equals 28.35 avoirdupois grams. One gram of coke I'm sure still costs a hundred bucks or there-abouts. Three pounds equals forty-eight ounces. Forty-eight ounces comes to 1360 grams." I drink from my beer. I think about Fagen's drainage bag and wonder exactly where the thing rests—against the right or left thigh, wrapped around his middle like one of those new dieting devices, all the way down into one of his tube socks he buys two pair for three dollars from a vendor with a monthly indoor table. "If Johnny Maroni's selling cocaine, then he's making $136,000 every Saturday. I don't think he'd be driving a new used Geo with that kind of money."

Hassett says, "He's got to deduct the cost of his action figures."

"There's that, and then there's the money for gas coming back and forth from Florida," says Weigel. "I know I've sold enough gator heads to drive something better than my Econoline. But if I do that, no one's going to buy from me. They'll think I'm only slumming, or that I don't really need the money."

"The last thing you want in the flea market business is people thinking you're just an eccentric, like some kind of idiot from a wealthy New England family who don't need to work nohow," Joe Ray says.

Heidi stretches her left leg my way and runs it up my inner calf. She doesn't correct Joe Ray's double negative out
of habit. Heidi's celebrating a half-dozen hobnail candy
dishes she's sold, and wants a room with Magic Fingers
tonight.

We sit quietly as Fagen starts up a game of quarters with
the college boy. Fagen's added a new rule that includes bodily emissions of any kind. His competitor's got a good mal-
leable bladder and hasn't shown the first sign of needing to
relieve himself, which, by the way, is a constant crossing of
legs. Weigel says to me finally, "Hey, you the man with all
the devices. How much are calipers going for these days? I
keep getting people wanting to know exactly how wide
each alligator head is. I think there are people out there
wanting to somehow knock out bricks, and mortar gator
heads into their houses so it looks like they got a special security system."

I say, "Calipers. A thousand dollars," and wait for his
counteroffer.

WE GO OUT picking country people in our own
way. Heidi walks right up to mudrooms and back-door
added-on kitchen entrances and asks the wife if she has any
vases, candy dishes, and ashtrays stored away in the attic
collecting dust, any old gathered items that the farmer's
wife might want to sell off at a fair price. Me, I go straight
toward any barn or work shed and find the man, ask the
same questions about measuring devices. Usually I run into
Joe Ray or, if Joe Ray got there before me, get yelled at

about how a man hardly has time to work what with all these gypsies asking questions. I'm not sure, but I think Hassett drives straight into new construction areas with Weigel and, while Weigel's showing some poor carpenter's helper or gofer a big gator head, scoops up any levels scattered around the premises. I can't be certain. I just never see him inside barns or garages.

Bad economic times work in our favor. Upcoming holidays work in our favor, too, seeing as people want extra cash for Christmas, and later on at the flea market customers feel gratified to buy something that doesn't have the high and necessary overhead markup it would at a Kmart, Wal-Mart, Target, Home Depot, or Lowe's.

Father's Day moves my wares. My other big holidays are only Christmas and Valentine's Day. Sometimes St. Patrick's Day brings out drunks not thinking how they don't need to measure the thickness of leather, cardboard, tin roofing, or wood. Near Veterans Day I might sell anything manufactured in America during the Second World War.

Weigel sells his gator heads the week before Halloween. Fagen sells his Davy Crockett hats around the Fourth of July—as if Davy Crockett had anything to do with our independence—and sporadically whenever a middle-aged man decides to buy a convertible and reenact his younger days. Weigel could've retired had he stocked up a couple years ago when some rap band came out wearing coonskin hats, but he only sold out of a dozen and by the time his reorder came in the band was off the charts and forgotten. Hassett plays his one-dollar-bill trick on people year-round, and says that as soon as people brighten up enough, he'll quit altogether unless he thinks of a new trick to prove himself smarter than the masses.

As Father's Day nears I step into Joe Ray's territory, but he understands. I place screwdrivers, socket sets, framing hammers, drill bits, pipe cutters, pliers, and vises right up at the front of my table. Every Elvis shot glass I'd ever picked up for a dime now goes for fifty cents.

I move in Fagen's merchandise, too: fuzzy dice.

The gun dealers always do well near Christmas and April 15.

Heidi gets Mother's Day easily, and if the floral industry ever pushes a Gay Pride Day onto the calendar she'll mop up.

Thanksgiving doesn't seem to matter to any of us. Easter doesn't quite work out anymore.

HEIDI RUNS OUT of a house near Forty-Five screaming, an old white farm woman behind her with a cleaver. I stand in the doorway of a giant springhouse admiring ancient rusted ice picks the farmer's bought or made over the years, old RC Cola thermometers, ice tongs, and well-bucket retriever hooks. Heidi says, "I didn't mean it that way, I didn't mean it that way," and circles around a fig tree.

Joe Ray's behind the woman saying, "I can go as high as two dollars on that cleaver."

In the van I say, "What'd you say to her? Goddamn, I was about to get about a hundred dollars' worth of good shit for ten bucks."

Heidi says, "She had some carnival glass. I pointed out that it'd been handled so much that it seemed more fragile than normal. You know how I always say that in order to get the price down."

I say, "I know."

"As it ends up, her mother and father worked in some traveling fair or circus, and she took what I said to mean that carnival people were more fragile than normal—like she came from a long line of psychopaths or something."

We drive past a statuary of lawn jockeys. We drive past bent men bent further between tractor and plow. We drive past a trio of barefoot children standing in front of somebody's makeshift sign advertising shoe repair/notary public/fresh strawberries. Heidi and I decide to drive on back to the flea market and set up for the morning, maybe play some hearts or spades all night, maybe read, maybe sit in the front seat of my van and stare out at traffic moving toward Florida or New York. I say, "A long line of psychopaths. That's funny."

Heidi says, "I didn't want to point out to her that she had a classic sloped head, that she probably emanated from a gene pool so shallow you could walk across it in a pair of shower thongs and not get the soles of your feet wet. I didn't want to go into that old joke about a one-limbed family tree."

We drive past a row of men on the roadside, all carrying half-filled plastic yard bags, pretending not to pick up aluminum. I throw out an empty Schlitz can without slowing up whatsoever.

On good days we hurt no one's feelings, and expect the same from mere strangers, onlookers, cops, and scammers.

JOHNNY MARONI'S GOT every teenaged boy's birthday. He has the anniversary of the Branch Davidians in Waco siege and the Oklahoma City bombing disaster—as do the gun dealers.

I say to Johnny Maroni after weighing-in his miniature men, "It'd be interesting to look into the causes of death for professional wrestlers. I bet they don't ever die of lead or asbestos poisoning. I bet they don't have trouble with allergies, either. Have you ever seen one doing manual labor outside the ring? I wonder if the masked ones wear another little white mask over their faces when they do something hazardous."

Johnny Maroni says, "Man, when are you going to get a life?"

I look across the table to Heidi. She doesn't blink. Fagen, Weigel, and Hassett all nod. When Johnny Maroni looks down the walkway in the opposite direction in search of prowling delinquents, I grab two handfuls of plastic action figures and toss them fifteen feet across, arcing toward my friends. When Maroni turns back around I say, "You're starting off today with a little over two thousand nine hundred pennyweights, Bubba."

One of the gun dealers sees me, but says nothing outside of "Pull!" from habit.

• • •

WE EACH KEEP one item on our tables in hopes that a believer might linger, a customer obsessed with any object touched by Hollywood, a dead head of state, rock star, or serial killer. More often than not we've talked ourselves into believing, too—convinced that our rarest piece of merchandise deserves a respect usually reserved for wonders of the world if not a hundred times its real worth. Fagen keeps one coonskin cap atop a Styrofoam wig display, forever telling the curious how either Fess Parker wore it on TV or Daniel Boone wore it himself. Fagen pretended interest in a 9mm one late afternoon and shot the hat in order to help authenticate his prize. On good days Fagen sticks to his original asking price, $1,700—which he promises as fair, the exact amount a similar hat worn by Moe Howard went for at a Christie's auction. On bad days, after a night surrounded by frightened, nongambling college sophomores, Fagen wavers his way down to a couple hundred, still to no interested buyers.

Heidi has an eight-piece cut-crystal set of water glasses used for props in *Gone with the Wind* and has a still photograph to prove it, or at least prove that she owns something worthy of Tara. Joe Ray's flattest sledgehammer once belonged to John Henry. Hassett claims he owns one level used by Frank Lloyd Wright—which is believable, seeing as if he sets it down on a flat, flat stainless-steel operating table in the hill-less regions of Nebraska it still registers a half-bubble one way or another. He swears that in his possession is a level used by the set designer working on *The Cabinet of Dr. Caligari,* but all the German's worn off. Weigel's largest alligator head supposedly came off the body of a trained animal named Sir Andrew that acted as a crocodile in a dozen Tarzan movies, but Weigel always fucks up and tells people it's the old, old Tarzan—the Olympic swimming champion, Johnny Wisenheimer.

I own an Italian ruler expertly wielded by a nun on the knuckles of Pope Pius VI, an Egyptian square handmade and used by Cheops, the original scales of justice, Archimedes' lever, the first tire-tread-wear gauge fought over by Goodrich and Firestone, and a barometer off Amelia Earhart's airplane.

I own Albert Einstein's first slide rule.

WE WANT MORE every day. Each of us lives to surpass that one big sale, steal, mix-up, or miscue. Our conversation invariably retreats to the past. Fagen always says, "I wish to God more people joined the Moose, Elks, Shriners, Masons, and Lions clubs, and that they'd have their retreat somewhere in the nearby hills. Hot damn I never will forget when all those old boys showed up drunk one morning wanting two coonskin caps apiece. They wanted one for the day and one for night, is what they said. I made over five hundred dollars that day alone."

Weigel comes back with the time he met a group of Haitian tourists who believed that their personal loas resided in alligators. He says, "It seems to me that your personal good luck charm can't be all that good luck what with its body that far misdirected from its head. But I didn't complain. I don't know where they all got their money, but that day I made something like six hundred dollars clear," which isn't true. The first time I heard Fagen tell his story he'd only made two hundred dollars, and Weigel came back with two-fifty or thereabouts. "I don't understand people having animal parts for good luck charms," Weigel says. "A lot of people don't understand why I don't carry a line of rabbit-feet key chains."

Heidi tells the story of a woman who came along crying, and then bought her out of every piece of Depression glass she had on the table, plus what was in the back of her van. Heidi got the woman's name and number, went to auction that night, and bought every piece of yellow Lorain, pink Doric, green Colonial, and iridescent Aunt Polly that came up for bid. She called the griever and turned around every butter dish, berry bowl, sherbet plate, creamer, coaster, cup and saucer for four times its worth the next morning when the sad woman showed up in a 1969 Rambler before dawn. She says, "I made so much money I couldn't even keep track. I made so much I wouldn't want to let anyone in on it should they become my enemy later on and call the tax man."

Joe Ray says, "One time I sold two turn plows and two axes to the same man at the same moment. He said he was so mad at his mule he wanted to work her hard, then hit her upside the head with one ax. He said mules are smart, though, and spectral. He said a good live mule knows it's been hooked up to a dead mule's plow."

Johnny Maroni never tells stories, maybe because he doesn't come out drinking with us later. Me, I tell the story about the midget who bought me out of metric yardsticks. He said he wanted them leaning all over the house so he could look at them at eye level, see the number 72, and feel six feet tall always.

But late at night, after we've spent money we shouldn't have, after all the stories and lies have been told, as the bartender flicks the lights to let us know it's last call, someone —and it's as if we subconsciously take even turns on this— tells the story of Frank McNutt and his little boy, Jacob, the king and prince of flea market legends. Frank only sold vacant dilapidated Sears and Roebuck Silvertones. Frank's child—and I'm not sure how he ended up with custody unless his wife was nuts—crouched down inside the things while holding a small transistor radio. I'm sure they gave each other cues or signals, but we never saw any. A prospective buyer always walked up to a Silvertone as if he expected the thing to jump out and grab his leg, and then looked up to Frank without asking a question. Frank said, "It works fine." He'd point how he had the thing plugged into a power strip that hooked up to the battery of his small stripped-down RV, then turn a knob clockwise and from the desolate guts of the once-proud machine we'd all hear the radio jump through all of the AM stations. Then Frank worked it back to the 550-on-the-dial area. He'd switch over to FM, say something about the thing needing an antenna, and repeat the process.

Of course Frank always set the radio right up against his van, so that once the customer bought the thing little Jacob could crawl out from underneath and hide between two axles. He stayed down there most of the day, too, waiting for his father to pull out the next model from the back of the van. I say, "It's the perfect example of teamwork. It's the perfect example of why we need to unionize."

Heidi says, "It's a shame we don't have them around with us anymore."

If a stranger sits with us, or a newcomer to the flea market business, or maybe even the bartender should we sit as close as possible to the bottles, he or she asks what happened, thinking some drastic and execrable event must've taken the McNutts from our lives. I say, "There were a hell of a lot of pirates, alchemists, plunderers, and con men from previous lives who unfortunately escaped in order to inhabit ours," and then go on to tell how Frank and Jacob now run an infomercial program between about three and four in the morning, usually between channels 50 and 69 in most cable markets.

HEIDI'S FIGURED OUT that she can eat on less than six dollars a week, outside of her Sunday porterhouse. At each flea market there's a man who specializes in overturned food—not expired—bought from truck lines and freight cars. Heidi says she absorbs seventy-five thousand calories a month. She stays away from snack cakes but can't resist Yoo-hoo calcium-enriched chocolate drinks, canned lima beans, Hormel chili, and odd-brand chopped spinach. She says, "What they need is a flea market in every county of every third world country." She says, "You can do a lot worse than day-old bread and dented Veg-All with the label intact."

At each flea market there's a man I swear is the same guy. My colleagues say it's a different one each time. He rents a table, offers up no wares, and only sits. He wears sunglasses. Some people say this guy just quit drinking and only wants to be in a place like a bar, filled with drunks but without the temptation. Some people say he lost his wife and children in a fatal car crash and that he's not been the same ever since. Fagan believes that the guy is blind, and some trickster friend of his brings him out saying that they're at a drive-in movie.

I tell everyone that he's an ex-alcoholic who lost his wife and child in a fatal *bar* accident, then stabbed his own eyes out from the guilt. Heidi takes the guy fresh peaches in the spring, and he eats them directly so as not to have anything on his table.

HERE'S A LESSON: never set up a table within a hundred yards of a man who brings his daughter along to watch him sell her pet pony. If a radio's nearby playing old country songs, go ahead and put a pistol to your temple.

WHEN NO ONE buys it's as if people come to the flea market drawn by mystical powers, as if the ghost of every fitness expert has come down and commanded the locals to walk in circles and never stop. The antique vendors don't even show up early to find inexpensive hidden Roseville, Edgefield, or Jugtown pottery brought out by desperate unknowing folks in need of cash to pay the month's electric bill. Antique dealers say they can't sell, either.

The only difference in an antique dealer and a person

like me concerns optimism and general health. An antique dealer feels as though he'll live to be a hundred—old enough to see his early buys actually quadruple in value. Fagen and I have talked about it before—we hope to live long enough to unload what we bought a week earlier. Antique dealers think nothing of boxing up a Beanie Baby and storing the thing fifty years before taking it out for auction.

I go to Madame Tammy and say, "I got this idea. I'm having a hard time making table rental, much less food and gas money for the next market. When you're reading people's palms, why don't you tell them that you see a measuring device in their future. Just come right out and say something like, 'You will live a long and happy life if you go two rows over and buy a tape measure from that man.' Then tell them to mention to me how they got sent by you, and I'll give you ten per cent of the gross on it. At the end of the day I'll come over here and let you know how much I sold, and give you cash money."

Madame Tammy says, "How much do your tape measures cost?" She has a fake accent that doesn't come close.

"Anywhere from two dollars to ten. You can say antique yardsticks, too. Or micrometers. I'll make a list of what I carry so you'll know. So you can vary your advice from client to client."

The air hangs as thick and musty as two yokes in a wet barn. Madame Tammy says, "That's only from twenty cents to one dollar. Listen. I don't know your name, but I must tell you that I have pride. I have built trust over the years."

I say nothing about how she should know my name if she's a crystal-ball-reading psychic palm reader, et cetera. I say, "You give hand jobs to men in the front seat of your old car."

She says, "So why would I bring up rulers and yard-sticks?"

HEIDI AND I sleep together under one table. It rains, but we've found a solid metal top as opposed to the one-by-six slat tables that have bowed over the years. Hassett once punched out the table collector after telling him how he couldn't sell a fucking level on a table that looks like a prairie schooner's naked ribs. Heidi says, "I don't even remember my last sale. They always say that when you can't remember your last sale it's time to move on."

I say, "They say that in hopes that you do move on. Hey, it'll get better. Not everyone from Florida's come up yet to escape their own heat. It's still cool down in the Miami area."

Heidi says, "They always say that once you start getting attached to what you have in front of you, it's time to get out of the business, too. If you can't sell what you own, you know. If you can't sell what you own, and you don't feel like you own what you sell, then it's time to get out. That sounds good. I made it up myself."

I roll over and pull a plastic twist-off bottle cap from my back. I say, "You should paint it on a sign and ask a dollar for it."

Heidi looks away, at someone's campfire on the other

end of the lot. She says, "I have a sister living in Oregon. We used to be close." She clears her throat. "You don't have one of those gizmos that tells a person how long it'll take them to drive somewhere, and how much gas it'll take, do you?"

I say I don't, then. I secure our tarp down better, for privacy, and in the middle of making love with Heidi I realize that in time I'll find a way to talk myself into believing that she left because she'd become overly attached to me, that if she didn't care about what was closest to her whatsoever, she'd've stayed. Later on, I'll have theories. I'll have pertinent information and asides, should anyone want to listen. It might not be easy talking Fagen and Weigel into believing my side, but they won't interrupt me in the bars late at night, seeing as I know all their measurement tricks, too.

Page-a-Day

Walter Inabinet stands in the center of his four-hundred-square-foot work space — a shingle-sided ex–slave cabin — conjuring up his alter persona, lowering his intelligence quotient, emptying his brain of the formal training he'd received in tenth-grade art class. He waits for visions and the voice of God to tell him what to portray next. Since leaving his regular job selling pharmaceuticals four years earlier Walter's scrawled his new name, "Seldom," daily, grown a beard, properly torn and smudged his clothes in a manner befitting a primitive artist, and sold enough flat paintings of the baby Elvis, the baby Jesus, the baby Henry Ford, and the baby Robert E. Lee to get his work inside art galleries across the Southeast and on the Internet. He's not had to withdraw money from his retirement accounts. Rather, he's had time to perfect his accent, mannerisms, and squint. He's learned to buy latex paint at the Habitat for Humanity thrift store, and to gather tin after healthy windstorms.

Walter does not imagine that at this moment his wife, Emmie, hand prints scurrilous and defamatory remarks about him on calendars. She works, selling calendars, at a place called Get a Date! that's open only Thanksgiving to the end of January. She sells regular wall-hanging calendars with pictures of kittens, naked men, Vermont mountain scenes, naked women, Humane Society dogs, swimsuit models, teen-boy bands, teen-girl pop stars, thoroughbred horses, the multicolored houses of Charleston's Bay Street, and the diners of Route 66. She peddles word-a-days, crossword-a-days, horoscope-a-days, cartoon-a-days, find-your-spirit-a-days, cryptoquote-a-days, and regular generic desk calendars on her job, located a block off King Street in the fancy, tourist-ridden section of downtown Charleston. On each calendar she turns to April 15—the day her husband, Walter, quit his job in 1997 and became Seldom—and writes "Seldom Inabinet is a Phony," clearly, in indelible ink, hoping that whoever buys the calendar will notice it, keep the thought, and never buy primitive works from the man. On occasion Emmie writes, "Seldom Inabinet Ran away from Wife, 1997" or "Seldom Inabinet Leaves Human Race, 1997."

Emmie took the job because, as she told her increasingly distant husband, "I can't count on you bringing in money like you used to when you lived by the vows we took." At least once a week she says, "I loved you better when you were a drug dealer."

In the center of his work space amid tin and plywood cutouts, waiting for the simplest of ideas, Seldom forgets about his wife. He looks out the window into a copse of pines that hides him from the subdivision where he lives most nights, a mile away. He walks to his workplace each morning before daylight hits, before Emmie has time to remind him of the days when they could afford a new car biannually.

He's about to replace a blade on the jigsaw when he hears someone shuffling up the gravel road. He expects it to be Junius, an old black man who brings discarded items for sale, the occasional stray dog, or trapped raccoons. Seldom hears, "I need your help," from a woman, but no knock. "I need your help for my baby, sir."

He opens the heart-pine door to find a disheveled woman he's not seen before in these northern swamps of the county, a white woman aged anywhere from eighteen to forty. She holds a pretoddler against her chest, wrapped in a thin, beige, cotton curtain. "Hey, come on in and get out of the outside." He pulls her up the two-foot step.

"They say you can breathe on babies and rid the thrush," she says. "My little girl's got the thrush real bad."

Thrush, Seldom thinks. *Thresh? Thrash?* "What?"

She tips forward and sticks her finger in the child's mouth, pries its lower jaw open as if pressing a piano key. "It's got bad," she says. "I got some money. If you could breathe on her and fix it I'd be beholden." She tilts her daughter's head so Seldom can look down the girl's throat.

Seldom knows that she's not one of the art gallery owners visiting, hoping to buy work for a deal, wanting to go back to Atlanta with a story or two. He reverts to regular

Walter Inabinet and says, "Jesus Christ, lady, you need to get your kid to a doctor." The woman's child's throat looks as if someone poured Elmer's glue down it. There are lesions on the mouth and lips, and when viewed from above, it does not look dissimilar to squeezed milkweed, or a latex volcano. "Come on. I can run over to my house and get the car. I'll take y'all to the emergency room or something."

She pulls her baby back. "I ain't got the money. They say you can breathe on people and cure their ills. They say you got a way with the thrush. And warts."

Walter thinks it's a prank—who speaks like this anymore outside of extras on *The Real McCoys* or *The Andy Griffith Show*? He says, "I think you might have the wrong address." He tries to think of some codger up or down Pinkney Mill Road who might have compatible skills and/or breath. Inabinet wonders if one of his old pharmaceutical salesman buddies drove this woman over and let her out of the car. "Let's take this baby of yours to the hospital."

"Breathe on my baby," she says. "I don't even have money for Gripe Water. Please just breathe on my baby." The woman tears up, then screams so loudly that Walter wonders if his neighbors down the road can hear her: "Breathe on my baby! All's I'm asking is for you to breathe on my baby!" She falls on the sawdust-covered floor of Seldom Inabinet's visionary-art work space. "In the old days people breathed on babies without having to be ast," she sobs out.

Seldom looks past her at a rusted, blank tin cutout and sees a white circle in the spot where a mammal's mouth goes. He thinks, They say I can breathe on people and cure them. He thinks, What the fuck's Gripe Water?

EMMIE TOOK THE JOB at Get a Date! in order to stick money in a savings account that garnered two-percent interest. Her husband supported the decision, seeing as she might be able to pilfer little things that would aid his primitive art: boxes, certainly, but also damaged spiral binders, Magic Markers, and cash register tapes. Emmie worked for one year as a high school English teacher before she and Walter realized that he made enough money in pharmaceuticals to support both of them.

Emmie volunteered for the Human Society soon thereafter, and drove into town to fix twenty-gallon cauldrons of potato soup at the food bank. She wrote members of Congress about recycling, air quality, and the changing roles of women in society.

Her life had felt complete initially. Walter held her hand when they ventured out on walks. They talked of children, a house on the beach, retirement by the time Walter reached fifty. Emmie framed new pictures of them monthly down the hallway of their house. She didn't say anything about how, increasingly, she skipped her volunteer work and returned to bed after Walter left for work. Emmie never mentioned how she turned to the Yellow Pages' list of psychologists but never gathered enough courage to call. She read Dear Abby, flipped through cable channels in search of a segment that featured something resembling her condition, and watched every talk show. As best she could figure, she had postpartum depression without the baby. She thought, I have pre-postpartum depression. I have pre- and postmenstrual syndrome. Each year Emmie thought, This will end when spring comes around. It'll end in April. She thought of April as the only month of hope. They had married in April, on a day that the local weatherman said might've been the most perfect day ever recorded in the history of the heavens.

Then, in 1997, Walter quit. He took to primitive art for no logical reason, such as having God come down and tell him to construct simple pieces. Later on in life he would tell people that he'd had a dream, and in this dream he foresaw everybody in his life addicted to pharmaceuticals that never worked. He would tell people later, "I don't think it costs more than a nickel to manufacture most pills that cost two bucks each. I couldn't live with myself."

Walter began his new life by sitting around trying out new names, starting with the biblical: Moses, Nimrod, Nadab. He stood in front of a mirror and imagined introducing himself by country names: Lester, Jethro, and Zeb.

"You're seldom around here anymore," Emmie said one late evening after Walter returned from a seminar, before he'd decided to let his wife in on his change of plans in regards to lifestyle. And he thought, I am Seldom around here. I am Seldom, around here. I am Seldom.

EMMIE RETURNS FROM a half-day of work to find her husband holding a child that isn't one of their nieces or nephews. He says, "Lookee here what I got," and holds the baby out as if it were a medicine ball. "Lookee here."

Emmie drags inside an eight-foot one-by-ten piece of yellow pine she found in the alley behind Get a Date! that she
figured Seldom might use later. She says, "No." She doesn't
say anything about how they can't have children of their
own. She doesn't say anything about how they'd already
decided not to adopt children. She says, "No, Walter. No,
Seldom, whichever."

He stands up and joggles the woman's baby on his hip.
"It ain't mine, or anything. The mother's back there sleeping," he says, jerking his head toward the guest bedroom.
"This isn't what it looks like, Emmie. Look at this." He
pulls the baby's bottom lip down to show the thrush.

"There's a woman sleeping in my house?" Emmie says.

Walter walks toward his wife. "The people around here
are saying I can breathe on babies and heal them, I swear to
God. They're saying I can breathe on people and get their
warts to fall off. Mark this day on your calendars, Emmie.
That's what they're saying." He bobs the baby up and down.
"Her name's Jeannie, just like the TV show. I got her to a
doctor and they fixed her up with some kind of penicillin."

Emmie points to the bedroom and says, "Her mother's
in there?"

"Oh, she's as country as they come, honey. Don't worry.
I was in the middle of painting a cutout of Adam with a
snake and this woman knocked on the door. What could I
do? I did what I could do. Listen, I know that they say I can
breathe on people and cure them and all, but I thought a
doctor might be the best option. To be honest, I'd never
heard of anything called 'thrush.'" He struts around with
his not-baby cradled, acting the martyr.

Emmie holds out her arms for the child. She asks no more questions. "Thrush is a bird," Emmie says. Holding the baby, she walks from the den and down the hallway. She puts her ear against the guest-bedroom door, then knocks softly. Emmie opens the door as if expecting to see an anxious cur huddled against the wall, then swings it wide without holding the knob. "Where'd you put her?"

Walter looks at the window. It's closed, but unlocked, and the screen's been replaced haphazardly. "Man, this is like something out of Hollywood. She abandoned her kid with us." He doesn't say it in an excited tone. He doesn't widen his eyes like a community-theater actor trying to pull off incredulity.

Emmie says, "We better call the police, or the social services people," thinking about how she'll have something new to write down on customers' brand-new calendars. She hands Jeannie back over.

WALTER DOESN'T HAVE a car seat. He lays Jeannie out on the back floorboard, then drives toward his work shack. The secondary road has no intersections for a mile either way, outside of old logging roads that dead-end into ex-swamps, trails manned only by illegal hunters and the deer they follow. He decides to drive five miles one way, then backtrack.

Jeannie's mother sits on the front steps of Seldom's shack, smoking a cigarette and looking the other way. Walter closes his car door, then reopens it, rolls down every window, and leaves Jeannie in the back. "What're you doing, woman? You can't just abandon a baby like that. My wife's calling the authorities."

She blows a smoke ring unintentionally. "Maybe I wanted you to come back there and breathe on me. Maybe I got tired of waiting and let myself out to see if you cared." She stands up. "Wife."

"You damn right. She's pissed off that I'd let a stranger in our house in the first place. Then you just take off. What the hell."

"Where's Jeannie?"

Seldom probably would have said, "Oh, she's right in back here sleeping off thrush." Walter says, "I don't know what un-underpinned trailer you crawled out from, but we don't think you're the most suitable mother for that little girl. We're going to let DSS decide what should happen to the baby."

The mother seems unaffected by these pronouncements. She opens the unlocked door to Seldom's work space and jerks her head once. "What you make in here, anyways? I looked in and it looks like the work of the devil, to me. Maybe I ought to be the one calling po-lice on you."

Walter walks up, reaches inside his building, and turns the lock. "Go on and get in the car. I'm taking you back to the house."

The mother smiles; she has perfectly round holes between each of her top teeth, as if carpenter bees had set in and drilled between each space, halfway through one tooth and halfway through its next-door partner. Walter can only think how she'd let out a strange whistle should she smile in a windstorm. "Sounds to me you could take a tonic of what water my baby girl needed. You come off a little bloated. Maybe we should've had you talk to that doctor, too." Jeannie's mother nods her head up and down like a panting dog.

The baby lets out a noise that sounds as if she's popped a giant mucus bubble. The mother looks toward the car. "I knowed you wouldn't leave her there with a wife. You brought her along with you. That proves a little something."

Walter squints. "What's your name again?"

"I never told you my name. My name don't matter none. Jeannie's name matters, but not mine."

A car slows on the road and turns down the pine straw–strewn one-lane. Walter doesn't turn to look. He figures it's either Emmie in their other car, a sheriff's deputy, or a social worker. "Mr. Seldom?" comes a voice, and Inabinet turns to see Margaret Flythe from the Margaret Flythe Gallery, a woman who buys Seldom's cutouts for twenty-five dollars each and then sells them to wealthy Charlestonians for upwards of a hundred. She steps out of a new SUV. "I've come for another load. I've sold out what you gave me two months ago."

Seldom says, "Hey, Ms. Flythe," as slowly as he can, remembering to put on the aw-shucks drawl. "How you doing?"

"Well I hate to bother you. I know how busy you are."

"This here's a model I got working for me," Seldom says, pointing to Jeannie's mother. "This is Jeannie's mother."

Margaret Flythe nods politely. She says, "Nice to meet you, Jeannie's mother."

"That's all she goes by," Seldom says. He opens the door to his shop. "I don't know if I got anything you'll find sightly, but go on in and pick up what you think other people might need."

Margaret Flythe enters. Seldom looks at Jeannie's mother with an eye that says, Don't talk while she's here.

Jeannie's mother says, "Let me get on my way. I won't say nothing if you let me on my way."

Seldom raises his voice. "I'll be in directly, Ms. Flythe," then walks Jeannie's mother to the car.

EMMIE TALKS WITH a deputy in the driveway, then gets in the front seat with him. She says, "They've been gone more than an hour. I assume my husband has her down at his work."

"Is your husband having an affair with this woman?" the deputy says. "I hate to be so callous, but a lot of time a man will make up a long-winded story like this only to fool his wife. Good lord I've seen men act and lie in ways that I can't even mention to a beautiful woman."

"No," Emmie says. "My husband barely pays attention to me. He couldn't handle a mistress." She realizes how this sounds. "I mean, I come home all the time to find my husband alone. I come home early and I come home late. There's no way."

"I believe if I was your husband I'd be home all the time when you showed up." He shakes his head slowly and offers her a shy curl of his lips. "Now exactly what does the woman look like?"

Emmie detects a slight blush on the officer's skin. She thinks about how Walter showed such signs when they first dated. "I've never seen her. She was asleep in our guest bedroom, and then she went out the window."

The deputy says, "Huh," and follows Emmie's finger to the right, out of their driveway. "Where do you work?"

Emmie looks straight ahead. "I work downtown at Get a Date! It's a calendar store."

"I've been there. I know it. When our chief retired we got him one of those gag calendars where every day says Saturday. The numbers are right, you know, but every day says Saturday."

Emmie looks at his hair and notices how it's perfect, maybe one centimeter all the way around. He looks as though he's carved exotic blond wood, she thinks. "We sell a lot of those. I bet if we stayed open year-round we'd sell a bunch to people in May or June, when teachers retire."

The deputy wears a pistol on his right side. There's a shotgun clamped upright to his car's dashboard. "I bought a few calendars for Christmas presents this year. You didn't wait on me, though. I wouldn't forget you."

"My husband's not having an affair, I promise. That's all I have to say. To get back on the subject," Emmie says.

The deputy drives no more than twenty miles an hour and looks toward the right-hand ditch, as if for footprints. "You know your husband better than I do," the deputy says. "Probably. I only know profiles of people. They teach us those kinds of things at the academy." He makes no eye contact; he looks at the berm, using the heel of his left hand to move the steering wheel. "I don't want you killing the messenger, but I'd bet my pension that he's messing around. I'm sorry."

Emmie's chin quivers. "He might be. No. No, no."

The deputy nods. "I've probably met half the women in this county. You're the most stunning one I've encountered, confused or not."

Two miles past Seldom's shop Emmie learns that the deputy's name is Loris Treen. She begins to cry, he pulls over and brings her torso to his and says for her to let it out. Her head's against his right pectoral, an inch from his name tag. At first she flinches, but then she allows his right hand inside her panties, his middle finger moving in slow circles. Deputy Treen pulls back onto the asphalt and barely touches the accelerator. He looks forward. They pass Jeannie's mother and Jeannie walking along the tree line, but both of them pretend not to see her. Emmie cries. The officer consoles her in his own way.

SELDOM ASKS MARGARET FLYTHE, "Have you ever heard of Gripe Water?"

She picks up, then sets down, an unfinished tin cutout that could either be Ronald Reagan or Gumby. "It's a brand name. It's given to babies with colic. Why do you ask?"

Seldom shuffles across his sawdust. He looks at a metal cutout and thinks how he'll paint a circle of white in the middle of the head. "Gripe Water sounds political."

Ms. Flythe sets aside two Adams, two Eves, a dozen baby Elvises, and a John the Baptist that Seldom made when he accidentally lost control of his tin snips. She reaches into her purse and says, "I'd like to get these if three hundred and seventy-five dollars will be enough."

He thinks about how it took around two hours' work for fifteen pieces and that the paint didn't cost two dollars. "I shore could use about four hundred, ma'am."

From afar he thinks he hears his wife yell out. "Well, you got me," Ms. Flythe says. She hands him three hundred-dollar bills and five twenties. "Now don't you go drink this away or anything."

Seldom runs his left hand through his hair and holds out his right. "No, I won't. I might get my teeth fixed."

Margaret Flythe holds what she'll sell for upwards of two grand. "Mr. Seldom, as always, it's good doing business with you. Have you ever thought about doing a series of conjoined twins? I think that would go over well. Or people with prehensile tails. There are people nearby, you know, with tailbones sticking out of their backsides. We need to keep alive the folks we have living among us, it's my belief. We have more Siamese twins born here than any other place in the world. At least that's what I read."

Seldom nods. "I'm pretty much consumed by the woman just left. I got to get my drill working right to finish her off." He thinks about how he needs to make life-size works concerning people that he helped to take Prozac, Xanax, Ritalin, Valium, and extra-strength Motrin back when he sold.

Flythe says, "I don't see where you have any bad teeth, Seldom. Let me look at you smile."

She sets her artworks down on the floor and reaches toward Seldom's mouth, all thumbs and forefingers. She wants to pull back his lips. He says, "Don't do that, ma'am."

"I'm serious. I never thought about it before, but your teeth are strong."

Because Seldom has never thought of Margaret Flythe in a sexual manner he holds two palms forward, as if for a shield. She presses her body against his and flips his upper lip back as if looking for a tattoo on his gums. Her breasts surge into his upper stomach, and from where he stands against the back wall Seldom can see where she needs to redye her off-red hair. He mumbles out, "I was borned with good teeth."

"I've always been infatuated with creative people," Margaret Flythe says, breathless, pulling Seldom's zipper down. When she falls on her knees and Walter feels the building shake, he knows that he must go beneath it soon to reenforce the floorboards, the joists, the foundation that he stands upon more often than not.

EMMIE TAKES HER FOOT down from the spotlight attached to Loris Treen's passenger door. She says, "It might not be how you got me to start thinking. My husband might be innocent."

"No husband's innocent," the deputy says. "Believe me, again. That's one thing I've learned on this job. I've been a cop for ten years. Before that I was in the Marines, over in Beaufort. I've learned some things I'm not proud to admit as true."

Emmie pulls her panties up from her ankles. What the hell am I doing? she thinks. "You better turn around and go the other way. It's obvious that that woman hasn't gone this far." For the first time she thinks about what would've happened had they driven by Walter.

Loris Treen hits the brake. He doesn't turn one way or the other. "It's kind of obvious that you're in a bad marriage, and that you and I get along good. Emmie. It's kind of obvious." He lifts his right hand hard against her crotch. Then he releases his hold, and means to grab the back of Emmie's neck. When Loris Treen tries to pull her face down into his lap, he pops her upper lip by accident.

Emmie says, "You son-of-a-bitch." She opens her car door and steps out.

"I didn't mean to do that," Loris Treen says through the window. "I swear to God." He puts the patrol car in reverse and tries to keep up with Emmie, but she shoots off shoeless into the woods, running, holding her skirt with two hands in front of her. She thinks, This is not April, this is not April, this is not April—nothing else.

When she hits the stagnant water of a cold, shallow swamp, Emmie pulls her skirt higher, then looks for cypress knees and occasional rocks on which she can go from one point to the next, not thirty feet from the roadside.

• • •

Seldom makes admissions. "I'm not the person you think I am. To be honest, I have a college education."

Margaret Flythe lifts her eyes. She shakes her head and gets off her knees. "You're a phony primitive artist? Like Tubby Burt? Oh, that makes you more important than ever."

"I don't want to be important, Ms. Flythe. I just wanted to make people laugh."

She straightens her dress, shoos sawdust from her legs. She hands Seldom another hundred-dollar bill. "Let's keep this between the two of us," she says. "I mean, about you being a fake and all that." She picks up her purchases. "I'm a writer, too, by the way. I'm betting that I could write Seldom's life story one day, if you want. We could make some money."

Walter Inabinet thinks about his wife. He thinks, This is a day that shouldn't have happened.

When Emmie passes Jeannie's mother holding Jeannie, they look at each other as two specters might. Emmie's farther in the swamp, choosing a makeshift trail that turns from creek bed to muck to flattened saw grass where deer bed down nightly. Jeannie's mother carries the child as if she were a thin bag of gum erasers, closer to the drainage ditch on the side of the road. Emmie knows it's the woman who escaped the house, but Jeannie's mother only thinks that she's finally met a woman worse off than herself.

"Tell me you're not having an affair with my husband," Emmie says from fifteen yards away. She stops and leans against a live oak. Her bare feet sink into what's not mud or water, not dry land or the detritus of splintered limbs and fouled fern. "Or tell me that you are."

Jeannie's mother turns her baby away from the woman. "You live in the swamp? I ain't never seen you."

"You were at my house. Where's Walter?"

"You the swamp witch they talk about? You the woman conjures up healing?" Emmie shakes her head; she shakes her head thinking about Walter, and about Loris Treen. "Are you the one they all talk about lives in the House of Fog over past Ringworm Creek?"

Emmie looks toward the road. She hears Officer Treen's cruiser accelerate and imagines him driving hard toward nowhere, hoping that she doesn't file a complaint. "You and your baby were at my house. You know that and I know that. Tell me where Walter is."

Jeannie's mother stares at Emmie, then looks down at the other woman's submerged feet. When she jerks her head, Emmie can't tell if it means "back there" or if a bank of mosquitoes has risen. Jeannie's mother walks away on a path that isn't visible, recorded, or known to reptiles or mammals. When Emmie gets to the road she thinks she hears Jeannie's mother call back, "No man knows where he's going, either."

EMMIE SHOWS UP at Seldom's shack looking much the same as Jeannie's mother had. Emmie doesn't so much collapse on the front step as give up completely, as if each muscle inside her frame relaxes. Walter sidles up to her and sits. He puts his arm across Emmie's shoulders. "I take it you went looking in the swamp."

His wife turns and buries her head into his left armpit. Although she has never been a deeply religious or philosophical person, Emmie says, "There are some things we cannot explain, right? There are some things we can't figure out."

"I've been back and forth to the house twice looking for you. Where'd you go? Did the cops ever show up?"

Emmie stands. "I know I complain all the time about you giving up a regular job." She doesn't say, "But I'll quit," or "You were right and I was wrong." She says, "I realize."

"I know you've been shoving money into a bank account," Walter says. "I don't want you moving out, but I could probably understand."

Emmie almost says, "I have something I need to tell you." She turns her body ninety degrees and looks down the path. Instead, she says, "What a weird day. Here's a day I might mark down on my own calendar, you know."

Seldom wants to go back inside and work on a series of tin cutouts that incorporate conjoined babies with prehensile tails, white-white open mouths, and wedding bands on their ring fingers. He says, "Margaret Flythe showed up when I came back here looking for that woman. She bought four hundred dollars' worth of shit." He reaches in his right front pocket and pulls out the bills. "It wouldn't be a bad idea for you to open up an art gallery and sell work from Seldom. Goddamn. I could reinvent myself into some other visionary artists, too."

Emmie says, "That's not a bad idea. That's not a bad idea until we get caught. Maybe later on, after we're both dead."

In the distance a feral cat screams. Sporadic traffic veers along the winding rough asphalt of Pinkney Mill Road. Walter Inabinet thinks about his wife on their April wedding day and how she looked coming down the aisle, eyes filled with an exuberance known only to a woman wearing blinders to what pains may burble up like swamp gas into a marriage.

Richard Petty Accepts National Book Award

Let me say right now that this couldn't've been done without the support of all the good Hewlett-Packard people. The Intel Pentium III, 550 megahertz with 128 megabytes of RAM done us right. There for a while we thought a 20-gigabyte hard drive wouldn't be enough for what we had to say, but hot almighty model 8575 chugged along and took the curves. I'm happy to say that we moved over from the 40x/CDRW CD-ROM to the CDRW/DVD CD-ROM—not that we couldn't've wrote what we wrote without it, but hey—we never felt like we was either too tight or too loose in the curves, or like we didn't flat-out have plenty of get-go when we felt pressure from all the other fine writers who published books this year. It's no secret that modem speeds in actual use may vary, but I got to hand it to the HP people for the way they kept me constant. There weren't no surprises, is what I'm saying.

I'd also like to thank the people at LaserJet Laser Paper

for the strong, smooth, twenty-four-pound white paper that won't curl up and wilt, even at Darlington. We done some high-speed copying, and the ink and toner stayed consistent throughout. The extra weight and brightness always assured crisp text, which is important for résumés, brochures, report covers, newsletters, press releases, and the Great American Novel. Ninety-six brightness can't be beat when it comes to LaserJet 4050 Series printers, which gave us the ability to go seventeen pages a minute. We liked the 1200 by 1200-dpi resolution, and the fifteen-second start-up time probably kept us in business the same way my pit crew did down in Daytona Beach all those years—fast, fast.

Oh I know I'mo forget somebody.

I can't say enough about the people at Martin Computer Office Grouping. Our credenza, hutch, two-drawer lateral file, deluxe executive computer desk with return, and print tower made it easy as coming down pit row at forty-five miles per hour every day when we set ourselves down to type and write each morning. We'd just pull our deluxe ergonomic manager's chair with pneumatic and independently adjustable seat height right up to the desk without even having to think about lumbar support, knee tilt, or durable fabric upholstery. Weavetek 100 percent Olefin put us in a good Dusty Rose 541 pattern that suited what we needed to say about the human condition, plus left us comfortable and dry during those humid summer afternoons of conflict between protagonist and antagonist.

Listen, the Great American Novel don't come all at once, and we'd like to thank the Greencycle Recycled Steno Book people for their high-quality six-by-nine-inch green-tinted, Gregg ruled pads, where we took notes and drew charts up about conflict and plot. Let me say to all the aspiring writers out there that I wrecked a good twenty pads before finding the groove on the outside of the home office, I tell you what.

Now I know a lot of the rest of the field went with Uni-Ball Roller Grip pens because the steel point added strength and resistance to smears, but I got to tell you—toward the end there we just decided to take a chance on Papermate stick pens in black medium. The durable ballpoint tip withstood everyday office use there down the stretch. I can't say for sure I'd've made it another couple chapters, but the team made a decision and stuck to it. For those of y'all not acquainted with the nuances of composition, it's a lot like taking on two tires at the end of the Coca-Cola 600 instead of opting for four new Goodyears.

I ain't too proud to admit that I partook of the Webster's New World dictionary put out by Simon & Schuster. I ain't too proud to admit that on those cold winter nights when we couldn't even think of a good character's name I got some support from Jim Beam and Jack Daniel's and George Dickel, not necessarily in that order.

Listen, sometimes it takes a wreck to understand a work of art. That time I rolled the wall—and y'all seen the clips on ESPN—the whole time I only thought, Well, the main character has to grow some by the end of the story.

We can't forget the Xerox remanufactured cartridge people. I don't know how many nights I called them people up and said, "Hey, I need a remanufactured laser-printer cartridge pronto up here in North Carolina." They'd work all night long so I wouldn't have to start next day at the back of the pack, which ain't easy. Ask any driver in Rockingham, Richmond, or Pocono.

I remember one time at Bristol when I couldn't keep up with what went on. Back then I could've used a printing calculator with twelve-digit fluorescent display and mark-up/mark-down function. We couldn't've kept up our pace without the AC-powered Canon MP25D, just to let us know where we were in the novel, what with chapters, and scenes, and pages, and sentences. And words. Finally on the hardware front I got to tip my hat to the people at Acco for their smooth, nonskid, regular and jumbo paper clips.

And the people at Brown Kraft recycled clasp envelopes, whose envelopes I used to send my first chapters off to the agent.

Now I know y'all in attendance might think writing the Great American Novel don't take much more than one idea and a support team like I done mentioned. Somebody famous said oncet, "Clothes make the man." Well, it's true. I don't know if I coulda finished up my pivotal climactic scene without the support of the people at Wrangler jeans. Combed cotton is the way to go having to sit on your butt six hours a day. Same goes for our people at authentic Dickies workshirts—another 100-percent cotton product made o'vair in Bangladesh. We couldn't finish a minor scene—much less a chapter—without the good work of the people down at Stetson. And Dingo boots. And Ray-Ban sunglasses, naturally.

And, more than anyone else, we want to thank Mrs. Louise Gowers, who taught us how to type back in high school. F-R-F-R-F-R. J-U-J-U-J-U. Don't look down at the keys. Ruler on knuckles. A lot of people think it only takes "Once upon a time" or "It was a dark and stormy night" or "Call me" whatever that guy's name was on the boat, but I'm here to tell you that it all starts with a ruler on knuckles.